Ruthless Heart

Ruthless Heart

EMMA LANG

BRAVA

KENSINGTON PUBLISHING CORP.
www.kensingtonbooks.com

BRAVA BOOKS are published by

Kensington Publishing Corp.
119 West 40th Street
New York, NY 10018

All Kensington titles, imprints and distributed lines are available at special quantity discounts for bulk purchases for sales promotion, premiums, fund-raising, educational or institutional use.

Special book excerpts or customized printings can also be created to fit specific needs. For details, write or phone the office of the Kensington Special Sales Manager: Kensington Publishing Corp., 119 West 40th Street, New York, NY 10018, Attn. Special Sales Department. Phone: 1-800-221-2647.

Brava and the B logo are Reg. U.S. Pat. & TM Off.

ISBN-13: 978-0-7582-4750-6
ISBN-10: 0-7582-4750-8

First Trade Paperback Printing: July 2010

10 9 8 7 6 5 4 3 2 1

Printed in the United States of America

Prologue

Eliza squinted at the numbers she'd noted in her journal and cursed her poor eyesight. She'd left the data alone for two solid days and could not for the life of her remember what she'd written. There was no help for it, she'd have to ask for help, a dangerous proposition to be sure.

She pushed the glasses up on her nose and sighed. Her sister Angeline was the only one she trusted to assist her. If their papa caught her performing experiments again, the rage would be unimaginable. One of the reasons she was up at three o'clock in the morning checking on the data.

A knock at the door startled her, and she nearly fell off the bed. Eliza shoved the notebook under the blanket along with the pencil and hoped it was Angeline out there, because there was no way she'd be able to hide the potato peeler she'd built last week.

Eliza made it to the door without tripping over anything in her path, not the first time but certainly a rare occasion. Just as she reached it, someone knocked again, this time in a staccato rhythm as if telling her to hurry up.

She pressed her ear against the door.

"Who is it?" she asked in a harsh whisper.

"It's me. Open the door."

Her sister Angeline had been blessed with everything that had not been bestowed upon Eliza. Where Eliza was plain, dark hair, dark blue eyes, average height, terrible eyesight, Angeline was tall, blond, willowy, simply stunning in her beauty at seventeen.

Eliza opened the door, and Angeline darted in wearing her nightdress, her hair in a big braid. Her eyes were swollen and red as if she'd been crying. The girls had been very close when they were young, and then as they grew older and Eliza was shunned by the other children in their ward, they grew apart. Eliza had been reading scientific books and journals, no less, which warranted painfully severe punishment. She learned to hide her passion, but the damage had been done to her status in the community. She was an outsider even in her own home.

Angeline coming to her room in the night could be dangerous for both of them, yet Eliza did love her sister. From the look of her, she needed help.

"What's the matter?"

Angeline opened her mouth and closed it, then folded her arms across her chest and shook her head. It was a parody of something. "Josiah has made an offer for me."

Eliza couldn't stop her mouth from dropping open. "Josiah? The Josiah who already has two wives, who's older than Papa? That Josiah?"

Angeline nodded jerkily. "I don't know what to do. I must be obedient. I must do as Papa says, but I was so hoping Jonathan would make it back from his mission and offer for me."

Angeline and her beloved Jonathan had been inseparable as children. A few years older than her, he'd gone off to fulfill his mission before coming back to the ward and marrying, which was the way of the followers of Latter-day Saints, what she referred to as LDS. Some people called them Mormons, after Brigham Young and his ideals. Regardless of what they were called, Eliza did not follow the LDS beliefs. Angeline sat

down on the bed and for the first time noticed the contraption on the floor.

"Oh, Eliza, if Papa catches you . . ."

Eliza knelt on the floor in front of her sister. "Forget that.
We can't help who we are, we can't help who we love." She
took her clammy hands, her heart breaking right along with
Angeline's. "What did Papa tell Josiah?"

Angeline's mouth twisted into a grimace. "What do you
think he told him? He accepted. We're to be married. Eliza,
I . . . I have to be obedient and listen to what Papa says, but
my heart belongs to Jonathan." Tears coursed down her cheeks
in the path left by the dozens before them.

Although it had been years since they'd sat side by side and
shared secrets, Eliza finally realized it had been her choice to
stay away from Angeline. Maybe to shield her younger sister
from the ridicule heaped upon Eliza. Now Angeline needed
her.

Eliza sat on the bed beside her sister and put her arm around
her. "What can I do?"

Angeline looked at her with great sadness in her blue eyes.
"You're already doing it."

"What am I doing?"

"You're being my sister again. I've missed you, Eliza."

This time it was Eliza who began to cry, knowing that
Angeline was fated to be third wife to a man high in the LDS
community, a man who wielded power, a man not to cross.
None of it mattered. She'd do her best to stop Angeline's im-
pending wedding.

Chapter One

October 1872

Eliza nearly dropped the glass on her foot. Her heart pounded frantically as she held back the scream of fear that threatened to explode from her throat. She forced herself to set the glass back against the wall as quietly as she could.

The men were in the living room, sitting by the fire and talking in whispers. Eliza had discovered if she put a glass against the wall and then her ear against the glass, she could hear conversations in the next room.

A handy skill to have when her sister's life was at stake.

As she listened, she pressed her hand against her aching chest and closed her eyes. For the past week, Eliza had thought her sister had disappeared at the hands of her husband, Josiah. However, from what she just overheard, Angeline had run away, *run*! To where, Eliza had no idea, and she was still worried beyond measure.

Josiah Brown was in there along with her father. They were talking about Angeline and how to find out where she went. Eliza was still reeling from the news Angeline had run away, and she needed to know more.

"We need to send someone after them." That was Josiah. "I will not be made a fool of by two of my wives."

Two? That meant Lettie probably went with Angeline. Good for her! Josiah was a horse's ass and a mean one at that. He deserved no wives, much less three.

"I know of a man." Her father spoke slowly, as if the words were being pulled from him. Eliza wished she could see his face. "He will track her for a price."

"How much?"

"Two hundred dollars. He's not a man from the ward. He's an outsider with a great many, ah, skills." Her father made a funny sound, and she realized he was sucking on his pipe. A disgusting habit she abhorred.

What kind of skills did the man have?

"You will talk to this man and tell him we will not be hornswaggled. I want him to find them, find *her*. Punishment is required for an infraction such as this. She is not a godly woman, Silas." Josiah's words were sharp, scathing.

"I know that now, old friend. She was raised without a godly mother, and the devil has obviously inhabited her soul. I suspect it might be too late to save Eliza, too."

What? Save her from the devil? Oh, for pity's sake, she was a scientist not a devil-loving heathen.

"What is his name?"

"Wolfe. Grady Wolfe."

The name struck a chord deep in Eliza's soul; it resonated through her, raising goose bumps in its wake.

Grady Wolfe.

He sounded like a predator, a man sent to track human beings. She didn't like him already.

"Don't worry, Josiah, we'll find them. Angeline will know God's wrath for her misdeeds." Silas spoke of his daughter as if he hated her, as if she was a scourge on his family name.

Eliza wanted to punch him.

"When will he begin his quest to find them?"

"Tomorrow. He will wait for the money at the saloon at dinnertime."

"Then I will sleep better tomorrow in knowing the Wolfe

is chasing the runaway bitches." Josiah coughed or perhaps laughed, she couldn't tell which, but footsteps sounded and she realized her father was coming into the kitchen.

She ran to the stove and stirred the stew, realizing too late the glass was still in her hand. She slid it into the folds of her skirt as her father came near.

"When will supper be ready, Daughter?"

"Shortly, Father. I only need to take the biscuits from the oven and set the table." She kept her voice steady while her body nearly shook with anger and fear for Angeline.

"Set a place for our guest. He will eat with us." Without another word, her father left the room.

Eliza slumped and let out a huge breath she'd been holding. They were sending a man after Angeline, which meant she'd be dragged back here for her punishment. Eliza couldn't let that happen. She'd have to find her sister before the bounty hunter could.

How, she had no earthly clue, but her books could help her. After supper, she vowed to find a way to help Angeline. Eliza hadn't been able stop the wedding, but she'd die before she failed her little sister again.

Eliza breathed slowly through her mouth to avoid the stench in the alley. She never imagined anything could smell worse than an outhouse, but apparently she'd been wrong. The darkened stretch between the two buildings was the ideal place to wait for the man she was following. However, she was loath to admit, even to herself, her courage was beginning to wane. It was dark, obviously smelly, and there were numerous noises around her she couldn't attribute to anything human. Her heart thumped madly as the reality of the world around her assaulted her senses with each passing minute.

She nearly gave herself away when something dropped on her head, yet she held in the screech with effort, managing to squash the offending insect with only one long shudder as she wiped her hands on the grass beneath her. The man had been in the saloon for at least an hour. All she had to do was stay put until he left, then follow him. It was a simple plan.

Eliza felt anything but reassured by the simpleness of it. What she had decided to do, what she was currently doing, she'd never even dreamed of, and that was saying a lot. Eliza had spent too much time dreaming of so many things, she'd forgotten to step outside that world.

Now she was completely out of her element and scared. She had no experience in tracking or hunting. Realistically, she'd never been more than ten miles of where she'd been born nearly twenty-one years earlier.

Yet here she was in the town she'd been forbidden to be in, alone, with a borrowed horse and as much courage as she'd ever been able to muster. All she had to do was remember her sister Angeline, and Eliza's fear seemed petty and unimportant. She pushed her glasses up on her nose and shifted her feet to relieve the cramping in her legs. All she could do was hope the man she was waiting for would appear before her entire lower half went numb.

Just as she began to wonder if the stranger would ever leave the saloon, aptly named the Drinking Hole, a man emerged through the batwing doors. The light behind him silhouetted him, making him into a dark unknown. However, she recognized him from earlier when she'd watched her father pay him. Mr. Wolfe was tall and rangy with a loose-hipped walk that made him stand out in the small Utah town. His clothing was as black as the night around him, along with his hat and likely his heart and soul as well.

Eliza chided herself for jumping to conclusions about the man. There was no reason to judge him just because he'd been hired to hunt her sister. Or maybe there was a reason, but it wasn't Eliza's business. She really didn't care about why he accepted the money, just how she could use him to find Angeline. Eliza had to be smart enough to follow him without his noticing her. Definitely easier said than done.

He lit a cheroot, a flash of orange and red in the velvety blackness around him temporarily lighting his features. He looked like a creature of the night, a predator. It sent a shiver down her spine. What was she doing? Eliza lived her life in books, never venturing farther than she could walk, and there she was about to jump off a proverbial cliff. She had no experience in being on the trail, couldn't hunt or fish, and the only knowledge she had came from books and her own experiments.

Panic clawed at her belly as the stranger stepped toward his horse. She either followed him now or she lost the trail to find Angeline. This was the moment she decided if her sister's life mattered more than hers, if comfort and familiarity, even if it included unhappiness, was better than the unknown danger awaiting her.

Tears stung Eliza's eyes as she thought of Angeline, the sweet blond girl who had trusted her father to keep her safe, to always make sure she was out of harm's way. He'd failed at his job, failed Angeline completely, and left her to her own devices, as limited as they were. Now it was up to Eliza to help Angeline, and she'd never been so frightened in her life.

His boots scraped on the dried mud on the wood-planked sidewalk, loud in the quiet surrounding them. Fear coated her tongue, but Eliza rose, keeping her eye on him as she held on to the reins of the horse behind her. Melba was mostly a plow horse, but her father had ridden the gelding for the past ten years. Another reason he'd be furious with her, but at that moment Eliza didn't give a fig for what her father would say. He lost his rights as a parent as far as she was concerned.

Silas Hunter wouldn't have recognized his elder daughter, not that he'd ever really seen her clearly. She had not only found her way to town, she'd also found the man called Grady Wolfe. The stranger scratched his bay behind the ears, earning a wuffle and a nudge from the horse's big snout. The stranger murmured something Eliza couldn't hear, then unhitched the horse and mounted quickly with an agility that surprised her. He obviously hadn't had too much liquor or he would've been a lot less graceful. Or perhaps he was always that athletically gifted.

Just because he was thin didn't mean he wasn't muscular or agile, that much was obvious. As a scientist, Eliza admired his skills. Then she reminded herself he was now trotting away as she stood there like a bespectacled fool wondering which muscles he'd used to get on the horse. She'd remind herself later to look it up in the anatomy book tucked in her bag.

Eliza threw herself up on Melba, with significantly less agility than the stranger, and started after her prey. Although not a regular rider, Eliza always had a good seat and rode astride whenever Papa wasn't around. She'd even made one of her skirts into a split riding skirt a few years earlier, which came in handy when she'd been readying for a life on the run. And now here she was riding into the night alone, following a man hired to find Angeline.

It was frightening and exhilarating. For at least the first fifteen minutes. Then the lights from town faded from view and the cloak of darkness settled around her. She recognized the sounds of the birds, frogs, and insects, as well as the constellations in the sky. Much as she enjoyed nature in all its fine glory, her thighs and fanny would never forgive her.

Two hours into her adventure, Eliza questioned her own sanity for embarking on it. As the cold seeped into her bones, she shivered, not realizing just how cool the night would get. Her bag bumped against her knee with the constant jarring motion of the horse. As her breath came out in small puffs, she shifted in the saddle because her behind was numb, along with her thighs. How long could the man ride? God help her if he planned on riding all night.

Grady had known someone was following him. Whoever it was didn't know what the hell he was doing, that much was obvious. The idiot didn't have the common sense to be stealthy as he plodded along behind him. Since he didn't know why he was being followed, he kept riding longer than he would normally have before stopping for the night.

His human shadow stayed close behind him, apparently determined to freeze to death right along with Grady. He prided himself, and heavily relied, on his instincts. They were standing up and howling like a pack of coyotes right about then.

The moon was high in the sky before he stopped near a thicket of trees. The sound of water nearby masked his movements as he jumped off the horse and crept over to wait for whomever was trailing him.

Apparently oblivious to Grady's movements, the stranger kept riding along. Grady crouched, his heart beating steadily as his muscles readied themselves. He sprang at the other rider, knocking them both onto the ground. As they rolled in the tall grass, he held on tight to the bastard until he heard him speak and realized he'd caught himself a woman.

"Oh, my goodness, unhand me." She had a husky voice, but it was definitely and unmistakably female.

Grady reared back and peered at the face beneath the floppy hat. "What the hell?"

"Did you just curse at me?" She pushed at his shoulders. "I'll thank you to take your hands off me, you ruffian."

He couldn't help it. A laugh burst from his throat, rusty and sharp. "Ruffian?"

"Scoundrel. Rogue. Miscreant. Choose your favorite, just do as I say." She pushed again, this time managing to shift a rock, which promptly dug into his hip.

"Ow. Jesus Christ, woman, give me a minute to—"

"I would prefer now instead of waiting a minute." She sounded like a damn schoolteacher scolding him. Her vocabulary spoke volumes about the young woman who followed strangers around in the middle of the night. She didn't belong, so what the hell was she doing?

Before he could ask, she tried to extract herself and this time used her legs and feet as weapons connecting solidly with his balls.

Pain ripped through him, and his stomach ended up somewhere near his throat. He rolled to the right, releasing the she-devil and trying to find a manly way not to throw up all over himself. It had been years since anyone had gotten the drop on him and gave him a kick to the nuts. He'd forgotten just how agonizing it was.

Grady heard her scramble to her feet, then brush off her clothing with sharp strokes. He wanted to toss her in the mud.

"You had no right to attack my person, sir. I am sure you'll apologize for your behavior."

"You're fucking loco, lady," he gasped out between the pulses of pain.

A gasp of breath was her only response. He got to his knees, almost anyway, and pressed his forehead into the cool ground. His breath was uneven as it escaped from his mouth. One hand cupped his crotch—there'd be no more riding that night—while the other slowly pushed himself up.

"You're out here in the middle of the night following me, then you kick me in the balls and you want an apology?" He snorted. "Not a fucking chance."

"You have an interesting vocabulary, sir. I'll thank you to stop using profanity."

"And you talk like an uptight woman who spent her life in books. God help me if you're ugly, too." He expected a reaction, but certainly not a poke in the back. "Did you just poke me?"

She ignored him. "I have no qualms about lodging a complaint with the local authorities."

Grady gritted his teeth against the incredibly annoying woman and managed to get to his feet. "Then make sure you tell them how you kicked me and poked me."

His vision was a bit blurry, but he was able to finally get a good look at her. She was kind of short, barely brushing his shoulder, with long dark hair, pale skin, and spectacles shining in the moonlight. Damn she looked like a schoolmarm, which really begged the question as to what she was doing. He was damn sure going to find out.

"I did no such thing. I simply extricated myself from your attack." She folded her arms across her chest and stared.

Grady finally made it to his feet and sucked in a big breath. "How about we just call it even?"

"What do you mean?" She peered at him, her brows knitted.

"You go on your way, and I'll go on mine." Not on a horse until at least morning, that was for sure. Damn girl had feet like rocks.

"B-but I don't understand."

Grady realized two things at that moment. First, since the woman had definitely been following him, it would be a good idea to keep a close eye on her. Second, she had no idea what she was doing. She had on a thin cotton dress for pity's sake. The nights went down to near freezing in the fall. He wasn't one to have a soft heart, but she'd likely be dead in a day or two if he didn't at least get her to the next town before he was rid of her.

"What's there to understand? You obviously don't want to be around me, so be on your way." He made a little shooing motion with his hand.

"It's late and dark. I was going to stop here at this clearing for the night." She sounded quite sure of herself, or perhaps she was just a really good liar. Grady would put good money on her being the latter.

"What clearing?" Grady peered around, still trying to focus on where they were.

She pointed to the left up ahead of them. "That one there. I hear a source of running water, and there is a line of boulders to block the wind."

Damned if she wasn't right, the little vixen. It was the perfect clearing to stop for the night. He'd be a fool to continue on with throbbing balls in the pitch dark. She turned her back and retrieved her horse, leaving him standing there beneath the tree.

"Suit yourself." Grady limped over to his horse, and by the time he made it over to the clearing, she'd already settled in and somehow unsaddled and hobbled her horse. The schoolmarm was currently building a ring of stones, presumably to make a fire.

He stepped toward her and she stopped, looking up at him with those spectacles winking at him. "Are you planning on sharing my campsite?"

"I'm planning on stopping for the night and resting my balls. You kicked them clear up to my throat, woman." He ignored her disapproving cluck and hobbled his horse. As he uncinched the strap around the saddle, he kept an eye on his strange companion.

She created a perfect circle from the rocks, placing them so tightly together no sparks could get under or over them. Then she set about gathering twigs, and he was so amused, Grady sat down to watch her. Like a little chipmunk, she used her skirt to gather as many twigs as she could find in the moonlight clearing. She sat down on her haunches and built a triangular-shaped bundle in the middle of the ring of stones.

Grady wondered where the hell she'd learned how to make a fire. He'd never seen such a thing before. "Do you know what you're doing?"

Again, she ignored him and continued on her task. She reached into a travel bag and pulled out what he recognized as waterproof matches. He honestly expected her to be there for at least another thirty minutes before she gave up and asked for help.

The fire flared to life, making his eyes sting at the sudden brightness.

Hell and damnation. She sure didn't look as if she could take care of herself, but she'd just showed him that was untrue. Maybe she was much cleverer than he gave her credit for, or perhaps she was a confidence man, er, woman. Grady watched her with a new set of eyes.

There was still the matter of why she'd been following him, and why she was sitting there pretty as she pleased making camp with a man she didn't know, alone and unprotected. It was the strangest situation and it didn't sit right with him, which meant it was wrong.

"What's your name, honey?"

This made her stop in her twig gathering to stare at him. "Pardon me?"

He leaned back against a rock and folded his arms, assessing the little wren. "Your name? Or is that a secret?"

"You may call me Miss, uh, Eliza." It was the first time he'd seen her ruffled. The hunter in him assessed his prey, and she was not as confident as she appeared.

"Eliza what?"

"Just Miss Eliza." She arranged her skirt in front of her, then began feeding larger sticks from the pile beside her into the fire. It flickered merrily enough to make him want to throw sand on it. "And you, sir, what is your name?"

"Wolfe. Grady Wolfe."

She glanced up at him, pushing her spectacles up her nose. The firelight danced across the glassy surface so he couldn't quite see her eyes. "As in the big bad?"

Grady couldn't help the annoyance mixed with amusement that raced through him at her wit. The woman definitely had a brain and a sharp tongue. "None other."

"I read the Brothers Grimm once. Perhaps I am the hunter instead of the helpless girl." She continued to feed the fire, seemingly uncaring of the verbal game she was playing with him.

"You sure as hell don't look like a hunter." He watched her closely; her reactions would tell him a lot of exactly what his short charlatan had up her sleeve. "And more like a helpless girl."

"Should I be afraid you're going to swallow me whole then?" She rose to her feet and put her hands on her hips looking like the damn schoolmarm again.

Grady's gaze raked her up and down, taking in the frumpy clothes, the dark hair, the ugly shoes. He didn't know what to make of Just Miss Eliza yet, but he would. She could count on that.

"I'll be grabbing some shuteye then. Much obliged for ah, building the fire." He pulled his hat down low and blocked her out.

Eliza thought for certain he could hear her knees knocking together. She never thought herself a thespian, but after that performance, she was ready for Shakespeare. Her heart thumped so hard, her throat vibrated from the force of it.

Various parts of her body ached from the tackle and then the fall. The man had a body harder than an oak tree, she could attest to that fact. Grady Wolfe was larger than life, and he scared her to pieces. Eliza had dug up courage from somewhere near her feet to pretend she was unaffected by him.

However, that was far from the truth. She shook with her body's reaction, whether it was fear, excitement, or just plain shock. Thank God she'd read the book on how to start a campfire. It was the only thing she remembered as she stood there quaking like a little girl in front of the exceptionally tall, strong man. The closest she'd ever come to touching a man was handing her father his clean shirt. Yet she'd been pressed against Grady Wolfe from head to toe, and it had frightened her as much as it excited her.

She must've convinced him that she had been planning on stopping at the clearing. It was blind luck there had actually been a clearing and that it was a good spot to stop for the night. Eliza had been miserable enough to stop an hour earlier, so the clearing was a gift she was quite thankful for, and glad it was suitable.

When a lizard darted near her foot, she bit her lip to the point of pain to keep the screech from popping out. Mr. Wolfe had apparently decided to sleep, and she didn't want him to wake up anytime soon. It would take her most of the night to recover from her first encounter with the man.

She needed to keep up appearances, to convince him she was simply a fellow traveler so he would maybe offer to travel with her. That was her master plan anyway; whether or not it would work remained to be seen. What good would she do Angeline if she gave up so easily?

She fed the fire with some larger wood, still surprised it was crackling so nicely. Doing mundane chores almost as if she was keeping house definitely helped, too.

She retrieved her blanket from the saddle and a book from her bag. Reading always relaxed her, and she certainly needed relaxing. Eliza picked her favorite, Jules Verne's *Journey to the Center of the Earth*. It transported her to a world outside her own, and Professor Von Hardwigg reminded her of Ephraim Monroe, her mentor and friend who had taught her so much. She laid out her blanket up against a smooth rock and sat down, stifling a groan. After she managed to get her boots off, she couldn't control the sigh that escaped. It felt so good to sit and not be bouncing up and down on a horse.

"You know if a man hears a woman sigh like that in bed, he'd know he did something right."

Eliza squeaked before she could stop herself. It sounded so silly and childish, bringing a heat to her cheeks she could only hope he attributed to the fire.

"I don't think that's a subject we should speak of." Eliza nearly cringed at how prim she sounded, almost like the mothers in her ward who used to chastise her.

"Obviously you ain't spent a lot of time around campfires and cowboys then, have you?" He peered at her from beneath his hat. "Bedsport is what they jaw about."

"Ah, well, it's a very good thing I am not a cowboy then. I didn't mean to bother you. I just wanted to read before I retired for the night." Her mouth was drier than sand, and she wondered if she would ever feel comfortable around Mr. Wolfe.

"Are you a schoolmarm or something?"

Eliza couldn't stop the chuckle that erupted from her throat. "A schoolmarm? No, definitely not. I am a student, not a teacher." She had no patience to teach anyone, especially the LDS teachings she didn't agree with.

"Who is your teacher then?" He pushed up the brim of his hat to stare at her, his dark eyes more intense than the deepest embers of the fire.

"He-he died a while back. I continue on learning though." She again tried to distract the man. His unceasing perusal made her want to squirm, so she looked away and loaded the fire with wood. "I'll just put my book away so we can both get some sleep then." She managed a weak smile and tucked the blanket around herself, turning her back on Mr. Wolfe.

His gaze was palpable, burning into her skin like the fire she'd built. It seemed like hours until her eyes finally closed in exhaustion, and her dreams were plagued with uneasy images of dark creatures and danger.

Chapter Two

"**Y**ou're going to have to wake up some time, so it might as well be now."

Eliza started awake, momentarily confused by the cold morning air, the unfamiliar surroundings, the hard ground beneath, and the man standing over her with the biggest knife she'd ever seen.

A gasp flew from her mouth, and she was instantly and completely awake as if she'd had a bucket of cold water thrown over her. Heart pounding like a bass drum, she finally got a clear view of Grady Wolfe. He was tall and whipcord thin, with wide-set shoulders and long limbs, likely giving him a great reach, agility, and speed.

She stared at his face. Each piece was nothing special, but together made Grady absolutely striking. He had the darkest eyes she'd ever seen, barely a distinction between the pupil and the iris. They were velvet pools of dark ice set in gaunt cheeks with at least three days' worth of whiskers. A dirty hat covered waves of brown hair brushing his collar. His lips were set in a tight line, almost as sharp as the knife in his hand.

Grady Wolfe was positively frightening.

"Mr. Wolfe?" Eliza didn't know how she managed to actually form the words with her stiff lips. And she had thought she had been scared last night. Obviously she had no idea what being truly scared really was.

"What the hell are you doing, Just Miss Eliza?" He frowned fiercely, his eyebrows slammed together so hard she almost heard the snap.

"I don't know what you mean." She sat up, pushing hair out of her face and trying to appear normal, whatever that meant. The last thing she should do is cower like a little mouse facing a big cat.

"You were following me, don't deny it. I want to know why." He fingered the tang of the blade, sending a shiver up her spine at the caress.

"I-I wasn't following you. I was traveling alone and you happened to be riding ahead of me." She didn't even believe herself.

Apparently he didn't, either. "You were in the alley near the saloon. I saw you. Then when I left town, you were right behind me. Don't shovel any more shit at me."

Although she was shaking hard enough to rattle her teeth, Eliza knew she couldn't admit what she had been doing. Something told her giving into his bullying would be the absolute wrong thing to do.

"The fact you saw me in town doesn't mean I was following you. That's ridiculous logic." She rose to her feet, intent on holding her ground, feigning ignorance. "I wasn't being disingenuous about my intents."

"Using a five-dollar word ain't gonna change a thing, woman. You need to get your ass back on your horse and go back to town. There must be some foolish man out there looking for you."

Eliza held back the blush by force of will. If only he knew her father didn't care about her other than his meal being late. No doubt he had all kinds of punishment scheduled for her, including penance on her knees for days.

"I assure you, there's no one worried about me. I am traveling in the same direction as you, a pure coincidence." Hoping he didn't notice the trembling in her hands, Eliza tried to pick up her saddle, but found herself on her fanny in the dirt instead. It didn't occur to her that the saddle she lifted off the stall wall the day before would be heavier when lifted from the ground. It was simple science, of course, and Eliza was embarrassed she hadn't come to the conclusion earlier.

"That just proves to me you don't belong out here, Just Miss Eliza." He picked up her saddle as if it weighed nothing and plopped it on the horse's back, dead center on the blanket. The man was stronger than he looked. After cinching the saddle with expert speed, he grabbed her bags, then immediately dropped the larger one. "Jesus Christ, what's in here?"

Eliza forgot to be scared for a moment when her most precious possessions were in danger. "Be careful! That contains my books."

He poked the bag. "Books? You're out here with coyotes and scorpions and you got a bag of damn books? What the hell is wrong with you?"

His words should have stung, but Eliza was more annoyed than insulted. "I'll thank you to give my books the proper respect, Mr. Wolfe. These are very precious to me." She pulled the bag across the dusty ground, away from the toes of his boots.

"Go back to town, or I'll tie you to a tree and leave you here." He slid the big knife into its scabbard on his hip.

"I'm heading west, Mr. Wolfe, whether or not you want me to." She swallowed the big lump in her throat with effort.

He stalked toward her, that lean-hipped swagger making her want to turn tail and run. Leaning in close, he puffed out a breath, which smelled like coffee and tobacco, the heat a strangely welcome feeling in the cold morning air.

"What the hell do you want, Eliza?"

It seemed strange to have any man use her given name, much less a man like Grady Wolfe. She was used to being called Sister Hunter or Daughter, but only Angeline called her Eliza. The reminder made her courage return in equal measure to combat her fear. Then her imagination took over and saved her.

"Fine then, I'll tell you the truth. I'm a widow with no means to support myself."

"You could sell the books," he mumbled under his breath.

"My husband's family threw me out of the house, so I took what I could carry and left." She gestured to the bags. "The books are all of what's left of Ephraim." Her throat closed up at the truth of her words even if she was using the memory of him to tell a falsehood.

Grady stared at her in that intense manner of his. Eliza wanted to squirm, but she didn't even reach up to wipe her eyes.

"You have no other family?"

"Some distant relations." She was at least being somewhat honest about that since Angeline was physically distant.

"Where are these relations of yours?" He fingered the grip of the pistol hanging on his hip. Her gaze was absolutely glued to the small gesture. She doubted a man like Grady touched his gun for effect—when he touched it, it was for a purpose.

She only hoped she wasn't that purpose.

Eliza attempted to swallow her dry spit. "West, but I'm not sure where. I was hoping to find them without help." Now that wasn't the entire truth of course.

"Glad to hear it. Stop following me and stay out of my way." He threw himself into the saddle with the agility she recognized from the night before. Without a backward glance, Grady Wolfe rode away hard, leaving Eliza alone.

"Phooey," she whispered, suddenly more nervous than she was when she started following him.

Grady had never met a woman like Eliza, if that was even really her name. She talked like a professor, rode around with twenty pounds of books, and could build a campfire like nobody's business. Yet she was as innocent as a child, had a sad story about a dead husband he didn't believe for a second, and seemed to be waiting for him to invite her along for his hunt.

He snorted at the thought. Grady worked alone, always and for good. There sure as hell was no room for anyone, much less a woman like Eliza.

He had damn well tried his best to shake the woman, but the blue-eyed raven-haired fool wouldn't budge. Truth be told, he was impressed by her bravado, but disgusted by his inability to shake her off his tail the night before. Rather than risk having her do the same thing again, he decided to ride like hell and leave her behind. He should have felt guilty, but he'd left that emotion behind, along with most every other, a long time ago. Grady had a job to complete and that was all that mattered to him.

The only thing he was concerned about was finding the wayward wife he'd been hired to hunt and making sure she regretted leaving her husband, at least for the five seconds she lived after he found her.

Grady learned as a young man just how much he couldn't trust the fairer sex. His mother had been his teacher, and he'd been a very astute pupil. No doubt if she hadn't drank herself to death, she'd still be out there somewhere taking advantage of and using men as she saw fit.

The cool morning air gave way to warm sunshine within a few hours. He refused to think about what the schoolmarm was doing, or if anything had been done to her. If she could take care of her horse and build a fire, she could take care of herself. Food could be gotten at any small town, but then again maybe she could hunt and fish, too.

Somehow it wouldn't surprise him if she did. The woman seemed to have a library in her head. Against his will, the sight of her unbound hair popped into his head. It had been long, past her waist to brush against the nicely curved backside. Grady preferred his women with some meat on their bones, better to hang on to when he had one beneath him, or riding him. He shifted in the saddle as his dick woke up at the thought of Eliza's dark curtain of hair brushing his bare skin.

Jesus Christ, he sure didn't need to be thinking about fucking the wayward Miss Eliza. If she was a widow, no doubt she'd had experience in bed with a man. It wasn't Grady's business of course, so he needed to stop his brain from getting into her bloomers, or any parts of her anatomy.

As the morning wore on, Grady's mind returned to the contents of her bags. The woman didn't have a lick of common sense and fell asleep, vulnerable and unprotected. Good thing he didn't have any bad thoughts on his mind or she wouldn't have been sleeping. She even snored a little, something he found highly amusing as he'd rifled through her things.

Her smaller bag had contained a hodgepodge of clothes, each uglier and frumpier than the last, a hairbrush, half a dozen biscuits in a tattered napkin, and some hairpins. A measly collection of a woman's life, and quite pitiful if that was all she had. Perhaps she'd been at least partially truthful about taking everything she owned and hitting the trail. Her husband must have been a poor excuse for a provider if this collection of rags was all she had.

The bag of books was just that, a bag stuffed full of scientific texts ranging from medical topics to some titles he couldn't even pronounce. In the bottom of the bag was a battered copy of *Wuthering Heights*. He didn't know what it was, but it was much smaller than the other books, likely a novel. She obviously put the spectacles to good use judging by the two dozen tomes she had in her bag. He wondered how she'd gotten it up on the saddle in the first place.

"Fool." He had to stop thinking about Eliza and what she was doing and why. Grady would never see her again.

As a child, Grady learned very early not to care or ask questions. It only bought him a cuff on the ear or a boot in the ass. A boy could only take so much of that before he kept his mouth shut and simply snuck around to find out what he needed to know.

As a young man, it served him well and garnered the attention of the man who taught him how to hunt and kill people in the quickest, most efficient way. Grady had learned his lesson well, even better than his mentor expected. When the job was put before him to hunt and kill the very man who had taught him those skills, Grady hesitated only a minute before he said yes.

The devil rode on his back, a constant companion he'd come to accept. He didn't need a woman riding there, too.

Eliza spent half an hour trying to get her bags onto the saddle and by then she was sweating and angry—at herself and at Grady Wolfe. He'd scared her, yelled then left her behind.

She'd been sleeping as if nothing could hurt her, somehow safe in Grady's company, although she'd been sure she was anything but safe. He'd left her and she had to follow.

Eliza spent the time to perform morning ablutions in the creek, so at least the sweat was off her body before she perspired again on the back of the horse. It didn't matter, though, she needed to get clean if only to feel normal.

After filling her canteen, she was returning from the creek when she saw the snake. Eliza's breath caught in her throat, and she froze, eye to eye with the serpent. It was light brown with a darker pattern on its back, and its head was diamond shaped. She was never more grateful to have read about snakes in Utah and knew the shape of its head meant the snake was poisonous.

Of course, that meant it could kill her with one strike of its fangs. Fresh sweat rolled down her face as she stood as still as a tree a mere twenty feet from her horse. The snake slithered toward her, its tongue slipping in and out of its mouth. As it slid between her feet, Eliza closed her eyes and pictured

Angeline. Her sister was all that mattered, and she had to be strong to help her. If Grady found her before Eliza caught up with him, there was no hope for either one of them.

A soft breeze caressed her face, almost as if someone had cupped her cheek as if she were a child. Her eyes popped open expecting someone to be standing in front of her, but there was no one there. She glanced down and realized the snake was gone.

Her breath came out in a gust, and she shook like the leaves on the small tree in front of her. She took a moment to make sure the snake wouldn't return and her legs would actually work when she walked. The last thing she needed was to fall and injure herself because of her own frailty.

Eliza made it to the horse and leaned into his neck. "I don't believe I'm saying this, but I'm glad you're here, Melba."

With equine understanding, he allowed her to hang on to him for a few minutes before he shook his mane. She took the hint and patted him. "Thank you, boy."

Eliza hadn't spent much time outdoors, but she had read many books, which she was happy to say prepared her to make a campfire. Perhaps it would help her to track Grady, too. There had been information about tracking animals, which should also work for a human animal, too.

She looked around until she found the tracks from the horse Grady rode in and around camp. The back right shoe had a nick in it, so she could easily see the direction he'd rode, and keep her on the right trail.

Grady had no idea how powerful books could be, but Eliza did. She had brought ones to help her, both with her adventure and with her courage. Ephraim's books were so important to her, she couldn't imagine being able to do this alone without his guidance in her memory.

Eliza took hold of Melba's reins and led him over to a rock so she could mount without making a complete ass of herself. As she slid up into the saddle, her behind and thighs groaned in protest. After the long ride the night before, there wasn't a place on her that didn't hurt. However, none of it mattered. She had to find Grady.

Eliza didn't care how she did it, but she was going to catch up to him and teach him a thing or two about bespectacled women. She gritted her teeth and started off west following the horseshoe prints.

The sun was high in the sky before Eliza stopped to eat. Food didn't seem important, but her stomach was yowling like a beast and had actually become quite painful. She knew it was partly due to anxiety, but if she got herself sick because she didn't eat, she wouldn't be good for anything or anyone.

Every half hour, she checked to be sure she could still see the horseshoe track with the nick. He was consistent in his riding skills judging by the horse's stride. Grady was obviously a man used to being on the back of a horse.

Eliza's backend had long since gone numb, along with everything below the waist. She had no idea just how physical riding a horse actually was—no book talked about just how hard the saddle was, either. Of course, the saddle she rode was meant for a man, and likely thirty years old if it was a day.

It was a sad realization, really, of just how much she didn't know. Books taught her so much, as did Ephraim, but the real world was full of lessons she still had yet to learn. Some of those lessons were hard, and she had a feeling they were only going to get harder.

The biscuits she'd put in her bag were barely enough to keep her going. In addition to being sore and tired, Eliza was hungry enough to eat one of her books. At least she had freshwater; that was a blessing even if the biscuits barely fulfilled a smidgen of her appetite.

Eliza had read a book about hunting and using snares, yet she shuddered to think about actually skinning and preparing a rabbit for cooking. That particular volume had not been put in her bag for that reason. Now she regretted it considering how hungry she was. No wonder people hunted for food, regardless of the blood and violence of it.

Eliza knew they lived in an insular society with the LDS church and the ward that surrounded them. Ephraim had been her neighbor and friend, a non-LDS resident who lived in a small cabin on the outskirts of town. She'd met him quite by accident when she'd been out looking for raspberries one spring seven years earlier. Angeline had stayed at the house because she'd been feeling poorly.

Of course if Silas had known Eliza had gone out on her own, he would have tanned her hide. Ephraim, however, had saved her life that day. She'd been picking berries she thought were the raspberries common to the woods behind their house. Yet they'd been poisonous and Ephraim had stopped her before she finished chewing the first bite.

With a patience Eliza had never known in an adult male, Ephraim, white-haired even then, taught her the difference between the berries. Then he taught her about what she could eat in the forest, what was dangerous, and what she could use every day for things like cleaning and curing headaches.

He was an amazing font of information, one she visited as often as possible. His books became precious to her as he taught her about science, inventions, and the world around her.

Her father never knew of Ephraim's teachings, and for that lone fact, Eliza was grateful she could lie. It wasn't a skill she had used in her life until she realized Silas Hunter would never let his daughters be exposed to anyone who did not believe what he did. The LDS church had no room for nonbelievers, and as a prominent man in their ward, her father had a reputation to uphold.

Eliza had no such qualms. At nearly twenty-one years old, she had long since given up on God and the LDS teachings. Science and all its glory had shown her the true meaning of what surrounded her. She'd always questioned the entire concept of faith, but had kept quiet for fear of embarrassment and ostracism.

She'd been right in doing so, because once she became a scientist in truth, and began doing experiments and building inventions with Ephraim, she would have been expelled from her family and her life if discovered. As it was, Silas had found her doing experiments, or constructing inventions, on six occasions. He'd been beyond furious and had forbidden her from performing the devil's bidding, destroyed her work, and beaten her until she'd been bedridden for days afterward. Eliza remembered each and every one very clearly.

Angeline was the only one who accepted her as a whole person, never judging Eliza or condemning her for beliefs she didn't share. Eliza's younger sister was the angel her name implied. She was sweet, obedient, and seventeen years old, and she was out there in the world with only another woman for company.

Eliza had to find Angeline before anything horrible happened. She'd disappeared nearly two weeks earlier along with Lettie Brown, the second wife to Josiah. Angeline was wife number three. Eliza might have believed Josiah had murdered both of them if it weren't for a conversation she overheard in her own house.

Josiah had hired Grady Wolfe to hunt down the two women. Eliza knew then she had to find Angeline before Grady did or her sister would have to return to the life she had run from. Knowing how much Angeline followed the LDS teachings and how obedient she'd been all her life, something horrific had happened. Eliza knew a great deal of what had happened in Brown's house, how Josiah had beaten his new wife, and she could only wonder what truly horrible thing he'd done to send the two women out into the world alone.

Eliza had never been so frightened in her life. Angeline was her baby sister; she'd practically raised her from the time they were girls and their mother passed away. Eliza had always thought it was due to unhappiness with her life, since

Margaret Hunter had been a convert to LDS, never quite fitting into the community. Her girls had been her life, and her death had deepened the bond between them.

There wasn't anything Eliza wouldn't do for Angeline, including setting out on a dangerous adventure she had never imagined doing. Now here she was alone in the middle of nowhere riding a horse and chasing a bounty hunter.

If it weren't true, Eliza might have thought she was reading about it in a book. That thought made a chuckle burst from her dry throat. In another hour she might start talking to herself, and that would be not only embarrassing but worrisome. She needed to keep her wits about her. Grady Wolfe was a smart man, exceptionally smart.

The moon had long since been hanging in the dark velvet sky when Eliza slid off Melba. The horse shook its head as if it was as exhausted and shaky as she was. The small campfire fifty yards ahead had to be Grady. It had to be.

If it wasn't him, she might lose whatever grip she had on consciousness and fall to the scrubby ground in a faint. Dramatic but sadly true. Eliza wasn't generally given to dramatics or frailty, but she had to accept she'd reached her limit and desperately required relief.

She secured the horse to a low branch on a tree, then took off her shoes to creep up on the fire. Grady might be asleep or simply waiting for her to get close enough to slit her throat with that enormous knife of his. Her breath came out in white puffs in the frigid night air. It seemed colder than the night before, but more than likely it was due to her complete exhaustion.

Eliza almost wept when she recognized his horse. She could hardly believe it, but she'd successfully tracked a professional tracker. Ephraim would be proud of her. She was proud of herself.

As she approached the small fire, nearly embers, it popped and snapped, sending Eliza's heart into a gallop. She stopped in her tracks and waited, but the still figure on the other side of the blaze didn't move. He lay on his side with his bedroll tucked around him, snug as a bug in a rug. Eliza debated what to do before she turned around and returned to Melba to unsaddle him.

She whispered an apology to the old but steadfast horse before she gave him a quick rubdown with his blanket and made sure he could reach the sweet, cool grass nearby. Eliza felt the sting of tears as she retrieved her own blanket and ignored the sheer agony in her legs.

The tiny fire called to her, offering sleep and warmth. Eliza followed the lure of the fire, knowing the man who slept beside it would likely be quite angry with her when he woke. Angry was probably a mild word, but that was the least of her concerns. Right then she felt as though she'd become a singular being with simple needs of heat, sleep, and food.

Eliza stumbled, nearly falling on her head, as she reached the edge of Grady's camp. After righting herself, she stepped around to where he lay on the ground. She put her blanket down on the ground next to him, then got to her knees and crawled in beside his big, warm body.

For the second time that day, tears pricked her eyes as she lay down and felt the heat from the fire on her front, and Grady's behind her. She was instantly asleep.

Chapter Three

Grady woke slowly in the gray predawn light, unusual for him, but he hadn't slept well because he'd dreamed of Eliza. In his dream, she'd been in his arms, pliant and soft. He woke up with a dick harder than an oak tree, pulsing and growling with need. Grady reached out and found he hadn't been dreaming after all—there was a woman in his bedroll.

He traced her luscious curves until he reached her round backside, which he caressed gently before he pressed himself against it. She moaned softly, and Grady continued his explorations past the dip of her waist.

Her breasts were round and full, the nipple peaked almost immediately in his hand. He tweaked it until it hardened perceptibly, and he had to taste it.

Conveniently enough, there were only six buttons on the front of her blouse, and he made quick work of them. He reached in to find a rough chemise covering his prize, but he pushed it out of the way until he found flesh.

It was softer than anything he'd ever felt, warm and inviting. Grady pulled her on her back and ducked beneath the bedroll to claim the best tits he'd ever held in his hand. The heat beneath the blanket was full of her scent, woman, and arousal. It sent a pulse through him, making his dick grow even longer. He breathed in deep, inhaling all of it into his body.

He nuzzled her and was rewarded with a kittenish sigh. Her breasts begged for his touch, and he was more than willing to oblige. Cupping one, he began licking the other, small catlike licks all around the nipple. He enjoyed the tight bud brushing against his cheek as he deliberately avoided it.

It wasn't until he could hardly stand it another second before he gently licked a nipple. He was rewarded with a sigh of pleasure, so he sucked on it; the sweet flavor of her skin made him groan. As he tweaked the other, she pushed up into him, filling his mouth with her breast.

Grady accepted the gift for what it was and nibbled at her as his hand crept down her body to the juncture of her thighs. Her heat penetrated through the clothing to his touch. Grady bit her and she jumped, bumping her head into his. Reality crashed down around him and he woke up fully as the pain from the collision throbbed almost as much as his dick.

"Oh, my."

That voice. He knew that voice.

It was *Miss Eliza,* the damn schoolmarm, under him, with her breast in his mouth and her pussy currently pulsing in his hand.

Holy shit.

He took his hands away slowly, almost as if she were a rabbit and he didn't want to spook her. She sighed as his mouth left her breast wet with his warm saliva. The nipple puckered even more as the cool morning air hit it. Grady told his dick to shut up, but it wasn't listening. It roared with frustration as he slid away from her body. He felt like a mouse backing away from a trap—the prize wasn't worth the risk.

Who the hell knew the schoolmarm had a body full of delicious curves and tits that would haunt his dreams for the next year? Not to mention her responsiveness, which was beyond amazing. Not many women reacted to a man's touch with such heat, such passion.

Of course his experience with women in bed was limited to whores, but some of them had been good girls doing what they had to do to survive. He had always done right by them, no matter what their circumstances. However, none of them had heated as quickly as the woman inches from his yowling cock. God, and it had to be Eliza for pity's sake. Why couldn't it have been a woman he could fuck and leave?

It dawned on him that he had actually left her the day before, and a long, hard ride was between them. So how in the hell was she lying by his fire snuggled up against him as if they were an old married couple? Was she a witch who flew through the air to taunt him with her curvy body? Or was he simply insane with thoughts of her that he called her to his side without meaning to?

Grady sat up and got a good look at Eliza in the murky light. She looked absolutely tempting, and it was a good thing he didn't like her or he might be doing more than scowling at her. Her dark hair was tousled as if she'd been well loved in a bed, and her eyes were heavy lidded with arousal.

Son of a bitch.

Grady stood and backed away from her. "Fix your clothes."

She smiled. "That was a lovely way to wake up, Mr. Wolfe."

He almost swallowed his tongue. There was no way she could be pleased with what had just happened. "Are you loco? I almost took you like a common whore on the cold ground."

"I beg to differ. There was nothing common about that. I thoroughly enjoyed it." She sat up, and one breast popped out of her gaping shirt.

"Jesus Christ, woman, put your damn tits away." He sounded gruff because he was beyond angry. In fact, he was furious with himself and her.

This time her smile disappeared, and he almost regretted snapping at her. She had it coming, though. Stupid female creature didn't have a lick of common sense.

"Well, that's not very polite of you." She buttoned up as she met his gaze.

Without glasses, Eliza's eyes were clear for the first time since the moment he'd met her. They shone like sapphires, accusing him of being the bastard he was. She had no idea just how much of a bastard he could be if he had a mind to.

"I ain't a polite person by nature, so don't expect me to be otherwise." He frowned as he noticed her old damn horse happily munching grass by his bay. "Now we start with the questions, Eliza. How did you find me, and what the hell are you doing here?"

She shrugged. "After you left, I regretted the fact we hadn't discussed a deal. I had thought perhaps we could travel together. There are many advantages to sharing our journey."

"That didn't answer all my questions, lady." He squatted down and stared hard into her innocent looking face. "How did you find me?"

"Your horse has a nick in the rear shoe. It was easy to follow your tracks." She sounded so matter of fact, as if every person in the world would notice the nick much less follow it thirty miles through the rough terrain.

Grady frowned harder. "You a tracker, then?"

"No, but I read a book about tracking." She picked up her spectacles from a rock nearby and brushed at her dress. "I'm afraid this outfit is nearly ready for the rag pile."

He decided it had been ready for the rag pile before she'd even put the damn thing on. "A book. Of course, a goddamn book." Grady paced for a few minutes as she sat there prim and proper with an innocent expression. He stopped and pointed. "So why did you follow me?"

She picked at the dirt on her skirt. "Well, as I told you I am traveling west and truthfully, I'm in need of a companion. A woman alone can be in danger."

Grady threw back his head and laughed, something he hadn't done in a very long time, if ever. Now she says she could be in danger. Who did she think he was, a Sunday school teacher? She was a completely confusing mix of smarts, innocence, and annoyance. He had to admit, though, she had more courage than most men, not that he'd tell her that.

"Are you planning on paying me? I ain't cheap, lady, and sure as hell ain't free." He didn't expect her to actually consider his services, no matter what the price. She didn't know him from a killer who would leave her for the coyotes.

"Of course I would expect to pay you. What would you charge to escort me to my relations, for perhaps a week or two?" She got to her knees and poked at the fire with a stick.

Grady wanted to poke her with the stick. What the hell kind of joke was this? No woman in her right mind would act like Eliza. Maybe she really was loco and she'd leave *him* for the coyotes. He dismissed the thought as soon as it entered his mind. Grady had an ability to read people, and although Eliza confused him, she was definitely not a physical danger to him or anyone.

"You couldn't afford it."

She calmly put more wood on the fire and stoked it. When she reached into his saddlebags for the frying pan, he could hardly believe his eyes.

"What the hell are you doing?"

"Making breakfast of course. I noticed you had some cornmeal, so I thought I'd make some corn pone and coffee." She blinked up at him like an owl. "Is that not acceptable?"

Truth be told, Grady had never had a woman other than his mother make him breakfast before. That sure as hell was a thought for another time. He didn't want to think about his mother at the moment, or ever really. She'd done enough damage to his life.

"It's damn odd, that's what it is."

She continued stoking the fire. "I am used to taking care of others."

Grady didn't doubt that for a minute. She sure as hell took care of herself.

"As to your price for being my escort. Well, would you

consider payment to be my, ah, cooking and keeping camp for you?" She sounded hopeful, and it made him cringe. He didn't want the woman to be pinning her hopes on him, that was for damn sure.

"Cooking and cleaning, eh? You don't know much about offering yourself do you?"

Surprisingly, she blushed, telling Grady in no uncertain terms that she'd never offered to pay a man in services before. "I would be happy to discuss details."

Grady snorted. "There's nothing to talk about. I'm not buying. Anything."

She nodded, and although he expected her to argue, she turned back to rifling through his bags and started fixing breakfast. The woman confounded him at every turn, and he couldn't decide if she was doing it deliberately or not.

The one thing she did well was cook. He sat down and watched as she expertly made coffee and corn pone. He'd planned on buying supplies before he set out, but by the time he'd left the saloon in Tolson, the store had been closed. Then he'd spent all day running from the woman who ended up in his bedroll with his hands all over her surprisingly sexy body.

It was like he'd entered a new world, one he was unfamiliar with, and it angered him to feel that way. Eliza might well have come with a warning pinned to her blouse that said "Dangerous."

She handed him coffee in the only cup he had, which meant she was used to being the last served. He took the cup without comment, and she busied herself looking around for something near the trees. When she found a plant with big green leaves, she picked two of them and poured water from the canteen, then patted them dry with her skirt.

Damned if she hadn't found them some plates for the hot cornpone. He didn't want to eat it, but it smelled heavenly and his stomach yowled from the scent. As they ate their silent breakfast, hers with water to drink from the canteen instead of coffee, he watched her.

Eliza did seem harmless at first glance. He had a sneaking feeling she'd continue to follow him, using her damn books to guide her, unless he allowed her to ride with him. Since he still wasn't sure exactly what she was after, it was probably a better idea to keep her where he could see her. Some old saying about keeping friends close and keeping enemies closer rang in his head.

He'd be wise to heed that warning and keep Eliza within sight until he figured out exactly what she wanted.

Eliza wanted to moan in pain and confusion, but she held it all in through sheer force of will. She had woken to the most beautiful pleasure she'd ever experienced, then it was taken from her instantly. Her body was excruciatingly sore, yet it still called out for Grady's touch.

She'd never thought much about the sexual act between a man and woman beyond procreation, and of course what she'd read in books. It was a simple physical act, or at least that's what she'd thought before now. There was nothing simple about what happened beneath her blanket.

His mouth, his tongue, and his hands. Sweet bliss with every second he'd touched her. Eliza wanted to weep from the perfection of those moments. As a scientist she appreciated the attraction between two bodies; as a woman she felt things for the first time.

Grady had been angry, as she knew he would be, but beneath the anger, she sensed confusion for him as well. He didn't know she'd be beside him when he woke, and she didn't fault him for his actions even for a moment. The bald truth was she enjoyed it too much to think badly of him, although she knew she should have. What they did was meant to be done between a man and wife, not two strangers under a blanket.

Perhaps his confusion was rooted in the same cause as hers—there was no reason for them to be attracted to each other much less find physical pleasure, yet they were and they did. Eliza had spent enough time around animals to recognize the signs when two creatures were aroused. That fact was undeniable as the erection in his trousers.

As she worked around camp cooking and cleaning up, her legs ached with pain, but she knew that muscles reacted to stretching to heal. Each time she bent over, she pushed herself to stretch even farther, until her body shook and she could hardly stand it. However, it was working, and each time she stretched, the better she felt afterward.

It was only after they'd eaten and cleaned up that she realized he hadn't answered her request to guide her or her offer to cook and keep camp for him. His bawdy suggestion about other services still echoed in her head. Her chagrin had been compounded by the fact she was embarrassed enough for her cheeks to heat. She couldn't remember the last time that had happened.

"If, and that's a big damn *if,* I let you tag along with me, we're going to have to set some rules." Grady's voice nearly scared a year off her life. He'd come up behind her as she rinsed off the pan using the sand in the creek.

"What sort of rules?" She wiped the pan and stood up. Since this was the first time they'd actually stood nose to nose, or rather nose to chest, Eliza was quite surprised at how tall he was. Their previous encounters had been at a distance or on the ground; she had no reference as to their full distance in height.

It was almost a foot.

Up close, his whiskers were nearly menacing in his sculpted cheeks. However, it was his eyes that told her the true story. In the morning light, they were dark brown with tiny flecks of gold that sparkled, topped with long, thick lashes. All in all, quite lovely eyes even if they were looking at her with impatience.

She stopped perusing him for a moment to realize what he said. He'd decided to take her with him!

"First, we ride when I say, how long I say, and you don't

complain about any of it. Second, you don't tell me how to do anything, no matter what any of your books say."

"Somewhat stringent rules for being a traveling companion." Eliza didn't want to tell him she wasn't sure she could ride at all, given the current state of her thighs and buttocks.

"It's going to be my way or nothing at all."

"Then your rules are accepted provided you agree to allow me to cook and make camp in payment for your services." She had to secure her own terms or he may think her too easy.

"My services? You make everything sound so fancy, woman."

"My name is Eliza. Calling me 'woman' makes me think of a Neanderthal who may grab my hair and club me." Eliza didn't know what possessed her to say that to him. It apparently surprised him as much as it surprised her. "What I meant to say was, please call me Eliza."

His gaze narrowed. "I think you've got a smart mouth, *Eliza*. I prefer my women a bit dumber."

With that, he turned away and walked toward his horse. "We're leaving in ten minutes. Be ready or get left behind."

Eliza wanted to shout with joy, but she kept it bottled inside. It would not do for him to see the victory dance in her eyes or on her tongue. However, it was a definite victory considering Eliza had spent her life in a small house in a small ward with a small-minded father. She'd broken free from the yoke forced upon her since birth.

She wanted to throw back her head and howl in triumph.

Instead, she walked over to her horse and began readying Melba for another day of riding. She got the blanket on just fine, but when she reached down to pick up the saddle, it was scooped up from her reach. To her utter astonishment, Grady put it on the horse for her.

"Cinch it." The man was used to giving orders.

Although Eliza wanted to respond that she wasn't a dog to

be ordered what to do, she knew it wasn't a wise idea. She didn't want to jeopardize that fragile agreement five minutes after it happened.

She did as she was bid and finished getting ready, even packing his saddlebags and bringing them to him. He frowned at her when she brought them over.

"I mean to keep to my word to cook and clean." Eliza went to retrieve her own bags, when he grabbed her arm.

There were few times in her life she'd been touched, and now three times in only a few days, Grady had laid hands on her. Once in anger, once in arousal. And now an almost innocent touch. This time she jerked as if she'd been scalded, and it shocked her into immobility. His hand was hot on her skin, in sharp contrast to the cold morning air. Yet it wasn't the heat that shocked her, it was her body's reaction.

As soon as they made contact, a sharp twang resounded through her body like the string of a violin being plucked. An echo of awareness that hadn't been there before they'd been intimate, or nearly so. Eliza wasn't expecting it, and she knew she looked as flummoxed as she felt.

He took his hand away slowly as if he were afraid she would protest. "What the hell just happened?"

"I-I don't know." She managed a small, strained smile. "Shall we be on our way?"

He stared into her eyes, peering into her soul, perhaps to find the desperate longing for more of his touch she was trying so hard to hide. She knew in moments she would blurt out exactly how she felt about his hands on her skin if he continued to gaze at her so intently.

"Should I bother asking you if you'll leave the confounded books behind?" He moved his gaze to her traveling bags.

Eliza's fascination with Grady's touch flew away in a millisecond. Her protective instinct reared its head. "Never."

"That's what I thought. I ain't picking them up for you, so I hope you can do it yourself; otherwise the rats will get them."

He turned his back and began securing his saddlebags to his own saddle. Eliza was full of righteous anger, and it helped her haul up the bag of books for what seemed like the hundredth time in mere days. She put the smaller bag on as well, then led Melba to a fallen tree.

When she stood on it to mount the horse, Eliza found Grady watching her. "I'm ready."

He shook his head. "I seriously doubt that, but let's go, Liz."

Liz?

Chapter Four

The woman didn't have much of a seat on the horse, but she had grit. Grady pushed her hard, intentionally past her limits and nearly to his. The only consideration he made was for the horses. He let them rest, the only break Eliza got. She looked exhausted with a pinched expression around her mouth. Even though she spent a good deal of time bouncing on the saddle, she didn't complain even once.

Hell, if she were a man, he'd say she had a pair of brass balls.

"What's your family's name?"

His voice apparently startled her because she let out a squeak. "I didn't think you wanted to speak at all." She met his gaze from under the brim of a hideous brown hat. "I appreciate the conversation."

"Liz, answer the question. Or maybe there is no family?" He actually believed her about the Ephraim fella, whoever he was, but knew there were other things she was hiding.

"My family's name is Hollingsworth. Why have you started calling me Liz?" Eliza frowned at him. "Do you dislike my given name?"

"I don't feel one way or another about it, just think Liz is easier to say." Grady mulled over her answer about her family's name. She didn't hesitate a second, which might mean she was telling the truth. For the moment he'd give her the benefit of the doubt.

"I suppose that's true. I've never been called anything but Eliza. It sounds, well, odd." She frowned at him.

"You'll get used to it. It won't hurt none to do something you never do." He was pretty sure everything she'd done over the past few days were things she never did. "When's the last time you heard from these folks?"

"Almost a year ago." She sounded wistful, an emotion he didn't think he'd hear from the staid schoolmarm.

"Where abouts were they living?" He would let Eliza think he was helping her find her family. However, his paying job was first and foremost on his mind. If they happen to find Eliza's kin, then it would likely be a coincidence.

"I believe it's near Raymer Falls. They own a boarding-house."

This time Eliza's words didn't ring true, and he wondered if this family was real or if she was just running from the supposedly dead husband. No doubt she would do what she had to. Wouldn't be the first time a woman had to find a way to survive no matter what it cost.

"It's about two hundred miles to Raymer Falls. That's a long way to be riding alone." He watched her reaction from the corner of his eye.

She glanced down at her hands on the saddle horn. "I'll go as far west as you're traveling. If you don't make it the entire way to Raymer Falls, I can proceed the rest of the way alone."

After all the trouble she'd gone to wiggle her way into riding with him and she was acting meek? He snorted at the thought.

"You are full of shit, Liz. You'll stick to me like a damn cocklebur until you find what you're looking for."

"I beg your pardon?"

Grady shook his head. "You heard me. Just be good and I won't leave you behind."

He was satisfied to hear her suck in a breath, but she didn't say a word. He had a feeling she wasn't used to being silent for any reason. It had been a while since he enjoyed anyone's company, but he was enjoying sparring with the fancy-talking Eliza.

It should have sent him riding in the other direction, but the memory of what she felt like in his arms stopped him. She was a combination of so many different and unusual things, he was challenged to find all of them.

And his body ached for more of what was hidden beneath the little wren disguise.

The sun was high in the sky before he spotted the edges of Bellman. It was a good time to stop for dinner, and he needed to get supplies. Now that he had a cook, they could actually eat more than stale biscuits and dried beef.

When they rode into town, for once people either nodded or tipped their hats toward him. Usually he received dark looks and folks avoided his stare. Grady knew it was because of Eliza. She looked respectable, even travel weary and covered with dust.

Until that moment, he hadn't recognized he found a tool to help him in his own quest. With Eliza at his side he would gain access to places he'd been unable to breach in his business. Folks didn't like gunslingers and made it clear he was unwelcome to even step foot in some places. She'd be a perfect companion for a man on the hunt who needed to find the scent of his prey.

Grady didn't pretend to be a good person, or a moral one for that matter. He shouldn't feel guilty; he *refused* to feel guilty about keeping Eliza with him for his own ends. She was using him to find her long lost family, or something like that. He suspected she was running from a husband who smacked her around. Either way, she was using him just as much as he was using her. Or at least that's what he told himself, then shut down the thought in his mind before it could go any further.

"Are we stopping here?" She sounded like she'd been gargling sand.

He tossed her his canteen, which bounced off her shoulder, but she caught it in midair before it fell.

"Take a drink, would you? Yes, we're stopping here for supplies and dinner. This will be the last time you don't have to cook for a while."

She moaned as she took a swig of water. The sound went straight to his dick. When she looked over at him, drops meandered down her dusty chin and he had the urge to lick them off. He was going loco for sure.

"That sounds lovely. I'm looking forward to it. I've never eaten at a restaurant before." She smiled, showing even, white teeth.

Two things hit him with the force of a slap. Eliza had never eaten at a restaurant and her smile completely transformed her face. Grady didn't let his reaction show even a tiny bit. If she knew how she affected him, he'd lose the power he wielded over their agreement.

He couldn't let that happen. He wouldn't let that happen.

Eliza was simply miserable. Every muscle in her body ached as if she'd been beaten with a thousand sticks. When Grady finally stopped in front of what appeared to be a mercantile, she almost wept with relief. He'd pushed her hard, to test her mettle, no doubt.

She'd risen to the challenge and rode until she had to conjugate verbs in Latin over and over in her head as a distraction. If she was fortunate, they'd spend a good deal of time in town so she could have more than a few hours' rest from riding a horse.

When Melba actually stopped moving, Eliza still vibrated from the motion. She tried to pull her right leg over the saddle to dismount, but she found her limb unresponsive. Biting her lip, she attempted again but to no avail.

She simply couldn't get off the horse on her own power, and she was loath to admit it. Grady dismounted with his usual grace and secured his horse to the hitching rail. He looked up at her and scowled.

"Are you planning on riding on without me? Or do you want to get down and get some vittles?"

Eliza clenched her teeth. "I would like nothing more than to get down and find vittles, whatever they are."

"So get down and let's get moving." He turned and walked a few steps toward the sidewalk before he stopped. Without turning around, he spoke again. "You can't get down, can you?"

She counted to five while she wrestled with her pride and her fear he'd think her weak. Finally pain and hunger won.

"No, I cannot. I would be much obliged if you would assist me, Mr. Wolfe."

"That's a fancy way of asking me to pluck your ass off that horse."

She didn't dare chastise him for his language, but the man used enough vulgarity for two people. "Yes, please."

He had her off in seconds, depositing her on the hard-packed ground on very shaky legs. When Eliza started to topple over, Grady pulled her against him hard. The impact startled her, then the feeling of his body pressed to hers took her breath.

Eliza looked up, and Grady pushed her hat back until they were eye to eye. His gaze moved to her lips, and she realized that although his mouth had touched her skin, they'd never kissed. She couldn't help but wonder what it would feel like if they did.

"Don't look at me like you want me to throw you down on the street right here and now." His voice was strained, and she felt his body harden, sending another shiver through her. He was so incredibly firm, more than any man she'd ever met. Most LDS men she knew were older and therefore soft around the middle.

Grady was nothing like those men. He was slender but muscled from top to bottom.

"I-I'm doing no such thing. My legs are stiff, that's all."

He put his finger on her chin and rubbed his thumb across her lips. She resisted the urge to encourage his behavior, even as his touch excited her, made her want more.

"Should we move before we attract attention?" She attempted to move away from him, but he held her firm. Since her legs were still full of pins and needles as the blood began moving through them, she was actually glad of the extra time in his arms. That's what she told herself anyway, even if it were only a half-truth.

"Don't worry, Liz. We want people to think we're married. If they do, folks are more willing to talk to us about things." He studied her face as he spoke, likely trying to read her expression and figure out what she was thinking.

"About things? Such as information we need?" She hadn't thought of that possibility, but it was a definite advantage.

"Exactly. You want to find someone, you have to blend in and make people trust you." He cocked one brow. "You might not be a beautiful wife, but you're a believable one."

The comment stung more than Eliza wanted to admit even to herself. She knew she was the plain, mousy dark-haired sister. A sharp contrast to the beautiful blond Angeline. She didn't need a reminder from a hunter like Grady, even if he meant it to be informational rather than cruel. However, it completely destroyed her current fascination with his lips and the close proximity of his body.

This time, she stepped away from him and forced her legs to work, pain tucked away until she had the time to handle it. Eliza had become very adept at putting things into separate places, particularly pain, anger, and hurt. She could not allow them to show or things could always get worse, and had.

"If you plan on posing as my husband, we should continue on with purchasing supplies and a meal." She brushed at the dirt on her clothes. "It would be nice if there were a place nearby I could wash away some of the travel dust."

He held out his arm. "Then let's find what we need, Mrs. Wolfe."

Mrs. Wolfe.

The very idea made a chuckle burble up in her throat. The man was hired to hunt her sister and drag her back to the bastard she'd run from. Eliza was there to rescue Angeline and stop Grady Wolfe from collecting his bounty.

Mrs. Wolfe indeed.

"Of course, let's proceed with our tasks." She took his arm, ignoring the silly way her heart fluttered at the gentlemanly gesture. It was all false, and she had to remember that. It wouldn't do for Eliza to confuse reality with a lie.

"You might want to tone down that fancy talk while we're in town. Folks don't usually take to people who are too different from them. You sound like a schoolmarm who spent her life in books."

"Well, I have spent my life in books, or at least half of it. And I'm not a schoolmarm." The very idea of wanting her to sound dumb insulted her, and the pride she'd already tucked away came roaring back. "You want me to sound unlearned?"

"Yep, think you can do it?" He stared hard, as if challenging her to tell him she couldn't, to quit and walk away.

Eliza wasn't giving up that easy.

"I know I can do it. All I have to do is sound like you."

She swore she heard him swallow a chuckle, but he didn't respond with words. Satisfied she'd gotten some of her dignity back, she walked stiff legged next to the man she was now going to pretend was her husband.

It seemed the universe had a sense of humor.

*   *   *

People never asked Grady why he did what he did, likely because they were afraid of him or his answer. Truth be told, he wouldn't know exactly what to tell them if they did ask. He'd always done whatever he needed to survive. When he'd started hunting people for money, it had been just that to him—money.

He buried what was left of his soul and his conscience at the ripe age of fifteen and faced the world alone. His natural skill for tracking developed into hunting, which ended up making his reputation.

Grady felt nothing for the money he put in his pocket. It was pure survival, a task to complete that paid a hell of a lot more than plowing fields or slinging booze. He had only one vice, and he didn't discuss that particular issue with anyone.

As he walked down the street with Liz on his arm, people didn't give him a wide berth as was the usual behavior. He didn't ever remember a time when that happened. He'd been right about having Eliza on his arm. She gave him something he didn't have—respectability. Without even trying.

They stepped into the mercantile, and the smell of cinnamon washed over him. He closed his eyes against the memory that shifted deep inside, a tiny flash of his father and life before it had burned into cinders.

"Looks as if the clothing display is, I mean, there's the clothes. You can do what you need to while I shop over there." She managed a tight smile and walked awkwardly toward the table laden with ladies' fripperies. Eliza was sore and stiff, that was for certain, but it didn't stop her from being bossy.

Grady frowned at her retreating back as he recognized the fact she had somehow taken control of their time in town. It annoyed as much as it relieved him. In between his guns and her strange speech, they might run into trouble. She didn't know a damn thing about getting out of trouble, but definitely knew how to find it.

"Can I help you?"

He turned to find an older man, balding on top with round spectacles perched on his hawklike nose. The sharp look in his brown gaze told Grady the man knew exactly who and what he was.

"My wife needs some clothes. We need trail supplies, too. Coffee, flour, bacon if you've got it, apples, crackers, canned peaches, and whatever else she wants. Some ladies' soap, too, something that smells good." He looked over and spotted the ammunition. "And I need two boxes of bullets for a forty-five."

The shopkeeper glanced at Eliza, then looked back at Grady. "I take cash only. We don't extend credit to strangers."

"That won't be a problem."

The older man nodded. "I'll get the goods together."

Grady walked over to Eliza as she peered at a purple dress. Her gaze was wide and her expression could only be called shocked.

"Never seen purple before?"

She shook her head. "I didn't know this existed outside of wildflowers. What an incredible scientific wonder! Whoever dyed this fabric is very skilled at what they do."

Grady again wondered exactly what cave Eliza had been hiding in all her life. "How old are you?"

"Hm? Nearly twenty-one. My birthday is October ninth."

Next week this woman-child would turn twenty-one. By the time he was that age, he'd already become hardened and lived in a world without innocence. At thirty, Grady was too much of a cynic to not be amazed at how much this book-learned creature didn't know.

"Have you been locked in your house for long?" He meant it as a joke, but judging by the stricken expression on her face, he wasn't far off the mark.

"I wasn't locked in. I, um, attended church and helped with sick neighbors in the, uh, town."

If there was one thing Grady knew it was when someone was lying. Eliza wasn't very good at it.

"You're lucky we're in this store, Liz, or I'd leave you behind in a second." He leaned in close, noting how blue her eyes changed, and were now the color of a winter sky. Then there was her scent, clean air and woman, that tickled his nose. Damn her anyway. "I'm letting you tag along, but that's temporary. If I wanted to you'd never find me again."

Never mind the fact she'd tracked him already.

"Grady, I-I was embarrassed by the fact I lived my life in books. There was nothing outside of my family except for Ephraim, and after he passed away, I couldn't be there a moment longer." Her voice cracked. "The last few days have shown me exactly what it means to live. Even with discomfort, pain, hunger, frustration, there was also passion, joy, and triumph. I-I couldn't imagine ever going back after this adventure is complete."

This time, Eliza's sincerity was apparent. Although miserable and apparently in pain, she wouldn't trade this adventure of hers for the safety and security of her life up until she took off on the ancient nag of hers. Grady wondered exactly what she'd experienced that would send her out into the world unprotected and unprepared, for the most part anyway.

Then again, her past was her business. There was no way he'd be telling her about his mother and her crimes. Or his own for that matter.

"Fine then, you either be honest with me or we will part ways." Before he thought about what he was doing, he grabbed the back of her neck and kissed her hard. Her lips were full and so damn soft beneath his, made him wonder what they'd feel like on other parts of his body.

Her initial surprise didn't give way to anger, so he softened the kiss, then pulled away. He didn't dare look her in the eye, so he focused on her red lips, which proved to be another mistake because he wanted to feel them again. Damn, he knew they'd be distracting, but he let his dick take control of his head.

"I'll be outside; just get whatever you need or want." For the first time in a very long time, Grady ran away from a challenge.

He stepped outside and took a deep breath. No need letting her know he was attracted to her to the point of distraction. Grady reached deep inside for his iron control and clamped it down on his randy lower half. Eliza was a passenger, someone to cook for him, no more. The money for his current job wouldn't mean shit if he lost focus over a woman.

Grady wasn't fooling himself for a minute. What he should have done was leave her behind, and he couldn't explain why he didn't.

Chapter Five

Eliza marveled at the colors of the fabric, wishing she had seen such wonderful materials before. Her clothing had always been brown or black, drab and drabber. She didn't want to spend any of Grady's money, but she simply could not leave the purple dress behind. It was well made and was delightfully just the right size for her.

The shopkeeper wandered over as she looked at the shoes. He reminded her a bit of Josiah, Angeline's horrible husband, and Eliza's instincts were making the hairs on the back of her neck stand up.

"Good afternoon, ma'am."

Eliza nodded at him. "Good afternoon, sir."

"You finding what you need? Your ah, husband said you was to get what you want." He jerked his head toward the door. "He's outside smoking."

While it was good to know Grady hadn't left her behind, the man's insinuation that her husband wasn't really her husband annoyed her. It didn't matter that it wasn't true; in truth they were traveling together as any married couple would. No doubt he thought Mr. Wolfe was a shady character beneath his regard. Eliza knew it wouldn't behoove them to have townspeople regarding him in such a manner—it would not help him find Angeline.

"My husband is very kind and generous." She managed a blinding smile. "I am the world's luckiest woman to have such a man as my mate. There is nothing he wouldn't do for me." She hoped she sounded convincingly enamored of him.

"Seems a bit dark, if you don't mind my saying." The shopkeeper frowned.

"He's just a quiet man." She held up a pair of boots. Perhaps if they spent enough, the man would change his mind. "These will be just what I need."

"Hope your husband has enough to pay for all this." He took the boots and dress and walked toward the counter in the back.

"Of course he does." Eliza had no idea if that was true, but it had better be. She looked at the pile of goods on the counter and reviewed the content. Grady had thought of all the staples, but not everything.

Eliza picked up a few more items and put them with the others. Grady obviously didn't know much about cooking, so it was a good thing she did. She glanced out the window and didn't see him. Her heart thumped hard as she realized he could have left her with a pile of goods to purchase and no funds to do so. In fact, Grady could have simply decided she was too much trouble and moved on without her.

"I will just go and see what's keeping my husband." She turned, remembering at the last minute just how sore her legs were. Hopefully the shopkeeper didn't notice how badly she limped.

The fresh air helped her breathe a bit easier, but the empty street stole that breath away. Where was Grady?

"I think your man has left you behind, if he was your husband at all seeing as how you don't have a ring and all." The cynical old man popped up at her elbow. "If'n you don't have money to pay for those goods, I'm going to have to turn you over to the sheriff."

"Considering that no crime has been committed, you have

no cause to file a grievance with the law." Eliza felt her ire rising as she spoke. "For that matter, I could file my own grievance based upon your unfounded belief that my husband is untrustworthy and maligning his character."

"Mal-what?" He backed away, his bushy eyebrows slammed together to make a caterpillar on his forehead.

"She just means you weren't nice." Another man appeared, this one sporting a shiny star on his leather vest. He was not much older than she was, with sandy blond hair and brown eyes. The kindness of his face was offset by his hand resting on the gun at his hip. "Then again, she doesn't know you're not nice to most folks, even if you know them." He tipped his hat to her. "Ma'am, name's Sheriff Brian Striker."

"Good afternoon, Mr. Striker. I'm Eliza Wolfe." She straightened her shoulders. "I'd like to say this gentleman, and I use that term loosely, was pleasant and helpful, but that wouldn't be true."

"Is that so?" The sheriff turned to the shopkeeper. "You scaring off your customers again, Abe?"

The older man crossed his arms. "I ain't scaring nobody about nothing. Her fella is right scary, has the look of a gunslinger to me. And they have thirty dollars' worth of goods to pay for and he's gone missing."

Thirty dollars? She had no idea the clothes and boots cost that much. That was more than she'd ever seen in her life, much less spent in one day. Grady would be furious with her, which did not bode well for her continued presence by his side.

"My husband has every intention of paying as soon as he returns." Eliza didn't mention her concern over how much he would have to pay when he returned. The lump in her throat told that story.

"Well, I'm glad to hear that." The sheriff smiled, one that didn't reach his eyes.

Eliza didn't know how to react to either one of these men.

They were outside of her experience, and truthfully, she hid her fear well, but she was afraid. The insular community of LDS kept her away from every type of person except the church people. The man called Abe was a bit unpleasant, and the sheriff made her nervous.

"Would it be acceptable if I went to find him?" She was relieved to note both their horses were still tied to the hitching post.

"Why don't I find him for you, Mrs. Wolfe?" The sheriff had another one of his pretending to be friendly smiles. "I'd be happy to assist a lady in need."

Eliza tamped down her discomfort and fear. There was no need to let the man know she was out of her element. "That would be very kind of you, Mr. Striker. I will wait here with the horses."

The young sheriff seemed to notice the horses for the first time, perhaps lending credence to her claim that her "husband" would return and pay the grumpy Abe.

Eliza could only hope it was sooner rather than later.

Grady needed a drink, or two. The past few days had strained every nerve he had, and Eliza was stomping on the last one. He needed a few moments away from her, especially after having kissed her.

Jesus, that was unexpected.

Or not. After all, she'd turned into molten heat in his arms that morning under the blanket. He should have expected her to be just as combustible when he kissed her. The truth was, he shouldn't have done it, but somehow since she'd gotten under his skin, he did things he normally would never do.

Maybe he ought to leave her behind in Bellman. She'd make her way to wherever she was going. The woman had enough books to either sell, burn, or use to find her way anywhere. She didn't need him except maybe to chase away snakes, even the two-legged kind.

As he sipped at the rotgut, it burned as it slid down his throat. He held on to that burn and savored it. Whiskey was familiar, it was grounding, it helped him regain focus, something he really needed.

Eliza's presence was disconcerting to say the least. He thought to use her to find information, yet he hadn't counted on the physical pull between them. Pull? More like a raging fire set to burn them both.

"You looking for some fun, sugar?" The saloon girl was a redhead with corkscrew curls, tired eyes, and perky tits. Her body smelled of other men and a bit of desperation. She pushed her large breasts into his arm and gave him a clear view of them.

Normally he would have taken a sample and perhaps bought the entire cow. They were impressive tits to be sure. She was a redhead, not exactly his type, but getting a relief from his randy state would help everyone, him first of course.

He licked his lips at the sight of a raspberry nipple peeking out from the top of her blouse. This girl may do nicely to not only satisfy his needs, but to find information about the woman he was hunting.

"What do you have in mind?" He ran his finger along her cleavage, pleased to see her nipples peak beneath the pink material holding them in.

"Dollar for half an hour, whatever you want." She reached down and cupped his balls, making his dick wake up. "For you, I'll suck you off for free."

Oh, yes, she was a nice diversion for sure. "Let's get moving then. I'll take fifteen minutes for a dollar."

Her green eyes lit up. "I'm all yours."

They walked toward the stairs, and Grady slid his hand down her round ass. Very nice, not quite as round as Eliza, but would do in a pinch.

"What's your name?"

"Joy." She squealed as he squeezed one cheek.

"Mm, well I hope we find some of that joy in your bed."
He hadn't planned on fucking a saloon whore, but he wasn't
about to change his mind.

"You know a girl named Angeline? Blond, about seventeen?"
He was going to find out what he could before he didn't have
to think.

"No, don't think so. She work in a saloon?" Joy wiggled
her ass a bit harder, likely trying to pull his attention back to
her.

"Nah, not Angeline. She's my little sister, and she's traveling with my aunt. I figured somebody might've seen them."
At the top of the steps, he looked around to see only four
doors, each likely leading to a room. The stairs were the only
entrance and exit, giving him the lay of the land, so to speak.
His time with Joy could be dangerous if he didn't pay attention.

"Yeah, likely that's where she is if'n she ran away. I don't
remember her none, though."

Angeline Brown must've found a different route; otherwise
Joy would have seen her. Bellman was a small enough town
that most folks knew everyone else's business.

Of course that meant anyone had seen him with Eliza knew
he had gone upstairs with Joy. Maybe even told her about it
already. Jesus, he hated small towns and small minds. Damn.

Grady pushed away the thought of Eliza waiting for him
at the mercantile. She'd know he wasn't going far—he'd left
the horses there. God knew the woman could take care of
herself, and he needed the escape. From her.

Joy's room was darkened by newspaper on the windows,
and the bed was at least neatly made with a dark blue blanket. The room was surprisingly tidy with very few belongings
marking it as her own.

She turned and closed the door behind him, then smiled,
revealing a few missing teeth. No matter, he wasn't there to
judge her beauty. Joy pulled him toward the bed, somehow

unbuttoning and pulling off her dress as she went. A neat trick he fully appreciated.

She was down to her knickers and a black peek-a-boo corset that shoved her nipples up for easy access. Before he could grab the pink temptations, she'd gotten to the edge of the bed and sat down. Her quick hands applied themselves to his trousers, and within seconds his dick enfolded in those hands.

He closed his eyes and reveled in the feel of her fingers running up and down his staff. She cupped his balls and tickled them as she leaned down to pull the tip of his erection into her warm, wet mouth.

"Joy," he breathed.

She didn't respond, but she sucked at him, licking around the head, teasing him. Joy knew what she was doing. He leaned toward her as she pulled him deep into her mouth. Grady closed his eyes, and in his mind, he saw another woman pleasuring him.

"Ah, Liz," he breathed, her blue eyes shining up at him. As he reached out to touch her hair, instead of the soft dark hair he found frizzy curls.

He pushed aside the fantasy and concentrated on the reality. Joy was giving him exactly what he needed, so why the hell was he thinking about Eliza?

Joy leaned back and spread her legs; smiling coyly at him, she crooked her finger. "C'mon, sugar, let's get busy."

Grady gritted his teeth and started to climb on top of her, until a banging started on the door.

"Joy, you in there? I'm looking for a stranger, fella by the name of Wolfe."

The man's voice made Joy's smile fall so fast, his erection turned to ashes just as quickly. He tucked it back in his pants and was disappointed to see his fifteen minutes of distraction close her legs and reach for her dress.

"Joy?"

"I'm here, Sheriff. Give me a minute." She gestured to the window and Grady nodded his thanks.

He reached down and kissed her cheek, pressing two dollars into her hand. With a sigh, he opened the window and glanced down into the dirty alley below. Not the first time he'd escaped through the back way.

As the door opened, Grady crawled out and hung from the sill for a moment before dropping to the ground. Somehow he missed the crates but landed directly on a pile of dog shit.

Oh yeah, a great time was had by all. What a difference from what he wanted to be doing.

With whom he wasn't going to think about any longer.

Of course the last thing he expected was a fist to come flying at him from the gloom of the alley. It connected solidly with his jaw, and then everything went black.

Chapter Six

"Excuse me? You've arrested my husband?" Eliza stared at the sheriff's seemingly boyish face. He wore a mask on the outside, and she could only wonder what lurked beneath it.

"He was sneaking out of the saloon without paying for his drink." The younger man tucked his fingers into his gun belt. "He was also, ah, found leaving the saloon from a back window."

Eliza's heart dropped to her feet. He was sneaking out of the saloon? What in the world would have possessed him to do something so stupid?

"I highly doubt that my husband would have left without paying. May I speak to the person levying the charges?"

The sheriff frowned. "Levying what?"

"Whoever said Grady did these things." She had to remember to use the vernacular instead of using her accustomed method of speech. People didn't expect a woman to be book learned, and she could not afford to appear any stranger than she already did.

"Ah, that would be Butch, the barkeep." The sheriff took her elbow. "I can take you down there now if you like."

"Please do." She didn't like the feeling of his touch and

couldn't say why. However, she endured it, as she was trained to submit to men.

They walked down the street with Eliza's head held high. She maintained her dignity and the illusion that she was a concerned wife. Truthfully, she was worried about him. Grady had money, she was certain of it, and it made no sense for him not to pay for a drink of whiskey. There had to be another explanation.

She stepped into the saloon, named the White Dog, and immediately wrinkled her nose at the memory. It smelled like the alley she'd waited in back in Tolson. At least she didn't flinch outwardly even if her stomach clenched at the noxious memory.

Then she spotted Grady.

His face was bloody and purpled on the right side. He was sitting on a chair leaning his elbows on his knees. She gasped at the small puddle of blood on the floor beneath him.

"Grady!" Eliza dropped to her knees in front of him and pressed the hem of her skirt to the open wound on his lip. "Sheriff, do you mind explaining how my husband was beaten?"

"Well, you see, ma'am, he resisted arrest."

Eliza shot the sheriff a dark look. "It would appear it was more than simply resisting arrest."

"He broke the law, Mrs. Wolfe."

She saw a burly, hairy man behind the bar watching her with an intense stare. "You, sir, are you the barkeep?"

One bushy eyebrow went up. "I sling the booze here."

"You are the one who told the sheriff my husband didn't pay for his drink?" She was alarmed by Grady's silence.

"That's right, ma'am. He went upstairs without paying, then jumped out the window."

Grady's gaze slammed into hers, and she realized the bartender was telling the truth. Her "husband" didn't appear apologetic, either.

"I paid Joy."

The barkeep snorted, and the sheriff leaned against the bar, crossing his arms. "That so? She didn't say a thing about that."

"Give me the money." Eliza whispered to Grady.

He frowned and reached into his shirt pocket to pull out bills, which he pressed into her hand. "I hope you know what you're doing."

"Me, too."

She rose, conscious of the bloodstains on her tattered skirt. "We stopped in Bellman to purchase supplies, eat a meal, and rest. The people of this town must not want any money in their pockets, because we've been treated horribly since our arrival. Our mission is to spread the word of God and you have sullied that mission."

Eliza was pleased to see the sheriff's smug look slide from his face. "What?"

"You heard me. We are missionaries here to spread the word of God." She pulled a small book from her pocket, a well-worn one that would be mistaken for a Bible. "We had hoped your town was not full of sinners, but it appears there is enough sin here to fill Satan's cup."

The barkeep backed up and headed toward the door. "I ain't dealing with no preachers."

"You want me to believe you are here to spread the word of God, when your husband was upstairs with a whore?"

Eliza flinched at the sheriff's harsh words, but she knew there was only one chance to save Grady from jail. "Did they fornicate? No, they didn't, and it was because he was testing just how far you sinners will go." She held up the Bible. "Heal them, God, for they do not know what they do. 'Nevertheless, as surely as I live and as surely as the glory of the Lord fills the whole earth.' "

"Oh, hell, I'm leaving, Striker." The burly barkeep disappeared behind a door beside the bar like a rat deserting a sinking ship.

"I forgive you, sheriff, for your transgressions as will God.

As the Bible says, 'Let the Lord judge the peoples. Judge me, O Lord, according to my righteousness, according to my integrity.'" Eliza managed a smile for him and held out the money. "We have funds to pay for everything we purchased, as you can clearly see."

"You two are loco." Striker held up his hands. "You need to turn your tails west and get the hell out of my town."

"Let the heavens rejoice, let the earth be glad; let them say among the nations, 'The Lord reigns!' Eliza stepped toward him, and the sheriff jumped back a foot. She bit back a smile. Who knew listening to the Bible study on Sundays would serve her well when she'd run away from it?

"Be on your way." Striker held the door open.

Eliza took Grady's arm and helped him rise. He leaned into her and whispered, "You are loco."

She smiled and walked toward the door with her bleeding, whore-visiting bounty hunter in tow. Just another day on the trail with Grady Wolfe.

Grady's head throbbed in tune with his jaw, his eye, and his knuckles. Jesus, that sheriff had fists like oak, and he was faster than hell, considering he blindsided Grady. Someone else was in the alley, too, likely that big son of a bitch behind the bar. He wanted to ride back into town and teach them a thing or two about ambushing someone.

He should be sitting in a jail cell instead of riding away with two dozen cuts and bruises on his face. Eliza surprised him, a feat she seemed to enjoy doing every hour or so. When she pulled out the Bible and started quoting scripture, he had to clench his jaw shut to keep his mouth from falling open.

She had looked like one of those Bible-beating preachers in a tent he'd seen on occasion in his travels. All full of passion and God, reminding him that the schoolmarm was so much more than the little wren.

"We should stop so I can provide medical assistance to your wounds."

Oh, yeah, there was the book head again. "You mean put some bandages on me?"

"Perhaps stitches as well. Don't worry, I have had experience with medical procedures before. We don't have, I mean, we didn't have a physician in town when I was a child, so there was always a woman trained in medicine and healing."

Interesting bit of information about her, one he wouldn't have guessed judging by what she carried in her traveling bags.

"You have medical supplies?"

"We do now. I had that horrible shopkeeper put some in with your purchases." She looked down at her hands, fiddling with the reins clutched in her slender fingers. "I apologize for spending so much on me. I never intended on it, and honestly I'm mortified by the amount."

Grady knew the dress cost around eight dollars, so he couldn't imagine what she would have spent so much money on, but he was damn curious now. Did she buy some kind of undergarments for her "services"? He'd handed over thirty dollars to the bastard Abe, and now he was mentally tallying what he'd put on the counter to buy. Somewhere in there, Eliza had spent another ten or twelve dollars.

Question was, what did she buy?

"There is a clearing with access to a stream. It's an ideal spot for us to stop." She pointed ahead, but when Grady turned to look, the world began to spin a bit.

Oh, shit.

He leaned forward and closed his eyes. As he wrapped his arms around the horse's neck, he hoped Eliza would be able to move his two-hundred-pound carcass when he passed out again. Damn sheriff likely cracked Grady's skull. Now he really had a reason to go back and kill him.

His stomach roiled as the world refused to stop spinning. He wanted to warn Eliza that they really needed to stop, but all that came out was a grunt. However, he underestimated Eliza yet again.

"Hold on, Grady. We're almost there."

Was that worry he heard? Wouldn't that be a neat trick. Someone actually worried about him. Although in the saloon she'd certainly put on quite a show when she had seen him beaten and bloody. Her voice sounded closer, then when her hand touched his back, he realized she'd ridden up next to him.

If he wasn't about to lose what was left of his stomach, he might think she cared about him. He snorted at the thought, then started to slide sideways and he grasped the horse's mane, but it wasn't enough. Then Eliza took hold of his belt and held on firmly.

She anchored him on the saddle and apparently took the reins from him. How the hell she could manage all that when she was short, soft, and round, he would never know. Obviously the woman had a spine of steel and muscles to match.

"Here we are."

The horses stopped and Grady focused on breathing and not vomiting.

"I'm going to let go of you for just a moment or two while I ah, dismount."

He knew just how graceful she was getting on and off a horse. Hopefully he wouldn't hit the ground before she did. Before he even knew she'd let go of him, she was by his side taking off his hat. Her cool hand touched his forehead.

"I believe you have a concussion, Grady. It's caused by a blow to the head, and I'm afraid it's quite painful, although you probably already know that." She talked faster with each word, and Grady knew then that aside from her fancy talk, Eliza did feel fear. This time it was for him, a unique and disconcerting thing.

"I've laid out your bedroll on the grass near the stream. I'm going to help you down off the horse and if we're lucky, I can get you over to the bedroll successfully." She cupped his cheek. "I apologize in advance if my clumsy efforts result in more injuries."

"Let's just get on with it," he managed to get out.

She took hold of his belt again and wrapped his left arm around her shoulders. He slid off the saddle, and the world began to gray around the edges. Eliza held him up like a tiny shadow pushing his chest. He knew he was likely crushing her, but he was barely conscious.

"That's it; now it's only a few feet. We can do it." Her breath came in pants as he felt himself moving across the ground, although his feet barely moved.

Before he realized she was dexterous enough to throw anything down, the bedroll was below them and slowly he got closer to it. She was holding his weight and sinking down until he was close enough to gently roll off onto the blanket. When he hit the scratchy wool, he saw her sweaty face with worry clearly written all over it.

"Don't worry, Liz. It's not the first time somebody's broken my head."

"Oh, Grady."

He would have sworn he saw a tear snake down her cheek, but it would mean someone was crying for him. Impossible really.

Everything went black.

Eliza pressed her forehead into the cool grass as she got her breath back. Grady was a lot heavier than he looked, not that she had any experience carrying unconscious men around. For a few moments there, she thought she'd collapse on the ground, flattened by his weight, and suffocate.

She had a mental image of the sheriff finding them both dead on the trail and feeling smug over his mistreatment of them. Eliza sucked in a deep breath and pushed away the silly thoughts floating around in her mind.

Grady needed her help. For the second time that day, *he* needed *her*. It was a different twist to their already strange relationship. Although she didn't want him to be wounded or in need of rescuing, somewhere deep inside her, she felt a spark of pride flare to life. Someone needed her.

Her back had already been in rough shape after the days of riding, and carrying Grady even ten feet had strained the muscles even further. As she got to her feet and straightened up, she groaned as a sharp stab of pain sounded through her. She never had this type of pain before, but she knew stretching would help.

After forcing herself to use her over-used muscles, she felt a margin better. Not riding for a day or two would be even more helpful, but she knew that wasn't likely to happen. As soon as Grady could sit on the horse, they'd be on their way. Eliza knew she'd go with him, and because the end result would be finding Angeline, her sore muscles meant nothing.

She retrieved the first-aid supplies from the bundled package on his horse and returned to his prone form. Other than to turn his head to the side so he could breathe, she hadn't moved him. He was unconscious again, which didn't bode well for his head injury. From what she'd read, forceful blows to the head could cause a concussion, which if left untreated, could be fatal. Grady couldn't die, he *wouldn't* die in her care. She had to find Angeline, no matter what, and well, she honestly didn't want him to die. She'd come to like Grady, to enjoy verbally sparring with him, not to mention kissing him.

After successfully starting a fire, and grinning stupidly at the little flames, she retrieved freshwater from the stream. With the shiny new pot, she boiled the water, then set it aside to cool a bit. The medical supplies included bandages, carbolic acid, and needle and thread. Since she held to Dr. Lister's theories on keeping patients healthy, she also used the carbolic acid to sanitize her hands, then finally settled down beside Grady.

His breathing was even, which was a good sign. She managed to roll him over onto his back, never forgetting for a second she had her hands on him. He was so warm to the touch, so alive. It was almost as if she couldn't stop touching him once she started. Eliza had spent most of her life being physically kept separate from other people, with the exception of Angeline, but even then they did not even embrace.

Grady had touched her so many times the past couple of days he'd become familiar to her body, to her hands. She ran her hands up and down his body, looking for breaks and other injuries. He moaned when she touched the right side of his ribs, likely bruised by fists or perhaps shoes.

His face and head had suffered the worst of the beating. His lip was split with coagulated blood in the wound, yet it was still seeping and would require stitches. Both eyes were swollen and bruised, as were both cheeks. There was a gash at the hairline above his right eye and a large lump above his left ear, which had dried blood crusted on it. That was the injury that had caused the loss of consciousness, she was sure of it.

"If you're done taking advantage of me, I'd appreciate a drink of water."

His voice startled her so badly she lost her balance and fell forward onto him. A soft oof popped out of his mouth as she pushed on his already sore ribs.

"Oh, Grady, I'm so sorry." She scrambled back up onto her knees and peered down at his battered face. "How are you feeling?"

"Like I fell off a horse, then got stomped by it." He tried to lick his lips and flinched when his tongue touched the open wound. "Shit."

"Let me get you that water." She opened the canteen before holding the back of his head and dribbling some into his mouth.

"I'm not a baby, Liz. Give me a goddamn drink already." He obviously felt a bit better if he was cursing at her.

"I can't give you too much or you may vomit. I believe you have a concussion, so we need to take care of your injuries." Eliza felt calm, but her heart still raced as she touched him, the person she'd been closer to than any other in her life. And he was the bounty hunter after her sister, the person she loved the most. What a tangle.

"What's a concussion?" His words were a bit slurred.

"It's what happens after a heavy blow to the head. It can cause dizziness, nausea, and unconsciousness. You also have a large bump above your ear caused by the scalp's veins leaking blood into and under the scalp. It may take days or even weeks to completely go down." She recited the medical text as fresh as the day she'd read it. Then of course she'd never met someone who'd been kicked in the head.

"Oh, that's happy news. And here I thought I just needed a nap after the sheriff and the bastard bartender beat the shit out of me." He swallowed more water, then met her gaze. "I've never been in debt to a woman before, but thanks for what you did."

Eliza felt her cheeks warm at his thanks. Not many people said thank you where she grew up, and if they did, it wasn't sincere. Grady was more than sincere; he grudgingly thanked her, which meant he was being truthful and grateful.

"You're welcome. We, um, are traveling together and I want to contribute to our success." Again, she sounded so awkward, tripping over her words like a fool. One day she might be able to sound like a normal woman.

He frowned, then winced again. "You talk so odd, woman. I wish you'd just get on with the tending."

Eliza inwardly cringed, after he said out loud what she'd been thinking. What she should do was listen to how he spoke and then mimic the cadence of his speech. She should have thought of it sooner. First she needed to tend to his medical needs.

"I need to wash and sanitize your wounds; then I'll stitch your lip. All of this is going to cause you pain. I mean, it'll hurt a lot." Eliza managed a small smile and was rewarded with what she was beginning to refer to as a "Grady frown."

"Understood, just do what you gotta do."

She set up the bandages and antiseptic on a clean cloth.

With a silent apology knowing she was about to cause him more pain, she cleaned his face with the hot water, paying special attention to the open wounds. He gritted his teeth, but didn't make a peep even when she put carbolic acid on the cuts.

After cleaning the needle and thread in hot water, she dipped it in the antiseptic. Although she'd sewn enough fabric to clothe ten people, she'd never stitched skin. The thought that she was about to pierce Grady's skin made goose bumps dance up and down her skin.

Eliza closed her eyes and thought about what could happen to him if she didn't stitch his lip. When she opened her eyes again, she felt prepared to do what she needed to. With surprisingly steady hands, she stitched his lip as if it were the seam of a very delicate fabric.

Each time the needle went through, she bit her own lip. She was causing someone else pain, a practice she had always strived to avoid. Yet she held fast to her science and her ideals, and did what she had to.

By the time she'd finished, his frown had disappeared and his gaze unfocused. He reached up and touched her lip.

"Don't hurt yourself, Liz. I sure as hell ain't worth it."

She managed to chuckle, although inside she knew exactly what he felt. It was what she always felt as well. Perhaps she and Grady were more alike than she thought. His touch made butterflies dance in her stomach.

"Kiss me before I change my mind." He sounded pained, as though he didn't want to kiss her, but rather *needed* to kiss her.

"But your lip." She didn't want to cause him any further pain.

"To hell with my lip." Grady tugged at her hair, pulling loose a long lock from the simple bun at the back of her head. He curled his hand around the long raven strands. "Softest thing I've ever felt."

Eliza felt their relationship shift at that moment, and the

earth moved beneath her. She was beginning to have feelings for Grady, and it frightened her more than riding alone across the Utah prairie.

Regardless of her fear, she bent down and kissed him softly on the left side of his lip. He groaned deep in his throat, and an answering howl sounded within her. This was arousal, lust, animal heat swirling around them.

It was positively exhilarating.

Her breasts pushed against his chest, making the nipples peak at the delicious friction between them. His hand reached up and cupped one, and the memory of his touch slid through her. She had been half awake the last time, but she was completely awake now.

"God, you taste good." He breathed into her mouth and she swallowed his breath into her own. "Let me see you, Liz, show me."

Eliza had never been closer to another person before, emotionally, physically, or in any other way. His heat surrounded her, enveloped her.

She hesitated only a moment before she unbuttoned her shirtwaist and was soon naked from the waist up. As she straddled his prone form, his eyes darkened as they roamed over her breasts. The dark pink nipples were tight to the point of nearly pain, but she recognized it as a need to be touched. Eliza was new to being aroused and tried to keep her scientific side in check to savor every second.

Grady reached up with both hands and traced the outline of her areole. She shivered at the contact of his callused skin against the delicate skin of her breast. It shouldn't send shivers through her, or make her body heat, yet it did.

There was something connecting the two of them together. She had no experience with anything like this, so she more or less let her emotions and instincts guide her. It was a unique experience, one she was unsure she'd ever have again.

Eliza gasped as Grady pinched her nipple. A jolt zipped through her, landing right between her legs.

She closed her eyes. "Oh, my."

A rusty chuckle sounded from below her. "Oh, my is right. Damn, girl, you have beautiful tits."

She'd never heard the word before, except from Grady of course, and the coarseness of it made the sensations that much more heightened. Eliza admitted to herself she was thoroughly enjoying the naughty aspect of what she was doing with the man.

"You have a beautiful touch."

"First time I heard that."

"Me, too."

He laughed again. "Let me taste them." He tugged at her waist until she was dangling above his mouth.

"Be careful of your lip."

"You stitched it up so tight, ain't nothing gonna happen to my mouth." Grady continued to pinch one nipple while the other grew ever closer to his mouth.

Eliza didn't know what to expect, but it wasn't the hot, wet heat that nearly overwhelmed her as he tasted her. She held her breath while his tongue swirled around the turgid peak and he sucked her into his mouth.

"Good gracious." She dug her nails into his shoulders. A heavy pulse started through her, pulling her deeper into the pool of sensations she could barely swim in.

"You taste like sunshine and woman." He was quite a poet, surprisingly enough.

"You feel like sunshine and man." Eliza didn't know what she was saying, so she decided to stop trying and simply enjoy his touch.

"Shut up, Liz." He said it gently, with an affection she hadn't heard before.

"Gladly, just don't stop what you're doing. I'm thoroughly enjoying it."

His warm breath gusted against her skin. "I plan on it."

She felt his cock hardening beneath her, and she wanted to feel more than that. As a woman knows a man, as a lover knows another. Eliza hadn't planned on copulating with Grady, but now she couldn't imagine not.

As she closed her eyes and enjoyed the sensations, his hand slid away, then his mouth was slack on her nipple. Popping one eye open, she looked down to find him unconscious again. "Phooey."

Grady woke with a pounding headache, but the dizziness and urge to vomit were gone. It was dark and the embers of the fire the only source of light around them. He was lying on the bedroll on his back, with a warm form pressed up against his right side, the fire on his left.

Eliza was shivering; that's what woke him up. She'd been sleeping between him and the fire, but obviously because he was injured, she swapped places with him. Grady wouldn't have done that for her, at least he didn't think he would have. The woman had him turned topsy-turvy.

He felt better, stronger than he had after the beating. She was a damn good nurse, his little wren. Grady sat up and poked the fire until the flames started up again, then he put a few more pieces of wood on it.

"Time for you to warm up, Liz." He scooped her up and set her closer to the fire.

She immediately rolled over and faced the fire with a contented sigh. Grady liked the sound of it, like a sweet candy rush on his tongue. He laid down behind her and spooned up against her.

Apparently not the best idea, because as soon as he was touching her, his body reacted. Strongly. His blood began pulsing through his veins, through his ears, through his balls and dick. Suddenly he was hot, more than hot, burning.

Why did he react so strongly to her? She wasn't pretty or even well put together, although her tits were fantastic. Did she actually dangle them over his mouth? It was a hazy memory, but it was there. He must have been hit on the head harder than he thought, because he would have taken her if he'd been himself.

Grady couldn't explain if asked what his fascination with Eliza was. Something about her, though, called to him at the deepest level, pulled him to her until he was helpless to stop his reaction.

He nuzzled her hair, breathing in her scent even as he inched closer to her, until he was flush against her soft, curvy form. God, he wanted her so badly. He was harder than an oak branch, straining against the buttons of his trousers.

Grady shouldn't bother her when she was sleeping, if at all, but he couldn't seem to help himself. The more she made little noises when he touched her, the more he had to keep touching her. He unbuttoned her blouse, pleased to find her undergarment bunched up, and her sweet breast completely unfettered. He couldn't help but groan as the soft skin filled his hand. The nipple reached for his palm, begging him to be tweaked.

When he pinched it, she sucked in a breath; that's when he knew she was awake. He was almost embarrassed, like a kid caught with his hand in the cookie jar, or tittie jar in this case.

"This is familiar." Her voice was hoarse from sleep. "I remember how lovely it was to wake up with your hands on me."

He figured that meant she wanted more, which was a good thing because he didn't think he could stop this time.

Eliza rolled onto her back and faced him. Her blue eyes glittered darkly in the firelight. She reached up and ran a finger down his cheek, then along the seam of his lips.

His tongue snaked out to lick the meandering digit. He smiled at the expression on her face, the way her lips parted in surprise. There was only one thing to do.

He covered his mouth with hers, fusing them into a hot mesh of lips, tongue, and teeth. She opened readily for him, dancing with his tongue even as his hand continued to pleasure her breast. The nipple was like a pink diamond in his hand.

She moaned sweetly in her throat as he moved to the other breast while he pushed his aching staff against her soft hip. They kissed for what seemed like hours, learning each other, learning themselves.

He pulled back long enough to get a breath, since he was getting light-headed.

She surprised the hell out of him by reaching down to cup him. Her small hand had strength he didn't expect, and it felt more than good.

He lapped at her, teasing her swollen lips, until her tongue did the same to him. Grady couldn't help but wonder what that tongue would feel like on his dick.

He grew about an inch just thinking about it.

"God, Liz, I can't . . . if you want to stop this, it's gotta be now or I'm going to fuck you." Better to be honest than not. She had to know what she was in for if they continued.

To his disappointment she sat up, and his entire body howled in denial. Damn, he'd have to go get himself off to get any sleep. Instead of leaving him horny and hard, she stood and slowly undressed, revealing alabaster skin in the moonlight on one side and golden warm skin in the firelight on the other.

Grady almost forgot his name.

Like a green kid having sex for the first time, he clumsily took off his boots first, although the right one got stuck and he thought about cutting his foot off. Fortunately he didn't have to and it came off, followed quickly by all his clothes.

She stood there, watching, with her deliciously curvy, delightfully naked body with its pink diamond nipples and dark triangle between her legs, beckoning him. Grady could hardly believe she wanted to do this with him now, but he wasn't about to refuse the gift.

He ran his hands down her soft shoulders and arms until their hands met. She smiled and reached up to kiss him, then surprised the shit out of him by licking his nipples.

He almost jumped out of his skin when her wet tongue pleasured his tiny nubs.

She looked up at him with concern. "Is this wrong?"

Grady choked on his own spit. "No, honey, it's not wrong. I was just surprised is all."

"It feels so good when you do it, I thought you might like it, too."

She was so childlike at that moment, unlike the brisk schoolmarm who was so matter-of-fact all the time. He liked this Eliza, the sensual siren who came out at night and into his arms.

"I did like it." He dropped to his knees. "And I'm going to do the same to you."

Eliza trembled as he held her waist steady and leaned forward to capture a nipple in his mouth. God, she was like honey, all sweet and hot, melting on his tongue. She made another kittenish moan, and his dick slapped her leg.

"He's hungry."

"So am I." Her response nearly made him stop what he was doing and throw her on the ground.

The only thing that stopped him was the notion it would be over way too soon. Grady wanted to enjoy every second for as long as he could.

He sucked her breast into his mouth, pulling and tugging until she filled him, then released her with a pop. He nibbled the hard bud, then licked it. His other hand crept down to her pussy.

She was wet.

That's when Grady knew she was as eager as he was. The truth was, he'd never been with a woman he didn't have to use his spit to moisten.

Eliza was wet enough for him to slide in to the hilt, to bury himself inside her until he forgot where he ended and she began.

Without another thought, he scooped her up and put her

down on the bedroll. Her legs opened for him and her center glistened in the firelight.

"God, you're beautiful."

"No need to flatter me, Grady. I'm yours."

He wanted to tell her it wasn't flattery, that he truly did believe she was beautiful. The most gorgeous thing he'd ever seen, lying there with her dark hair fanned out behind her, eyes darkened with arousal, her pale skin glowing in the moonlight, and her sweet cunny ready for him.

He couldn't imagine anything more beautiful than her at that moment.

Her arms reached up to pull him toward her, and he lost his balance, landing on her too hard. She laughed and opened her legs wider. Far from being embarrassed, Grady was trying to remember his fucking name as his dick pressed up against her wet flesh.

He braced himself properly and watched her face as he inched inside her slowly. Truthfully he wanted to get in so badly he was trembling, but for their first time together, he needed to take his time.

He went in an inch, then he pulled out and went in two inches. When he reached three, he realized there was something in his way.

She was a goddamn virgin.

"Liz, what the hell?"

"Please, Grady, don't stop." Before he could react, she grabbed his ass and pulled him so hard, he was completely inside her.

For a moment, he was unable to speak or even take a breath. She was so tight, so hot, so amazingly perfect, he lost the ability to do anything but close his eyes.

She didn't make a sound, no protests, no moan of pain, nothing. When he'd gotten his senses back, he opened his eyes and looked at her. Her expression was one of curiosity and unbelievably, arousal. Then she smiled and Grady knew everything was going to be all right.

"It's . . . so big."

He barked a laugh, but couldn't tell her that's what every man wanted to hear. His body commanded him to move.

"You ready, Liz?"

She reached up and pinched his nipples. "Yes, Grady, I'm ready."

He pulled out just a little, then slid back in, giving her time to get used to the movements, the sensations.

"Faster please."

Obviously he didn't need to go slow. Heeding Eliza's request, he began moving faster, pumping in and out of her pussy. She clenched around him with each thrust, squeezing him like a fist.

Her face displayed a myriad of emotions, from surprise to pleasure to beyond bliss. He reached down and touched her clit, rubbing the pleasure button between his fingers.

Her face lit up. "Oh, my."

Grady knew he wouldn't last much longer, his balls tightened as his release drew closer. He wanted Eliza to experience what he did, or at least try to anyway.

He pleasured her clit as his speed picked up. She started making all kinds of noises, likely scaring all the critters away, and he loved it. Her exclamations of pleasure echoed through him, made him go faster, deeper within her.

She screamed his name and bucked beneath him, squeezing his dick so much he came immediately. The orgasm whooshed through him so quickly he almost blacked out from the intensity of it. She scratched at his back as small yelps continued to pop out of her mouth.

Grady shuddered as the waves of pleasure rippled through him, then when he could get control of himself, he leaned down and kissed her hard, their tongues dueling in mimicry of their coupling.

"Oh, my," she repeated.

Grady rolled off her and lay beside her on his bedroll. "Holy shit."

Chapter Seven

Grady watched the sun rise as Eliza slept beside him. He hadn't meant to touch her, certainly hadn't met to take her, but he had anyway. It was beyond the crude act of fucking that had become the only human contact he had.

Eliza destroyed the vow he'd made to himself long ago. He didn't want to like her, but damned if he did. She was smarter than any person he'd ever met, that was for damn sure. Not only had the woman saved him from jail, but she'd also doctored him better than any sawbones.

She talked funny, was awkward and clumsy, but liquid sweetness in his arms.

Grady had to focus on his quarry, finding the woman he'd been paid to hunt down. It was his first time hunting a woman, and the experience was hard enough. Eliza was distracting him, and he had to do something about it. What he could do, he sure as hell didn't know aside from leaving her behind.

After all she'd done, it would be the lowest of the low to abandon her. It sounded easy, but the damn woman had woken up his long-slumbering conscience, not to mention his primal urges. He certainly didn't want all of it to happen, but it had and there was no going back.

In fact, he'd tried to leave her behind, and she had shown him exactly what she was made of and tracked him. Eliza would likely do the same thing if he left her again, and he'd ride with her ghost beside him.

Like it or not, he was stuck with her. And he didn't know anything about her other than she read too much and knew a hell of a lot about the Bible.

Grady had to know more. He'd stake his life that she was hiding something, otherwise she would have let more information out about herself. He was skilled enough in reading people to know she was lying, the question was why.

While she slept with a child's innocence snugly in her bedroll, he walked over on not quite steady legs to her horse. The poor thing had faithfully toted her damn heavy bags strapped to its saddle. It was a sturdy, faithful horse considering how much Eliza put the thing through.

Grady checked on both horses, then got to the business he needed to take care of. He'd looked through her bags before for weapons, but this time he looked for details about Just Miss Eliza.

He looked through the dozen book titles, some of which he couldn't pronounce. It was no wonder she knew so much about stuff if she'd read these complicated books. He had a limited education, more or less what he learned up to the age of twelve. After that his learning was done with guns.

Tucked away in a piece of fabric at the corner of the bag was a slate with chalk, a half-full journal, quills, and an ink bottle. Who took something to write with on a journey? Or maybe she was planning on staying wherever she traveled to. If that were the case, there would be more than a few articles of clothing, which were barely rags.

The purchases she'd made in town would double her wardrobe. He knew she felt guilty about spending money, and he understood why. Whoever had been taking care of Eliza didn't have two nickels to rub together or didn't care if she wore rags. Either way, she had next to nothing, except the books of course.

The journal intrigued him. Most times he let people keep

their secrets, but considering just how tangled they'd gotten, her privacy didn't mean spit. He needed to know more.

Grady looked over his shoulder and made sure Eliza slept on before he took the journal from the bag. He walked over to the boulder near the horses and sat down. If he was lucky, she didn't use fancy words he couldn't understand.

It felt as if he was peeking into her business, and damned if a smidge of guilt didn't creep across his shoulders. Grady shrugged it aside and opened the book. At first he didn't know what he was looking at, but then he realized it was a drawing of something with measurements and numbers. She had terrible handwriting judging by the chicken scratch next to the drawing.

He flipped a few more pages and found drawing after drawing, along with notes. It took him a dozen pages before he recognized what he was looking at.

Eliza was an inventor, by God. Each of the drawings depicted some kind of gadget and the notes detailed her tests. He could almost hear her speaking as he read some of them.

> *The gasket didn't perform well against the heat.*
>
> *Need to find another material to form a seal.*
>
> *The mechanism won't function correctly without it.*

She spoke the same way she wrote, so he knew for certain Eliza wasn't pretending to be someone she wasn't. The fact she was some kind of inventor had never crossed his mind. What the hell was she doing out in the middle of nowhere by herself? The woman needed to be at home with a husband and babies.

Then the picture of her at home with those babies made his jaw clench. She didn't belong there and he knew it. Eliza was as different as he was, standing out from everyone around her, singled out as unnatural. He could tell that by reading her invention journal.

Who the hell was Eliza? She obviously never had a husband, which would explain why she was still a virgin, or was until last night when he'd taken her on the hard Utah ground. Obviously the journal was important to her, a collection of her life's thoughts. Not many women had the brains or the education to think of even a handful of her inventions, much less a book full. His instincts told him she'd run from somebody or something—maybe a bastard who stuffed her into a corner and made her into something she wasn't. And she'd run because she wanted more than a simple existence allotted to women.

Grady didn't want to feel a kinship with her, but damned if he didn't. He wasn't someone who did what was expected, followed the straight and narrow path by rote, or listened to how he was "supposed" to live his life. He chose what he did, when he did it, and how he did it. Eliza may not have gone as far as he did, but she was obviously just as constrained by the role she played.

Grady closed the journal and rose to return the book to the bag. Eliza stood there fully dressed with her hands folded in front her and a frown on her face.

"I, uh, wanted to see. Ah, hell, I was just being nosy." He didn't want to feel embarrassed; it was a weakness he refused to acknowledge.

"I understand. May I have my journal back please? It's quite precious to me." She held out her hand without meeting his gaze.

Grady reluctantly walked over and set the journal in her hand. That's when he noticed her hands were trembling and she was pale as milk.

"You okay, Liz?"

She managed a shaky smile. "I find myself in uncharted territory."

He knew exactly what she meant.

"Are you hungry? I can make some food with the supplies we managed to get. You should be sitting down and resting based upon your injuries. And how is your lip?" She talked so fast he had trouble keeping up with her words. "Never mind, just sit down and I'll get the fire going again so we can eat."

He watched as she ran around gathering new kindling, poking the embers of the fire, then running to the saddlebags to get the cook pot. Then to the creek for water and back to the fire to poke at the embers again.

"Liz, what the hell are you doing?"

She stopped, startled and looking for all the world like a rabbit in the hunter's sights. "Making breakfast."

"You want to tell me why you're doing it like you're in a race?" He sat down and ignored the slight dizziness at the sudden motion. Damn head kick stole some of his strength.

"I find myself somewhat embarrassed about my behavior." Her cheeks flared pink. "I'm afraid you'll think me a loose woman based on how I threw myself at you."

Grady raised one brow. "You didn't throw yourself at me. What we do ain't no one's business but ours."

She stopped her manic work and stared, her eyes wide. "I've never done anything like this before. I mean, being with a man like you, well not like you, but someone who I've known less than a week." Eliza blew out a breath and covered her face with her hand. "I am a complete moron."

Grady snorted. "First of all, you had never been with a man before. Second if there's one person in this world who isn't a moron, that'd be you. You're the smartest person I've ever met, woman."

"Really?" She sounded so hopeful, so full of doubt, he again wondered just who'd been beating her down. He felt the insane urge to beat them down.

"I could hardly read most of what you wrote, and sometimes half of what you say makes my brain hurt. Yeah, I'm sure." He pulled a cheroot from his pocket and lit it, pulling in a drag as he watched her reaction.

"I, well, then. I don't know what to say other than thank you." She fiddled with the kindling in her hand. "I haven't had much support from others for my work except for Ephraim."

"Was that your husband?" He watched her face carefully as she reacted to his question.

"He was my teacher, my friend, my mentor. I miss him." A suspicious sheen twinkled from behind her spectacles, but she looked away so fast, he couldn't quite get a good look.

"But not your husband?" He pushed again.

She shook her head. "No, but I lost him almost a year ago and my life hasn't been the same."

Again, he believed everything she said. That meant she was running from somebody else, someone who likely beat her for using her brain. Maybe her father, which wouldn't surprise him in the least. Many men didn't cotton to their wives or daughters getting too smart.

"Your life sure is different now, isn't it?"

Her head snapped up, and she stared at him for a minute before the corners of her mouth twitched. "It couldn't be more different. An adventure to tell my grandchildren I think."

Grandchildren meant children, which meant husband. That image invaded Grady's mind again, and he pushed it away with a growl. Ridiculous how he got Eliza stuck in his head. Stupid even.

"What shall I tell them about you?"

Grady stopped and stared at her, wondering why it took her so long to ask and what he was going to tell her. "I keep my business to myself."

She shrugged and looked down at the little fire. "You know my business and why I'm traveling west. I thought you might want to provide me with similar information."

He wanted to tell her to go to hell, but he owed her something. "I'm looking for somebody."

"Your family?"

"No, just somebody I got paid to find." He wasn't sure how much to tell her. Truthfully he wanted to tell her nothing, that way she didn't pose a risk to his work.

"Can I assist you with your search?"

He still had trouble getting used to the way she talked. Woman sounded so odd to him.

"No. Just don't get in the way."

She nodded. "I will do my best not to get in your way."

Eliza almost shrank into herself so blatantly he could see it. He didn't want to take the place of whomever the bastard was that had beat her down whether with fists or words.

"That's not what I meant. I don't want you getting hurt because of my business, that's all." He fiddled with the cheroot, watching the orange tip as the smoke gently curled up from it.

Eliza smiled softly. "I appreciate your concern for my well-being. As I said I will do my best to stay out of your business."

He was struck again by how lovely she was. Most times she hid behind the spectacles, the ugly-as-shit clothes, and the fancy talk. Eliza was much more than the things she hid behind.

Eliza was still worried Grady wasn't ready to travel, so she convinced him to stay put until after dinner. He needed a few more hours to rest; although he seemed to be okay, he'd had a concussion. Aside from that she wanted to stay in their little hideaway longer than just a day, but she understood his need to be on his way.

He was looking for Angeline and she had to accompany him or lose her sister, and Grady, for good. They kept going west, and Eliza determined he was following a lead he must have gotten in Bellman. At least they'd gotten supplies and information in the den of small-minded bullies.

She'd never felt so angry as when she saw what they'd done to Grady. People in her ward at home did their beatings in private, and it stayed that way no matter who did the deed. The sheriff had thought nothing of leaving Grady in a dire physical condition and bleeding profusely. She wanted to ride back there and slap the men who'd hurt her Grady.

The very idea of thinking of Grady as hers sent a silly shiver through Eliza. He wasn't hers by any means and the act of copulating with him only bonded them physically, for a brief moment of pure bliss. He owed her nothing but had given her so much.

Eliza was afraid to admit even to herself that she'd fallen just a bit in love with the bounty hunter. He was short tempered, cursed quite a bit, and generally seemed to dislike everyone. Yet, she'd seen a side of him he didn't show most people. He'd been complimentary of her intelligence, and she didn't think he was merely being kind.

Grady was not the kind of person to be disingenuous, that was for certain. It meant he truly did respect her brain. Her! Eliza Hunter, the disappointment to her father and the entire church, was respected for her intelligence rather than her cooking.

It was positively liberating and left a smile on her face to accompany the twinges in her body as she adjusted to being a fallen woman.

She'd never had a better day.

"What are you doing?"

Eliza glanced up to see Grady scowling at her. "I decided to avoid singeing my hand on the open fire any longer and have been working on a device to assist me."

He sipped his coffee. "You don't want to get burned so you're making something for the fire?"

"That's correct." She held up some strips of leather from her traveling bag. "These will allow me to fashion a handle on the pan." She held up pieces of metal from the bottom of the bag. "And these will be a grate for the pan to sit on."

As she worked to fit the pieces together, he was quiet. Eliza always seemed better at thinking of inventions rather than building them. Her hands weren't strong enough to put the pieces of metal together in a lattice pattern.

On the fourth attempt, she nearly fell into the fire.

"Jesus Christ, woman. Give me the damn thing." Grady snatched the pieces from her and made quick work of a rather nice lattice pattern. "Is this what you wanted?"

Eliza told herself not to blush, not to look away as if she were embarrassed. "Yes, that's exactly what I was attempting to do. Thank you, Grady." She took the new grate back from him, pleased with the result.

As Eliza wrapped the thinnest leather strips around the grate to keep it secured, he picked up her journal and looked at the page with the drawing of the device. She wanted to take it from him, make him stop looking at what she'd invented, but she didn't. It wasn't as if they were the secrets of the universe; there was no need to be so childish about keeping them as such.

"Looks like a good idea." He glanced at the other strips of leather. "But I think if you braided these before you put them on the handle, they'd stay on better."

Eliza was startled, to say the least, because he was correct and because he had thought of something she hadn't. "You're an inventor, too."

He snorted. "Not hardly, just been on the trail too long with burnt hands." Grady picked up the leather and started braiding the strips.

Eliza could hardly believe it, truth be told. He was a bounty hunter, a man who made his living hunting other human beings, yet he sat beside her on the ground making a grate and handle for the cooking.

As she finished securing the grate together, he had already completed his task and was examining the handle of the pan. She set the grate down and picked up the braided leather. It was perfectly even and tightly done.

"This is marvelous work, Grady. I don't think I could have done a better job."

He narrowed his gaze. "I don't cotton to people talking down to me."

"I most certainly was not talking down to you. Your assistance with this invention is proving invaluable. I was being completely forthright with you." She bristled as if he'd insulted her rather than the other way around. Silly how she reacted to everything he said in the opposite way she should.

He watched her for another few minutes before he nodded. "Okay then, thanks."

"And please accept my thanks for your contribution. Now if you'll hold the pan, I'll secure the end and begin wrapping the braid around the handle."

Somewhat grudgingly, he picked up the pan and held it so the handle faced her. Eliza began tying the end knot and he harrumphed at her.

"That ain't no knot. It won't hold more than a day." He thrust the pan in her hands. "You hold this and I'll show you how to tie a knot."

Grady's font of knowledge was far greater than she suspected. He was actually patient as he taught her the intricacies of tying a secure knot. Although his hands were callused, his fingers were dexterous and strong enough to secure the leather braid to the pan.

She vowed to attempt knot tying later when he wasn't looking.

Grady finished wrapping the braid around the handle, then tied it to the hole on the end. "There, now stop fussing with the thing and make some supper."

Eliza examined the handle carefully. "This is quite marvelous work. You are a man of many talents."

His gaze glittered in the fading twilight. "You have no idea."

She shivered, although it was still quite warm outside. His insinuation was clear enough to even her untrained ears. She shouldn't be surprised; after all, she'd given herself to him already.

"Now let's see if we can make good use of our good ideas." She managed a smile, which he did not return, but his gaze slid to the pan and she thought she saw a spark of pride. It was probably something he didn't feel very often. Perhaps she should share her ideas for inventions with him more often.

Eliza made dinner using the ham she'd purchased at the store. The handle worked marvelously well, and she was able to move the pan to the grate at the side of the firepit when the ham was cooked. It served as a wonderful resting spot for the hot pan.

As they ate the ham and the canned peaches and drank coffee, the sun warmed up the air around them. She closed her eyes and listened to the wind and leaves, strangely at peace in the middle of nowhere with only a gruff bounty hunter for company.

Eliza couldn't remember the last time she'd been so content and wondered if it was because she was away from her father's heavy hand or because she was with Grady. She couldn't decide which idea appealed to her more.

After Eliza's careful cajoling, Grady agreed to wait until the next morning before leaving. She was glad of it, and although they didn't repeat their sexual encounter from the night before, both of them got plenty of sleep.

Eliza made only coffee for breakfast, and they started riding just as dawn broke. The cold morning air made her glad she'd drank the hot, bitter coffee. The saddle felt only marginally uncomfortable, which was a miracle since she had been simply miserable on it when she left Tolson. Apparently she'd toughened up her backside.

They stopped at a ranch just after dinnertime. It seemed to be a small cattle ranch in a valley with rich grass and bountiful resources. The sign over the porch, which was well swept, read DOUBLE B. It was a well-maintained property, which meant the owners had pride in their land.

A young woman poked her head out the door. "What do you want?"

Grady tipped his hat. "Looking to refill our canteens and set a spell to give our horses a break."

She peered at them from the shadows, first looking at Eliza, then at Grady. "That your wife?"

"Yes'm. This here is Eliza, and my name's Grady Wolfe. We're traveling to my kin over in Raymer Falls." Grady had gentled his tone. He definitely knew how to modify his ways for a softer audience.

"The men are in the corral. You're welcome to use the well pump out yonder." She closed the door before they could respond.

"Am I to assume I'll be introduced as Mrs. Wolfe while we travel together?" Eliza felt a little tickle in her throat when she said the inexact title out loud.

He grunted. "You have a problem with that?"

"No, I don't, but I thought perhaps we should discuss a decision like that or I might say something inappropriate. Particularly considering we are on our way to visit family." She sounded a bit breathless, as if she'd been running beside the horse instead of on his back.

"Good point. I ain't used to traveling with anybody." He dismounted and secured his horse to the hitching post. "Normally I just do what I need to without 'discussing a decision.'"

She'd venture a guess that Grady didn't tell anyone about his business. It was likely a result of being a bounty hunter and working alone for so long.

"That's a logical conclusion. I'd be happy to do whatever I can to assist you in your quest for the person you're looking for." She managed to disentangle her foot from the right stirrup, but before she could get off the horse, he was there plucking her off as if he hadn't had a concussion twenty-four hours earlier. "You shouldn't be lifting heavy objects."

He scoffed. "You're not heavy. Jesus, my saddle weighs more than you."

Grady set her on the ground, and they were standing together between the horses. His heat again reached out to her, and she closed her eyes, reveling in the sensation of being so close to another human being.

"You keep leaning into me like that and I'm going to think you didn't make a mistake with me." He touched her cheek with two fingers, running them lightly up and down the sensitive skin.

"That was no mistake."

His hand stopped at her whisper. Her heart kicked into a steady, thumping rhythm. She swore she could hear his beating in unison with hers.

"Can I help you folks?"

The man's voice made Eliza jump nearly a foot. She bumped into the horse, careened into Grady, then landed on the ground with a painful clack of her teeth.

"Jesus please us, Liz, are you okay?" Grady held out his hand and pulled her back onto her feet.

"Yes, I believe so." She rubbed her sore behind while she tasted the tang of blood from her tongue, which had unfortunately gotten trapped between her teeth.

They turned to find a man with a face that could have been twenty or forty, lined with years in the sun. He wore a blue shirt and brown trousers with his pant legs tucked firmly into his boots, which were covered in what appeared to be horse excrement.

"We just wanted to get some water for the horses and canteens." Grady put his arm around Eliza's shoulder.

"You're welcome to what you need." The man's gaze traveled down to Grady's pistols and back. "Where you headed?"

"Raymer Falls to my family. It's a long way, but my mama ain't doing well." Grady was able to tell fabrications at the drop of a hat. Eliza would do well to remember that while she was getting doe eyed over his sexual prowess.

The man studied them for a few seconds before he nodded. "Family's important. Glad to hear you're going to help out." He held out his hand. "Name's Gannon and this here's my little piece of heaven."

Eliza wanted to point out the patch of dirt was certainly not heaven, since she didn't believe it existed. However, the man seemed proud of his ranch and rightly so, it was well kept and seemed to be in good shape.

"Grady Wolfe and this is my wife Eliza."

Eliza smiled, and this time it was genuine. Each time Grady called her "wife" it sounded more natural than the time before.

"Pleased to meet you folks." He rubbed Melba's neck. "You got yourself one old horse here, Wolfe. This old boy ain't long for this world."

"I'll have you know Melba is the finest horse who ever lived." She sounded defensive and silly, but the horse had proven himself to be a stalwart friend to her.

Gannon smiled. "I'm sure he is, ma'am. If you need to visit with a woman, you're welcome to go up to the house. Mary is shy with folks, but she enjoys the company."

Eliza wanted to look at Grady for his permission, but decided against it. She wasn't really his wife and there was no need to ask him anything. No man would ever have a hold over her again—she made her own choices and decisions. She did not need to ask permission from anyone.

"I'd be glad of the female time with another." She stepped away from Grady and felt the barest hesitation in his arm before he let her go.

She headed for the house, leaving her "husband" to find out whatever information he could about Angeline. Exactly what she was planning on doing with Mrs. Gannon.

Grady wanted to snatch her by the collar and drag her back to his side. Of course, he had no right to and certainly didn't want to act the fool in front of the rancher.

What the hell would possess him to want to keep Eliza next to him was a mystery. She likely needed some time with another woman—maybe to ask a question or two about what had happened with him. Ladies were open like that with each other, made his feet get to walking.

"You have some trouble along the way?" Gannon eyed Grady's stitched lip and bruises.

"Ah, couple fellas in a town we went through decided I needed to meet their feet and fists." Grady touched the stitches, still amazed at how neatly Eliza had worked on him. "Eliza patched me up."

"She's good at it. Wish Mary had that kind of steady hand. She's a bit soft when it comes to blood." Gannon gestured to the canteens. "How about we get the water you folks need?"

"Much obliged." Grady walked ahead of the rancher, knowing the man was only protecting his own. After all, Grady was armed with two pistols and a knife. Any man worth his salt would be on his guard.

They walked around the side of the house to the pump marking the well. It was painted bright blue and shone like a beacon in the midday sun.

"You want to make sure you can see the pump in the dark?"

Gannon cleared his throat. "Nah, my boy loved the color blue, and after he passed on from a snake bite, the wife painted what she could see from the window blue. Blamed herself for not keeping an eye on him, so this way she always remembers."

Sounded like whipping herself for the rest of her life to Grady. Who was he to judge, though? He lived like that for a long time; then he trained himself to be numb. Maybe one day Mrs. Gannon may learn that lesson herself.

Grady didn't respond, because he didn't know how to. Instead he took hold of the handle and began pumping until the water started gushing out. It was cool and clear fortunately. He filled the canteens quickly, then ducked his head under to get the last of the water and get the dust off his face.

The rancher had moved away to the back of the house to watch him. Grady knew this was his opportunity to find out information about his quarry.

"I was also hoping you might have seen my sister and aunt traveling this way. She headed out a few weeks ago before we knew Mama was sick. Wondered if you might've seen her." Grady leaned against the pump in a relaxed pose.

"Maybe. We see lots of folks passing this way." Gannon pushed the brim of his hat back—a good sign. "What's she look like?"

"Eighteen, blond, pretty. Had to beat the boys off with a stick when she was growing up." Grady based his description on the old man's description only. He hoped like hell the girl was pretty. "My aunt has brown hair, about thirty, kinda plain."

The rancher rubbed his chin, his hand rasping on the whiskers. "There was a couple of ladies riding with Bill Parker last week. Saw them in his wagon headed west. They had hats on, but I remember thinking one of them had shiny blond hair that sparkles in the sun."

Grady's instincts kicked in although he maintained a very casual expression. "That sounds like her."

"Why is she traveling alone with your aunt?"

He expected the question. "She's a stubborn girl and wanted to get to Mama. She wired Pa she was coming and he made sure she had a chaperone, but he ain't heard from her and got worried, asked me to look after them." The lies rolled off his tongue as if the conversation had actually taken place with a concerned father. Little did the man know it was actually a furious husband.

"Sounds like what a pa would do." Gannon nodded. "I'd venture that was likely your sister and aunt I saw."

"You said it was last week?" Grady mentally calculated how far two women would get in a wagon with a rancher. Not too far considering he likely brought them as far as the next town.

"Ayup, it was Monday because that's the day my wife makes bread. I remember the smell of it chased the thoughts out of my head." Gannon smiled, which caused a sharp pain in Grady's chest. The man was obviously infatuated with his wife and it showed.

Grady wanted no part of it. Men who believed in love, who got trapped by love, were nothing but fools and deserved every bit of pain they got. He had no intention of opening himself up to that pain, no matter how stupid a woman might make him.

His mind immediately went to Eliza's expression when she reached her peak beneath him. If there was a female who could make him lose his focus, it might be her. She was the first one to be even more of a mess than he was, and had more courage than most men.

Grady realized the rancher was staring at him and that he'd been completely distracted by thoughts of *her*.

Hell and damnation.

"You fixin' to catch up with your sister and aunt?"

"Maybe, depends on whether we catch up to them before we need to turn north for Raymer Falls." Grady didn't think Gannon suspected anything other than a concerned brother was looking after his little sister.

He knew for certain that if Eliza hadn't been with him, there was no way he'd have been believable. The information may never have been offered, either. Much as he wanted to get some distance between him and Eliza, this only proved to him that he couldn't.

"Appreciate the water and the company. It's been a hard journey on Eliza. She ain't used to being in the saddle that long." Grady raised his brows knowingly.

Gannon laughed. "I can imagine that makes it difficult when you're in the bedroll at night."

The memory of exactly what went on in the bedroll nearly made Grady blush.

*   *   *

Eliza watched Mrs. Gannon as she flitted around the kitchen, seemingly without a specific plan of what she needed to do. Obviously having a stranger in the house made her nervous. She reminded Eliza of herself a bit, in the sense the woman was shy and reserved.

The journey had changed Eliza from an introvert into a woman who would track a man over twenty miles of rough terrain and lose her virginity by a campfire. Oh, no, she was definitely not the same woman who had snuck out of her house in the darkness only days earlier.

"You have a nice home, Mrs. Gannon."

"Mary." The soft-spoken word barely brushed Eliza's ears.

"My name is Eliza. Your curtains are quite lovely." They were a pretty pattern with blue flowers. "Your stitching is so tight and precise."

At this the woman stopped her puttering and looked at Eliza. The tiny woman had round owl-like brown eyes and wavy brown hair. Her heart-shaped face was marred by what Eliza recognized as grief. She felt an immediate connection to the rancher's wife, a shared deep grief over the loss of someone.

"Who did you lose?"

Mary's face drained of color. "I don't know what you mean."

Eliza held out her hands. "It's been almost a year since I lost my best friend, and there isn't a day that goes by that I don't feel the loss."

The other woman took her hands with shaking ones. "It's been a year since I lost my son." Her eyes shone with unshed tears.

"I'm so sorry." Eliza's throat closed up in shared grief.

Against all odds, the two of them embraced briefly, and Eliza found herself connecting with a new friend. A woman she never would have met without setting off on the adventure of a lifetime.

"Thank you, Eliza. I, uh, don't get much company out here.

I'm glad you and your man stopped by." She ducked her head and turned away, obviously uncomfortable.

Your man.

Little Mary Gannon had no idea just how untrue that was. He was no one's man, that much was obvious. Grady lived his life by his own rules and said to hell with everything else. He hadn't left her behind again, and had grudgingly thanked her for the help she'd rendered, but none of that meant he wouldn't pick up and leave her in the dust. Even though he'd been intimate with her and shown her exactly what bliss was like.

Eliza had spent most of her life wishing she were somewhere else, someone else. Here she was fulfilling that wish, and all she could think about was Grady. With all his gruffness and lack of social grace, he had become important to her. She didn't want him to leave her behind, and she had to admit to herself, it wasn't just because of Angeline.

The moment he discovered Eliza had been disingenuous herself, she knew their relationship would be completely over. Grady didn't tolerate liars, and although he might applaud her effort in finding her sister, he would hate Eliza then.

She dreaded that moment as much as she craved finding Angeline.

Chapter Eight

They left the Gannon ranch with full canteens and enough food for supper. Eliza found herself sad to leave Mary behind. She had never made a friend so quickly or one outside the church. Perhaps she may even make it back to the Gannon ranch one day; of course, then she'd have to explain why she had been pretending to be Grady's wife. That would be more than complicated and would likely end the new friendship.

Eliza had to accept the fact she would never see Mary again, which caused more than a twinge of sadness. There had been a bond between them, and that certainly didn't happen very often. She sighed heavily.

"You wanted to stay longer?" Grady didn't turn his head, he simply asked the question almost knowing Eliza's thoughts.

"No, just thinking I won't have the opportunity to see Mary again." She didn't want to explain why.

"Likely not. They were good people, which is why I didn't want to stay longer." Grady's tone was void of emotion, yet Eliza could hear something beneath the words. What it was she didn't know, but she assumed it had something to do with his opinion of himself. Although she would expect him to be confident and self-assured, perhaps he wasn't.

Eliza stayed quiet the rest of the afternoon. She didn't

want to talk or think, so she focused on the terrain. Although born and raised in Utah, she'd spent a good deal of time in a very narrow ten-mile radius. This adventure afforded her the opportunity to see much more. She could tell by the thickening of the trees they were getting closer to the mountains towering in the distance. The snow-capped giants were magnificent.

Grady must have wanted to keep his thoughts private as well because he didn't speak for hours. It was as if they'd come to the point where they were comfortable with each other, something Eliza found nearly unbelievable. Yet she didn't feel the need to fill the silence with inane chatter.

As the sun sank into the horizon, Eliza felt the day begin to slide through her. In its wake, exhaustion followed. The sharp tang of pine and cold temperatures surrounded her. She could hear running water in the distance and hoped Grady would make the choice to stop soon.

The ground beneath them became muddy the nearer they came to the water. In the distance, she spotted dark clouds and determined those had already gone past and left a soaking rain in their wake. She felt lucky they'd missed the rain since her coat wasn't particularly warm and she didn't have a slicker.

As if he read her mind, Grady stopped and dismounted near a grassy clearing. Unfortunately, to get there she'd have to slog through the mud. Her boots were new and she didn't want to ruin them; however, there didn't appear to be a choice. Not normally a squeamish or weak girl, Eliza found herself regretting the likely ruination of her new shoes.

She stopped and watched as Grady peered around the clearing with his right hand resting on a pistol. He took no chances at any point in time. The thought struck her that meant he never actually rested or felt comfortable enough to relax. What a lonely, tense life he led, something she never considered.

"Looks safe enough to stay. There are some tracks here, but they're not fresh." He walked back to the horses as Eliza began to dismount.

Before her feet could touch the mud, he scooped her up, earning a surprised squeak. He grunted as she settled into his arms.

"I'm trying to be a gentleman. I ain't done it much, so I don't know what's right and what's not." He deposited her on the grass, then turned to go back to the horses.

She should say thank you for his considerate act or even for saving her shoes. Yet she stood there watching him like a mute fool. Grady wasn't as mean as he appeared. He was like a cave deep within a mountain. Cold, dark, and forbidding on the outside, yet inside he was full of amazing sights, surprises, and needs. The trick would be to find a way to bring out some of these qualities into the light.

What was she thinking? It wasn't her job to help Grady out of his wall of solitude. She had no right to do so, and he likely would not appreciate the effort.

It didn't mean she didn't dwell on it and sincerely want to tear down that wall. Grady had become a part of her life and as such, she was inexorably linked to him, whether or not he liked it.

"You fixing on standing there the whole night or maybe you could build a fire?" Grady's harsh tone snapped her out of her reverie.

"Oh, you're correct of course. I'll begin now."

"Damn silly talk." He mumbled it, but she heard him anyway. Eliza wished she could relay the words and tone he wouldn't find so uncomfortable. She wanted the two of them to be as natural talking as they'd become when they were silent.

She found some appropriate rocks to build a fire pit, although the grass was wet enough to get the bottom several inches of her skirt wet. Eliza knew she'd have trouble finding dry kindling or firewood. Perhaps there were some places within the canopy of trees that may have escaped the rain.

Leaving the clearing behind her, she ventured into the woods. The sound of the rushing water was louder as it echoed off the pines that densely populated the area. She'd been right about the drier wood and found some to use as she meandered through the forest. As she gathered, her mind drifted to Grady and how she could break through his defenses. She shouldn't, maybe couldn't, but she knew she'd try.

Within a short amount of time, she had an armload of wood to use and felt a certain satisfaction that she'd accomplished a task he'd given her. Then she turned around and realized she was far from the clearing, the trees around her were now shadowed in the murk of twilight, and she had absolutely no idea where she was.

Grady finished unsaddling the horses, then rubbed them down. Luckily the grass was sweet and plentiful in the area, so he secured them at the edge of the clearing to feast. The horses seemed to be getting along well without any biting or fighting. He and Eliza could learn something from the accommodating equines.

They'd spent the afternoon in silence, strangely enough. He expected her to chatter as she'd been doing, but after the visit with the Gannons, she'd been as quiet as the horses. It was a bit strange for her, but he wasn't a talker by nature so he didn't start a conversation. Stupidly enough, he almost missed hearing her voice.

He put the saddles beneath a tree near the horses, keeping them out of the wet grass and mud. Then he took the bedrolls and laid them out near the circle of stones Eliza had put together. After he got the saddles unloaded and brought the various bags over to their camp, he was thirsty and hungry. He looked around and realized he couldn't see Eliza anywhere.

"Liz?"

The sound of rushing water in the distance was his only answer. Where the hell had she gone? A niggling smidge of worry danced up and down his spine. He sure didn't want to worry about her.

Damn.

Grady checked to be sure the horses weren't going to get loose, then stepped into the woods. The sound of the water was louder and could drown out his voice, or hers for that matter. She wasn't stupid enough to go near the river, that much was for certain. So where did she go?

He'd asked her to gather firewood; more than likely she had to hunt around to find some that was dry. She wouldn't be stupid enough to wander off and get lost. Eliza had more common sense for that, or maybe she hadn't read a book about not losing her way in the woods.

The longer he looked for her, the angrier he got. He called her name until his voice was hoarse, at least thirty minutes or more. The darkness got thicker with each passing minute. If she was stuck in the woods overnight in the cold that crept down from the nearby mountains, she could be in life-threatening danger.

Grady wanted to find her so he could strangle her for making him worry.

That thought made him stop in his tracks. His stomach flipped, then flipped again. He bent over and braced his hands on his knees to absorb what he just realized.

He was *worried* about her . . . Son of a bitch.

Grady wasn't even able to worry about himself, much less anyone else. He didn't have the ability to worry, and hadn't for a very long time, if ever. Damn Eliza for yanking him to the dirty pool of human emotion. He didn't want to be in there.

What he should do is go back to the clearing and wait until morning. If she wasn't back, he'd leave her horse and her behind. That's what Grady would have done a month earlier.

He wasn't the same person and he knew it. Eliza had changed him, whether that was a good thing or not. Grady wouldn't even consider leaving her lost in the woods to fend for herself. He continued calling her name, his entire body tightening with each minute that passed. Where the hell was she? Over the pounding of the blood through his ears, he thought he heard a sound.

Grady stopped dead and strained to hear. Closing his eyes, he put the sound of the water aside and pictured Eliza with her stubborn expression as she rode beside him.

"Where are you?" he whispered into the breeze.

"Grady?"

As if by magic, she appeared in front of him with an armload of firewood and enough dirt and twigs in her dark hair to build a second fire. Unbelievably, she was smiling. His anger returned with a whoosh, and he grabbed her by the shoulders, spilling the wood every which way.

"What the hell is wrong with you? I've been looking for half an hour for you. Are you stupid or something?"

He honestly didn't expect the slap, so it surprised the hell out of him. His cheek stung from the impact, almost as much as his pride. Nobody was faster than Grady Wolfe, and no one ever got the drop on him.

Until a mousy book-learned spinster slapped him in the dense woods of a Utah forest.

"How dare you?" Her voice nearly vibrated with fury. "I am a person and do not deserve to be treated like a dog who's gone astray. You have no right to speak to me like that."

Grady knew she had passion, but to see it explode from her was an amazing sight. Her eyes shone like sapphires in the dusky light, her breasts heaved with each breath she took, and her skin glowed with righteous anger. He would hazard a guess she'd never slapped anyone or raised her voice before.

"You got lost, woman."

"I realize that, Grady. I've been attempting to return to the campsite since I realized I'd lost my bearings." She poked at his chest. "That still does not give you the right to scold me so. I deserve your respect, not your scathing words."

He'd never been as aroused as he was at that moment. A howl rose within him, and he listened to the beast, shunting aside his reservations and common sense. He had to have her.

Grady grabbed her and slammed his mouth onto hers. She dropped the firewood and sucked in a surprised breath, giving him the opportunity to delve into the hot recesses of her mouth. His stitches pulled, but he didn't care; he couldn't have stopped even if blood streamed down his face.

Eliza should have fought him, but she didn't. Instead she wrapped her arms around his neck and pushed her breasts into his chest. He growled and pulled at her ass, grinding his hardened staff into her softness.

Her nails dug into his scalp and she pulled his hair. He couldn't believe that instead of being annoyed at her, the roughness actually made him harder.

"Jesus, Liz, I can't . . . I've got to . . ." He could barely get a sentence out.

"Yes, now." She seemed to understand what he was trying to say and pressed her lips to his neck. He groaned and backed her toward a huge tree. He wouldn't take her in the mud, but he couldn't wait even a second longer to have her.

She pulled his head down until her lips found what they were seeking. He ground his unbearably hard dick against her soft belly, with each movement growing harder and longer.

Grady pulled up her skirt and unbuttoned his trousers until he was finally free of the constraining fabric. The cold air did nothing to cool him down.

He picked her up until she was level with him, and she wrapped her legs around his waist. His staff nudged the entrance of her pussy through the slit in her drawers, reveling in the wet heat that met him. She grabbed at his ass, pulling him closer.

"Now, Grady." It appeared that Eliza had found her voice and intended on using it.

He wasn't about to argue with her since that was what he wanted, too. As he slid his dick deep into Eliza, the pleasure radiated up through him with each inch.

"Ooooh, it doesn't hurt." She sounded amazed, and Grady knew then she had been a virgin that first time. He regretted the fact he had taken her once on the ground, and now for the second time against a tree. What the hell was he doing?

"Oh, please don't stop. I'm enjoying this too much to stop now." She scratched at his back. "Please, Grady."

He was so far removed from himself and what he'd normally do, he took a deep breath and moved. That was all it took for his body to take over again. He slid out of her pussy and the cool air coated his slick skin. Then he plunged in again to be surrounded by the hot tight folds of her womanhood.

It was perfect, more than perfect; it was as close to bliss he'd ever remembered experiencing.

Her hot breath came in pants, brushing against his cheek as he thrust in and out of her. Her kittenish mewls echoed in the woods around them and through his body. He braced his arm on the tree, and the other supported her weight.

With more leverage, he fucked her hard, reveling in the sounds of wetness from their joining. She was as aroused as he was, enjoying the pure pleasure with him. Grady found himself actually enjoying the sex more because she was doing the same. Definitely unexpected.

Her breasts bounced against his chest, and he wished they were bare so he could lick and bite them. Eliza had gorgeous tits, and he'd never get tired of touching them, licking them.

Ah hell, he had to have them. Now.

"Open your blouse, Liz. Now."

She seemed to understand his urgency and quickly opened her shirt, pulling her chemise down so her breasts popped out. The nipples were already hard and begged for him. Grady leaned down with eager anticipation and pulled one into his mouth.

Yes, that was it. He sucked at the ripe nipple, then nibbled at it. She was salty and sweet on his tongue. Unfortunately, there was no way he could reach her clit to heighten her pleasure.

"Touch yourself."

"What?"

"Touch your cunt, Liz. You know where. C'mon, touch it." He wanted to see if she'd do it, this schoolmarm who'd turned into a wanton in his arms. How far would she go? Her eyes widened with shock, but she licked her lips and nodded.

To his utter shock, her slender hand slid between them and found her hot spot. She hissed in a breath as her fingers moved.

"That's it. You're nice and wet from fucking me." Far from being put off by him, she seemed to enjoy the dirty talk, the hot sex in the woods. "How does it feel to touch your cunt? Tell me."

"Mmm, it's . . . marvelous."

He smiled and sucked her nipple hard into his mouth as his balls tightened with release.

"I'm gonna come, Liz. Come with me, c'mon, you can do it." Her pupils dilated until her eyes appeared almost black. She licked her lips again, and then he saw the orgasm rip through her face. That was all it took for Grady to explode inside her. He pumped into her as the waves of ecstasy pulsed through him and her breathy pants echoed in his ear.

He sucked in a breath and realized his legs were about to give way. Grady dropped to the ground with his dick still inside Liz, and mud flew up around them. She landed on top of him with an oomph, and her soft breasts pushed into his chest.

"I should get lost more often."

His laugh echoed through the woods.

* * *

"I'm covered in mud." Eliza looked down at herself and realized that having sex with Grady against a tree wasn't the smartest idea. She wouldn't have changed her mind about it though—it was almost like a mating. She'd never felt more alive in her life.

He grunted and continued dressing.

"I need to wash the mud off myself as well as the clothes. I can't ride with itchy dirt all over me."

"So wash up." He was distant again, pulling away from her as soon as they parted. It was as if there was a connection between them only if she were physically touching him. That would make riding difficult on two different horses.

She gathered up her clothes and walked toward the sound of the rushing water. There was no need to stand around and wait for him to be rude to her again. Eliza still had trouble believing she'd yelled at Grady and slapped him. No matter how many times she wanted to do it to her father, she'd kept the impulse in check.

Grady opened up the passion she kept locked away inside her. For that she'd be grateful to him. That didn't mean she would allow him to speak to her in whatever manner he wanted. Eliza's self-confidence had reached new heights. She knew there was no way she'd ever go back to the life she'd led before embarking on this journey.

"Where are you going?"

She kept walking toward the river, which she could now see had a grassy bank. "I'm going to wash as you ordered." She couldn't keep the sarcasm from her voice.

"Liz, you can't just walk off by yourself. I thought you already learned that lesson." He was obviously following her.

"I'm fine, just dirty. I'll only be a few minutes." Eliza reached the river and walked right toward the water.

She yelped in surprise when she was again scooped off her feet. A shirtless Grady scowled at her.

"Woman, you're going to drive me loco. Do you even

know how deep the water is? Or how strong the current is?" He gently bounced her on his arms.

Eliza had to admit she hadn't thought of either of those things. The current in the river in front of her didn't appear too strong. However, after the bend twenty yards away, there were larger rocks and an incline where the river grew much fiercer.

"I was planning on finding out." She wiggled in his arms, aware of every inch of his skin against hers. They'd just finished an amazing sexual experience; how could she desire him again so soon?

"I'll bet you were. Now before you get swept away to Colorado, let me check it for you."

Very chivalrous and surprising. Eliza had never anticipated the gruff Grady would even come close to acting like a gentleman. He was the first to admit it, or rather bark it at her.

When he stepped into the river with Eliza in his arms, she took back the thoughts of how chivalrous he was. The water hit her heated skin, and she nearly screamed at how cold it was.

"Good gracious, why is it so cold?" She was absurdly grateful she hadn't jumped in alone.

"It's mountain runoff. This was snow a few days ago." He must be absolutely frozen considering how cold she was and the water was only touching a part of her body.

"Let me get cleaned up quickly then before we suffer from hypothermia. Please set me down." She didn't really want to wash in the cold water, but she didn't have much of a choice and she was already partially wet.

"You asked for it." He set her on the sandy river bottom and it took her a moment or two to get her balance.

The wickedly cold water swirled around her, instantly numbing her from the waist down.

"Now those are some diamond-hard nipples." Grady's voice was husky, making her shiver from more than the water.

She glanced down and realized the areole were so tightly puckered, there was almost no color left on the actual breast.

"I can't remember ever being so c-cold before." She wanted to explore the attraction between them further, but she really had to get out of the water before they suffered hypothermia.

Grabbing sand from the bottom, she scrubbed herself and her clothes as quickly as she could. He did the same, unsuccessful in getting his back cleaned off. She couldn't let him put on a shirt with that much dirt left on him.

Eliza stepped toward him. "Let me help you with your back."

He grunted, but didn't say no. She scooped up fresh sand and rubbed it between her hands before she started rubbing the mud and dirt off his back. Although he was lean, Grady had wide shoulders and upper back. She could hardly reach the very top, but fortunately that was the area he'd already cleaned.

His skin was smooth and tight. Truthfully it felt wonderful beneath her hands. Touching him was almost sensual, as if washing each other was an extension of what they'd already shared. She enjoyed it so much she took her time rinsing off the sand until his back was clean at least twice over.

"I'm done." Although she didn't want to be done touching him, she was frighteningly cold in the water, particularly considering their state of undress.

He turned back around and watched her as she finished cleaning herself. Standing there half naked with a man should make her uncomfortable, but it didn't. In fact, she felt sexy, an awareness of her body beyond its required needs of food, sleep, and daily ablutions.

Another first for the bookish Eliza Hunter, a shy creature who'd spent her life in the shadows was now a full-fledged woman in her own right. A surge of power accompanied the realization, and she smiled at the sensation.

"Something funny?" He sounded annoyed. "The water's

making my balls crawl up into my belly, so if you think this situation is funny, please tell me why."

"It's making your testicles crawl up into your belly?" She turned to look at his trousers. "That's an interesting phenomenon. May I see?"

She reached for him as he swatted her hand away, but she saw a twitch in the corner of his mouth.

"Finish washing up, woman, so we can go get warm." His lips were starting to turn blue, and her teeth were chattering so hard she was afraid she'd bite her tongue soon.

"Yes, sir." She almost saluted him.

Eliza made quick work of the rest of the mud, then found herself having trouble walking back to shore. Grady sighed, then threw her over his shoulder. All the breath whooshed from her body as her stomach was pushed against her spine.

She punched at his back, but he ignored her and slogged out of the freezing cold river. He didn't stop walking until they returned to the campsite, then he dropped her on one bedroll and wrapped the other around her.

"Stay." With that he walked back into the woods and left her shivering by the empty fire pit.

She wanted to be angry with him, but the truth was, she was grateful for the brusqueness of his methods. In this case, she needed to warm up badly, and he obviously knew it. The quickness of his actions might be protectiveness; it might have been self-preservation. Regardless of what his reasons were, she didn't move from her little cocoon until he returned with her pile of firewood.

"May I assist you?"

"No, just sit there." He had put on his shirt, but it was unbuttoned, gaping open to reveal his own hard nipples.

She was fascinated by the small flat discs with the tiny points in the center. She'd not had the opportunity to truly look at them until now. The urge to touch them, maybe even taste them, washed through her.

Grady had turned her into a wanton. The thought made her smile again, much to his consternation apparently.

"You'd better quit that or I'll toss you back in the river."

This time Eliza laughed out loud, so delighted to not only be alive, but to *feel* alive. She hid her smile behind the blanket as he expertly made the fire. If she wasn't careful, she could get very used to being around Grady Wolfe. A dangerous proposition indeed.

Chapter Nine

Two days after they had the marvelous sexual experience in the woods, Eliza found their relationship had changed. No longer aloof and uncomfortable in each other's presence, she and Grady were true traveling companions. She could hardly believe they had been together a week when she hadn't even known he existed two weeks earlier. And now she couldn't imagine not knowing him.

A routine developed, as they often do, where she would ready the campsite while he gathered wood—he simply refused to allow her that chore any longer. Then she would make food while he took care of the horses. As they ate their meal, she would ask questions about things they'd seen such as animals, rock formations, or interesting trees.

Surprisingly enough, Grady was very knowledgeable about the terrain and the flora and fauna. Eliza enjoyed learning from him as she was always hungry for new information. She hadn't felt as comfortable with a man before, except for Ephraim. The fact he was sixty-five somewhat limited their relationship to teacher and pupil.

What she had with Grady was as far removed from that as possible. She was ashamed to admit even to herself, but she'd been dreaming about him and their intimate experiences. And she wanted more and found herself watching him as he worked, as he moved, as he slept.

It was almost embarrassing the way she nearly ogled him, particularly when he sat astride Bullseye. Thank God he didn't notice, at least she hoped he hadn't. There wasn't much to do but look at things when they rode, and Grady was a very nice something to look at.

Amazingly enough, Eliza had stopped forgetting about how hard the saddle was, or how much she bounced on it. She was proud of the way she had become accustomed to being in the saddle for longer periods of time. Eliza was on her way to being a true horsewoman.

If only their journey would never end, if they could simply ride through the West together, enjoying each other's company and experiencing life. A silly dream, to be sure, but she was a romantic deep down. *Wuthering Heights* had opened her eyes to true love between a man and woman.

Perhaps she was on her way to feeling that kind of love for the gruff Grady. The very idea scared her because she knew the only direction their relationship could go was to a very quick end. Since she didn't want to think about ending anything, Eliza chose not to.

They stopped in another small town called Black Rock, which had a gathering of wood-front buildings, a smattering of wood-planked sidewalks, and three saloons. Eliza knew immediately this town was not one she would venture into alone.

Grady stopped at the building with a crooked hand-painted sign that read HOTEL. He frowned, then looked at her.

"Don't appear we'll be spending the night."

Eliza was glad of that fact. "I would say I regret not sleeping on a bed tonight, but I fear the beds in that building would be riddled with insects."

"Bugs would be the least of our worries." He shifted in the saddle and made sure he could reach his pistol. "We'd be lucky to not be robbed and left for dead."

Eliza shivered at the thought. Black Rock was definitely a dark place. "Should we simply leave?"

"Need to get a few supplies and see the smitty we passed." He started riding again, his gaze constantly moving as they made their way through town.

Eliza hadn't truly felt frightened until then. The idea that Grady was on guard meant she was ready to turn tail and run. She assumed he was looking for information about Angeline, but she hoped her sister had avoided this town completely.

They found the mercantile in a surprisingly clean building, so much so it seemed out of place in a town like Black Rock.

"Looks okay. You go on in and I'll stay out here to keep watch on the horses."

Eliza gaped at him. "You want me to go into the building without you?"

"Liz, you rode across the terrain alone with nothing but an old horse for company through Indian country, snakes, and likely scorpions, not to mention coyotes and other critters around you. Now you're turning yellow?"

When he put it like that, she did feel a bit sheepish about her reaction. She certainly didn't want to be a coward, and was generally not one to be so hesitant. However, her instincts were telling her to be afraid, so she was.

"You've told me to trust my instincts."

"Always. They'll save your life." His answer was quick and firm.

"Mine are telling me not to go into the store and to keep riding out of Black Rock without stopping." Her entire body was tense, as if she was waiting for something to happen.

"It's the cleanest damn building in this sorry excuse for a town. Besides I'll be out here the entire time. If you need me, just holler." He handed her the buttoned pouch. "Make sure you get whatever food you need, some saddle soap and liniment for Melba. His leg's looking poorly."

She glanced down now very concerned about her horse. "Is he injured?"

"Not yet, but he might be if we don't start taking care of the old boy. You know he ain't used to riding so long."

Grady was right, of course. She hadn't even considered Melba's pain or discomfort. Guilt washed through her, and she dismounted so quickly she surprised herself and Grady.

"Hell's bells, Liz, that was, well, damn impressive." He pushed his hat back and raised his brows.

She smiled and performed a curtsy. "Thank you, kind sir." When she turned to enter the mercantile, her amusement fled and she remembered where she was.

Black Rock.

As Eliza walked into the mercantile, she glanced back at Grady and realized he looked quite formidable on his dark horse. She felt marginally more secure with him watching her, but her stomach still jumped with fear.

A bell tinkled above the door as she walked in. The interior was as clean as the exterior, with very neat shelves stocked with many goods. She looked around but didn't see anyone, whether that was a good or bad thing.

The organization of the shelves made it easy for her to find the saddlesoap and liniment, then the canned peaches Grady favored. She placed the items on the counter and frowned.

"Hello? Is anyone here?"

The curtain behind the counter moved, and she jumped nearly a foot in the air. Gray hair appeared in the corner, then one wrinkled eye peered out at her.

"Whatchoo want?"

Eliza didn't know whether the speaker was male or female. "I need to purchase some supplies."

"Who are you?"

"My name is Eliza Wolfe. My, uh, husband and I are traveling to his mother's house and we need some supplies." She tried to smile to show she was friendly, but her face was too tight with anxiety to let her.

The person watching her made a grunting noise, followed by a horribly phlegmy one. Eliza managed not to grimace. From behind the curtain, a tiny little woman emerged. She couldn't be taller than Eliza's shoulder, which meant she was very short.

"Get what you need. Cash only." The older woman put a pair of spectacles on her nose, stepped close to Eliza, and examined her with her owl-like eyes. "You married?"

"Yes, ma'am. My husband is outside waiting." Eliza felt the lie becoming more than what it was.

"You got cash?"

Eliza didn't understand why the old woman kept asking her the same questions over and over. Perhaps she forgot things easily, although judging by the store, there wasn't a thing she forgot in there.

"Yes, ma'am, I do." Eliza breathed a sigh of relief when the old woman finally moved away.

"Get what you need then. Just be ready to pay for it." The tiny woman climbed up onto a stool behind the counter with, much to Eliza's shock, a shotgun across her lap.

First of all, she never even saw the gun. Second, it made her so nervous she forgot what she wanted to buy. She swallowed hard and tried to think of what Grady would do in the situation.

He certainly wouldn't be standing there cowering in front of an eighty-pound old woman with a shotgun she probably forgot to load. No doubt, he would take charge of the situation and get what he needed without quaking in his boots.

Eliza straightened her shoulders and focused on what she'd made for supper the night before, and for breakfast. That sparked her memory, and with Grady's ghost walking beside her, she stepped through the mercantile and got everything she needed.

The old woman watched her like a hawk watches its prey. Her stare made the hairs on Eliza's neck stand up, but she kept at her task until everything was on the counter.

With surprising speed, the strange shopkeeper tallied up the purchases. "Five dollars and thirty-seven cents."

Eliza counted out the money from the small brown pouch and paid the woman, frowning at the fact her hand shook. "Do you have a sack I could carry these in?"

"What's the matter, your husband lazy?"

Eliza just wanted to get out of the store, out of Black Rock, as quickly as she could. She gathered up everything she could in her skirt and turned to leave.

"No manners."

"I would justify that with a response, but that would bring me down to your level. I came in here with money to purchase goods, and you treated me as if I were a criminal." Eliza turned to glare at the woman. "If you're lucky my husband won't come in here and teach you manners."

A rusty chuckle followed her out the door. Eliza didn't know if she was amused or frightened by it. She was only glad to be out in the fresh air, out of reach of the woman's stare. When she stepped onto the sidewalk, she realized Grady and the horses were gone.

Grady wanted to shoot the damn blacksmith. The one-eyed old bastard simply chattered on about nothing in particular without answering Grady's questions. The one thing he did determine was that his quarry had not passed through town, or maybe the other man had lied.

Either way, he was ready to throttle the smitty. He needed to get Bullseye shoed and anyone would have thought he'd asked the old man to sing and dance.

"Listen, old-timer, can you shoe my damn horse or not?" Grady put himself between the grizzled smitty and the forge.

The man was old, but he was built like a tree with arms as big around as Grady's waist. If he wanted to, no doubt the smitty could simply break Grady in half and throw him in the fire. The heat from the forge almost burned his back from five feet away.

"You'd best move out of the way, stranger." His voice was soft but icy enough to make Grady believe the man had done more than work as a smitty.

"There's no livery in town, so you're the one who can shoe a horse. Just answer the question, and I'll move." Grady wasn't intimidated by the man, just aware of what could happen. His hand never left the guns slung low on his hips.

"Livery up and left last year after the owner got shot dead. Wife took off for her mama's house. Ain't nobody been there since."

More information about shit Grady didn't care about.

"Do you go somewhere else for shoeing?"

"Ayup, usually to Montgomery. There's a livery there." The smitty pointed at Grady with the hammer in his hand. "You look like you already tangled with a wildcat. I know you don't want to tangle with me. Now move."

Grady stepped toward the old man, tired of the foolish discussion and the threats. He leaned over until he was almost nose to nose with the smitty.

"Ain't too many men who can threaten me and walk away on two legs. Next time I ask you a question, answer it." Grady kept his coldest stare on the man for a full minute before stepping away, confident the smitty wouldn't give him a hammer in the back.

He had just made it to the door when a woman's scream ripped through the air. Grady's entire body clenched when he recognized Eliza's voice. He threw himself up on Bullseye and rode hell for leather toward the sound of her voice. It was only a short distance, perhaps three hundred yards, but it seemed to be a mile.

There didn't appear to be anyone on the street as he flew past, a streak of horse and man in the midday sun. He reached the mercantile and dismounted before the horse even stopped.

Eliza was nowhere to be seen, but the sidewalk in front of the mercantile was littered with cans, a broken sack of cornmeal, and liniment.

Eliza.

He looked around, furious that he couldn't see her. Although he didn't want her to scream again, without a noise there was no way for him to find her. There were alleys on either side of the mercantile. He had to take a chance and pick one. Each second weighed on his shoulders like lead.

Grady focused on Eliza's smiling face and then took off for the left alley because she favored her left hand when she wrote. If he were wrong, she might die because of it. The sun didn't penetrate the gloom of the alley. He stepped forward, straining for a sound, anything besides the scurrying of the rats.

His blood thundered through his veins as he put all his focus on listening. Rushing in might make her attacker panic, but creeping up might surprise him. Although it was the hardest thing he ever had to do, Grady crept along at a snail's pace. He kept his breath shallow and silent, letting no one and nothing know of his presence.

He reached the darkest part of the alley and stopped dead. There was nothing here but him and the rats. It was empty, which meant he'd chosen wrong. Where the hell was she? Grady's fury mixed with fear for her, a lethal combination for whoever had touched her.

There was no hope for it. He'd simply have to reveal his presence and hope she heard him.

"Eliza!" Her name was torn from his throat and echoed down the alley.

"Grady!" Eliza's scream made the hairs on his arms stand up. It was one of terror and pain—he knew it well.

He berated himself for not continuing to the end of the alley, because her scream had come from beyond it and behind the mercantile. Both guns were in his hands before he even realized he'd touched them.

His teeth were clenched so hard his jaw throbbed. When he burst around the corner, he found two men holding her down while a wrinkled old midget in a skirt had her hands all over Eliza.

Grady didn't hesitate.

He killed the two men with a single shot each to the head. The old midget continued to touch Eliza, but now that her arms were free, she could fight back. She stood up and started slapping at the hands that were all over her. A chilly chuckle burst from the old woman as the two of them started rolling on the ground.

Grady didn't want to hit Eliza, and he couldn't get a clear shot. He holstered the guns and reached in to try to separate them.

That's when he saw the knife.

His body turned into ice at the sight of the deadly blade a mere inches from Eliza's throat. They were moving so fast, she could be cut without either of them knowing it. Grady didn't like being helpless one single goddamn bit.

He could shoot the old woman, but if he tried he might shoot Eliza instead. He could separate them, but the knife was perilously close to killing her already. The women rolled around like two cats fighting, getting covered in dirt and blood from the dead bastards who'd held her down.

Grady stood there on his toes watching them, unable to help and unsure of what to do. It almost killed him to do nothing. He roared in frustration, then figured he had to do something. So he kicked the old woman as hard as he could in the kidneys, the first place he could reach.

She screeched and grabbed at her back. Eliza, being the foolish woman she was, took the opportunity to take hold of the woman's other hand. The one holding the huge knife.

"If you do not unhand this knife instantly, you old hag, I will skewer you with it." Eliza sounded so fierce, he almost didn't recognize her voice. Her lips were pulled back in a snarl. "Let go. Now."

She sounded so much like him, it was uncanny. Eliza was no longer the little wren. She was now an eagle.

With Eliza distracting the old woman, Grady was able to reach down and pluck the knife from her hand. Then he took the midget by the collar and dragged her from Eliza although she tried her damndest to hang on to his sometimes wife. He threw the old woman against a crate and she lay still, a tiny ball of gray hair and blood.

"Don't you even think about moving, you crazy old fuck. Nobody touches my wife. *Nobody.*" He wanted to shoot her in the head and end her miserable existence.

"Don't kill her, Grady. She's not worth the bullet."

Eliza got to her feet, visibly shaking, covered in dirt, grass, and blood. She met his gaze, and he was sorry to see the sparkle of life in her eyes had dimmed. It had been obvious she'd not seen the darkest side of other people before. Now because he'd insisted on stopping in Black Rock, she had.

"You left me."

Grady opened his arms and she flew into them, shaking so hard he could actually hear her teeth rattle. He held her tight, noting that his heart was beating just as fast as hers. Thank God he'd gotten there in time. He hadn't wanted Eliza's company, but she had definitely become a part of his world, like it or not.

The thought should have scared him more than it did, but he was too busy being grateful she was in his arms.

"I'm sorry, Liz. I thought it would only take five minutes to talk to the smitty."

"You left me," she repeated, her face against his chest.

He stroked her hair, picking out the debris as best he could. Eliza was a scrapper, a warrior queen who had shown him exactly what she was made of. He was proud of her.

"I should have listened to your instincts. Next time I will." He turned to leave the carnage behind them. "Now let's get the hell out of this place before something else happens." As they walked back to the front of the mercantile, she had her arm around his waist and his arm stayed firm around her shoulders.

Guilt was another emotion he didn't deal with very often, but he couldn't help but recognize it when it landed on him.

He told Eliza to listen to her instincts, and he didn't follow through on that lesson. Eliza was the smartest person he'd ever known, and she had just taught him a lesson that scared him almost as much as seeing her being attacked.

He cared about her, perhaps even more than he would admit even to himself.

Eliza returned from the creek with damp skin, wearing her purple dress and carrying her clean clothes, feeling much better. It had been a horrible day, and she was glad to have washed off the stink from Black Rock and all that happened there. Grady stood at the edge of the clearing with his back to her, looking out at the darkness.

The campfire flickered merrily in the twilight, leading her back. She wanted nothing more than to have a hot meal, then to rest. Although the riding had come easier, she was still sore and completely exhausted.

Grady didn't turn around, but lying on her saddle was a paper package, secured with twine. Her heart skipped a beat, wondering what he'd left for her. She laid out her wet clothes on tree branches to dry while her gaze kept returning to the package.

Common courtesy told her to wait until he turned around to open it. Perhaps he simply set it there without thinking. Or perhaps he'd left her a gift.

When he finally turned around, he picked up a skinned rabbit from the grass. He must've caught it while she was bathing. She forgot all about the package when she realized they'd have meat for dinner, hot and salty, exactly what she was craving.

"Oh, Grady, that's positively wonderful!" She hopped up and started searching for a few sturdy sticks to use for roasting the rabbit. "I'm sure we can fashion a spit of sorts to cook it."

With a little ingenuity, some blind luck in finding the right sticks, they made a spit for the rabbit to cook over the fire.

The smell of the roasting meat made her stomach yowl, and she laughed nervously.

"Hungry, Liz?"

"Most assuredly. I can't remember the last time I had rabbit. It's been years since—" She stopped, realizing she was about to mention her father.

"Since what?" He peered at her as he turned the rabbit on the spit.

"I never had the agility required to hunt rabbits, so we had deer when a neighbor brought us a haunch, and beef from the cattle we raised." Eliza found the story tripping off her tongue as if it were completely true. When had she become so adept at lying?

"That right? No man to take care of you?"

She swallowed the guilt for lying, silently apologizing to Grady for her falsehood. "My father was quite old and he didn't hunt."

A few moments of silence followed her thought, which had been the absolute truth.

"You look right pretty in that purple dress."

She glanced down. "It seemed too pretty to wear on the trail, but I had to wash the rest of my clothing." She didn't need to tell him why.

"You got it to wear, so why not wear it?" Grady was taking care of the fire, something she had been doing each night.

"Well, I'm just not used to wearing pretty things."

He snorted. "That's for damn sure."

"What does that mean?" She frowned, trying to decide if she was insulted by his backhanded comment.

"Your clothes are worse than rags, Liz. They're so damn thin, I can see through them half the time. Good thing your drawers are thicker, or you'd be showing a lot more than you think." He sighed and shook his head. "I didn't intend that to be mean, but it's the truth. And well, it's just, I wanted you to have something nice to wear."

Eliza took a moment to absorb what he'd said. She wasn't

used to nice things. Ladies in the LDS church didn't wear fancy clothes, especially the brilliant purple she sported now. She was glad she'd picked out the dress. It matched the new woman she'd become, rather than the one who'd been trapped by her upbringing and her own lack of self-confidence. She ran her hands down the fabric and smiled. Yes, she was definitely happy with her new frock.

"Thank you, Grady. I really do appreciate you paying for it, and I thank you for your generosity and thoughtfulness."

"I left you alone in Black Rock to get raped."

His bald statement made her frown. "It's true I was attacked, but their intent was never clear. I think they were actually trying to rob me."

"How the hell could they know you had money? I just told you the clothes you wear make you look like a beggar." He poked at the fire angrily. "I left you, and some bad things happened."

Eliza finally realized he was feeling guilty for what had happened. She moved closer to him and lay her head on his shoulder.

"It wasn't your fault. The old woman was the shopkeeper. She saw me with the pouch of money and decided to help herself to the rest."

"That thing was a woman?" He sounded as disgusted as she was.

A shudder ran through Eliza. "Yes, she was, I think. It was difficult to determine, but her hands were small like a woman's." She didn't want to think about the woman touching her, but the memory burbled to the surface anyway.

Grady put his hand on her cheek. "I'm sorry."

She looked up at him, at his dark eyes glittering in the firelight. "Thank you for rescuing me." Eliza placed her hand on his. "I've never been a damsel in distress before and had a knight save me from a dragon."

He shook his head. "You read too much, Liz."

She laughed and moved his palm to her lips, kissing the

roughened skin softly. Surprisingly a visible shiver raced down his arm at the touch of her lips.

He cocked one eyebrow at her. "Do you know what today is, Liz?" He rose and pulled the pot from the fire, then poured hot liquid into the tin cup.

"Thursday?"

He turned to pick something from his saddlebags. "It's October ninth."

Eliza sucked in a breath of surprise. It was her twenty-first birthday, and Grady remembered. Her throat grew tight at the idea he had tucked away the piece of information she'd given him earlier in Bellman, before they'd been truly intimate, when they barely knew each other.

"Happy birthday." He handed her the tin cup, which she took gratefully.

"Thank you, Grady. I had forgotten." Although warmed by the fire, and the sentiment, the night air was freezing cold. The warmth from the cup seeped through her hands. When she sniffed the coffee, she realized it wasn't coffee. "Is this tea?"

He held up a tea ball, which dripped onto the fire, making a hissing noise with each drop. "Yep."

"Where did you get tea? I don't understand." Truly, she didn't understand. Eliza was used to being the doer, the one who did everything for everyone else. He'd gone out of his way to remember her birthday, made her tea for goodness' sake, and all without her knowledge. She was at a loss to even absorb it all.

"I had the tin and tea ball from a while back, never used it. I figured you didn't like coffee being as how you make a face whenever you drink it." He shrugged. "I was looking for something and found the stuff at the bottom of my bags. It ain't new. Oh, and that's for you." He pointed at the package lying on the saddle. "Open it."

Eliza took a gulp of the hot tea—regardless of manners, she had to have some now—then set the cup down with some reluctance. Then she looked at the package and her excitement began anew. The day had been fraught with darkness, and now he'd brought the light back into her soul with his simple gestures of thoughtfulness.

Eliza's heart melted. "What is it?"

"Open it and find out."

With the enthusiasm of a child at Christmas, she put the package on her lap and carefully untied the twine. Grady made some impatient noises, but she didn't rush the experience. Eliza's hands shook as she finally unwrapped the paper to find a bar of lavender soap. The heavenly scent wafted up toward her, and she breathed in deeply.

"Grady, I don't know what to say." Her voice was hoarse with emotion. He had not only remembered her birthday and made her tea, but he'd purchased a gift for her. She didn't want to ever let that feeling go—the one where she felt more special than anyone else on Earth. For the first time in her life, she had a birthday gift.

She couldn't tell him that her church did not celebrate the day of anyone's birth. It was treated as any other day. Grady's gift, his thoughtfulness, was simply incredible.

"Thank you. Truly from the bottom of my heart, thank you." She looked up at him with tears brimming in her eyes.

He frowned. "It's just a bar of soap and tea, Liz. No need to get all weepy about it."

She shook her head. "It's much more than that. It's a gift, and I thank you."

"You're welcome. Now let's get to eating this rabbit before it gets overdone." He turned his back to her, but she wasn't finished yet.

Eliza set the soap aside and moved over beside him. She turned his face and took it in her hands, looking into his dark eyes.

"Thank you, Grady." She leaned forward and kissed him, softly, sweetly. His lips were soft and she kissed him several times before straightening up.

He licked his lips, as if tasting her essence. Her stomach

jumped at the sight of his tongue. She knew firsthand what that tongue could accomplish. She wanted to be with him again, to rub her body against his in heat and fire. To wash away the touch of darkness she'd been subject to.

"You keep looking at me like that and the rabbit's gonna be ashes." He sounded strained, likely as much as she was.

"The forest is full of rabbits." She captured his lips again, but this time, with hunger for more than food.

Without missing a beat, she started unbuttoning her dress.

Grady could hardly get his trousers off fast enough. He couldn't explain what it was about Eliza that made him nearly loco with desire, but she did. He nearly fell on his head when trying to yank off his trousers without taking his boots off first.

By the time he was naked, she was sliding off her dress. Her skin glowed in the meager light, and he again marveled at what was hidden beneath the little wren's disguise. His warrior queen, the eagle beside him and before him.

"God, Liz, you're like the damn stars in the sky." He didn't know what possessed him to sound like a poet, but the words were out and he couldn't stuff them back in his mouth.

"And you are a beautiful specimen of manhood."

Now her words made his cheeks heat. What the hell was that all about? Since when did someone like Grady Wolfe blush yet again?

Since he'd met Eliza no-name in the darkness of a Utah night and found his world turned sideways.

"Don't make me wait any longer." She lay down on the bedroll, spread her legs, and opened her arms. "It's my birthday after all."

Grady forgot about his confusion over resurrected emotions and focused on the beautiful naked woman in front of him. He slid up her warm, soft skin, hearing the gentle rasp of his body against hers. With heightened anticipation, he took his time as he moved, reveling in the feeling of Eliza until he reached the perfect spot on top of her. When he lay down fully and they were head to toe together, he groaned at the sensation. They simply fit together as if someone made them that way.

"This is simply wonderful." She ran her fingers up and down his back. "You're so warm and hard, and your hairs on your legs are quite crinkly."

Grady surprised both of them when he chuckled. "I don't think I've ever heard that kind of pillow talk before."

Eliza frowned. "I don't have a pillow."

This time it was a laugh instead of a chuckle. He kissed her, then looked down into her eyes. "You are a one-of-a-kind gal, Liz."

She opened her mouth to say something, but he was done talking. He captured her mouth again for one long kiss, then he pressed small kisses up and down her lips, nibbling at them as if they were raspberries ripe for plucking. She made a sound of impatience, but he didn't hurry.

Not the only impatient one, his dick pulsed against her, wanting entrance into the hot recesses of her body. Grady wanted to pleasure her on her birthday, even if it meant forcing himself to wait.

He had no doubt she'd never been pleasured before, and although he'd seen it done, this would be new for him, too. Grady's experience with women had been limited to the kind involving money.

She smelled so good, he breathed in her scent as he reached her neck and continued on his quest. Small kisses, bites, and licks ensued. She moaned, and he knew she had forgotten about being impatient. As he nibbled on her lobe, she sucked in a breath of surprise and wiggled her lower half. A sensitive spot he'd have to remember.

Grady shifted so he was on his knees and she was splayed out before him like a banquet of the gods. Her breasts begged for attention, the nipples tightly budded in the cool air, lightly kissed by warm firelight.

The crackling of the wood was accompanied by the symphony of the night creatures. They sang to Eliza as he began pleasuring her in earnest.

He licked her soft skin in circles around each breast, carefully avoiding the nipples. His hand made the same lazy circles around her pussy, teasing, tantalizing. Goose bumps broke out across Eliza's body as his journey continued.

Grady licked her nipples then, earning a gasp of pure arousal. Then when he blew gently on the wet skin, her gasp turned to a moan.

"Do you like that, Liz?"

"Oh, my."

He smiled and pressed a finger against her clit.

"Yes, yes, yes." She sounded so different, so fucking sexy, he could hardly stand it.

His fingers continued to tease her nubbin of pleasure as he finally took one nipple in his mouth. He sucked at her while his tongue lapped at the nipple, then he nibbled. When she didn't protest, he bit just a little harder.

She jerked in his arms but didn't tell him to stop. Apparently Eliza liked a little bit of pain with her pleasure. Grady switched to the other breast and proceeded to bite first, then lick and suck. She trembled beneath him, and he took a certain satisfaction from knowing he was giving her such bliss.

Shifting again, he pressed her breasts together in his hands and licked them both, then bit them, finishing with a kiss. The space between those beautiful orbs would fit his dick nicely, but that would have to be later.

Before she could ask him what he was doing, he had settled himself between her open legs and spread her pussy lips wide. The pink flesh glistened in the firelight; her arousal pleased him to no end. He blew on her again and she shivered.

"Grady, what—"

"Shhhhh, just feel and stop talking."

He swiped his tongue from one end of her pussy to the

other, her tangy sweetness coating his tongue. Grady wasn't prepared for the rush of pleasure that coursed through him. She was delicious and he wanted more, much more.

Pressing one finger into her tight hole, he began eating her in earnest. He licked, nibbled, and bit her clit, lapping at her as if he were a puppy finding a sweet treat. She moaned with each swipe of his tongue, each time his teeth closed, each kiss from his mouth.

Grady was afraid he'd come into the bedroll from pleasuring her. The more he tasted her, the sweeter she got. He sucked her clit into his mouth and tugged hard as he fucked her with two fingers. His dick pulsed along with her, humping the ground, shaking with the power of desire.

She screamed his name and bucked with more power than he thought she possessed. He held on, pulling every last second of her orgasm into his mouth. Her essence flooded through him and he closed his eyes, trembling with the sensation.

When he caught his breath, he kissed her pussy one last time, then rose up to find tears on her face. She smiled and opened her arms, inviting him to be with her. He didn't need to be invited twice.

This time when his dick pressed into her tightness, he groaned. Jolts of ecstasy slammed into him, and he knew in seconds he was going to come. Driving into her fast and hard, his orgasm began somewhere near his feet and rolled through him. Stars exploded behind his eyes, and a rushing sound filled his ears.

Grady vaguely remembered shouting her name as he came deep inside her. When he was able to form a coherent thought, he collapsed next to her, breathing so hard he felt dizzy from the lack of air. What the hell had just happened?

Never in his life, even as a teenager, had he dipped his dick and come within a minute. Yet Eliza's pleasure had driven him to the brink of orgasm. Grady didn't know what it meant, and he wasn't sure he wanted to know.

Eliza had obviously already gotten under his skin; he didn't want to think she'd gotten any farther than that.

She leaned over and kissed him, a sweet, long kiss. "Thank you for my birthday gifts."

Without even considering what he was doing, he tucked her under his arm so her head rested on his chest, then covered both of them with her bedroll. He closed his eyes and slept almost instantly.

Chapter Ten

Grady felt the shift in their relationship in the week following Black Rock. He was in uncharted territory, and it bothered him immensely. Eliza was so much more than he expected her to be, not that he wanted to get to know her better. It had just happened.

The wren had wormed her way into his life, and he resented it as much as he liked it. The sex with her was indescribable, more potent than any he'd had in his life. The truth was, he was hard for her almost constantly, something he hadn't dealt with since he left his teenage years behind.

He dreamed of her, watched her as they rode, hell he even peeked at her when she bathed. Her tits were so perfect, he wanted to touch them every time he saw them.

Grady didn't want to feel things for her, didn't want to be caught up in his fascination for a woman who was as plain as the brown clothes she wore. Yet she was anything but plain, and he knew it.

Beneath it all, she was amazing. Smart, brave, sexy, passionate, and patient. Grady was none of those things, he simply was what he was, a gunslinger with a fast hand and no conscience. Eliza was so much more than he was—it was a stark contrast he didn't forget even for a second.

However, he had to admit when he was in her arms that he

didn't think about a purpose for being on the trail. Eliza gave him the opportunity to not be a gunslinger with each second they were intimate.

It was a mistake and he knew it. Grady was not one to make too many mistakes, and he had to rectify the situation. The truth was, he should have left her behind weeks earlier when they'd first met.

Now he was almost too involved with her to simply walk away, which was exactly what he was going to force himself to do. First he had to stop fucking her every goddamn night.

Easier said than done, of course, since every time she kissed him, his dick stood at attention begging for her sweet pussy. Ridiculous that he couldn't control himself anymore, which is why he needed to pull away from her.

Grady steeled himself to do just that. They had stopped at a few more towns and traveled a number of miles, all without finding much except where his quarry wasn't hiding. Eliza didn't ask what he was doing or why, and he didn't offer.

Until they stopped in Emerson, that is. He told her they were stopping for supplies, even though that was the excuse he used each time they stopped. She was the smartest person he knew, and there was no way she believed that lie. They had enough to eat and plenty of supplies. Since she did the cooking, she knew it to be true.

Emerson was a sleepy little town with not much happening. Not dark and forbidding like Black Rock, or strange like Bellman, Emerson was a town built by the ranches that surrounded it. A central location for the cattlemen to meet and have social contact, not to mention the standard small-town needs such as a mercantile, a post office, and a jail.

The one thing Emerson did not have was a hotel. No matter, since he didn't plan on spending the night. It was late morning and they still had plenty of daylight left. Eliza had developed a better seat and rode without bouncing around in the saddle. She adapted quickly, and he realized it and was pleased.

Pushing aside his mixed-up thoughts about Eliza, he stopped at the mercantile.

Eliza looked down at him. "Why are we stopping here?"

"You need new undergarments."

Her cheeks flared red beneath the ugly brown hat. "Grady, that's hardly your concern."

"Yes it is, I want those fabulous, ah, parts to have softer material against them."

"Grady!" She glanced around, nearly losing her hat when she whipped to the right too hard. "You are incorrigible."

"I know that. I also think you need a better hat, one that fits you and doesn't look as if a horse shit it out its back end."

This time Eliza's mouth opened and closed, but she didn't say a word. She dismounted, secured Melba to the hitching post, and marched toward the mercantile alone. Her shoulders were back, thrusting her breasts out.

Grady couldn't keep his eyes off them. Damn, they were perfect. Much to his consternation, he wasn't the only one who noticed, either. Several men on the street stopped to watch her walk past, their gazes glued to those perfect tits.

With a frown, he dismounted and did his best to scare away the men who still watched the door even after she'd stepped inside the store. He growled as he passed one cowboy who was young enough he probably didn't shave yet.

"Mind not ogling my wife's tits, you little shit?"

The cowboy started and stared at Grady, the color draining from his face. "Sorry, mister." He skittered away down the street, looking back to see if Grady was going to shoot him in the back.

It was tempting, but Grady resisted the impulse. No need to get in trouble with the law again. Particularly since he was just healed up from the beating in Bellman.

As he walked into the store, he glared twice more at men who'd eaten Eliza up with their eyes. Damn, he didn't like this one bit. What the hell was that about? Eliza wasn't his wife in truth, but he sure was acting like she was.

He could tell himself all day long it was because she was supposed to be his wife. However, Grady knew the truth was much deeper than that. He'd become attached to Eliza, a bad move for a man who spent his life hunting and killing people for money.

He found Eliza talking to another damn cowboy. This one was older, likely Grady's age, with wrinkles on his face from spending so much time in the sun working the range. He was handsome, too, although Grady was no judge of other men. Eliza was smiling at him with a wide toothy grin.

Grady's body tensed, and he had to remind himself she wasn't his in truth, to keep his hand off his gun, and to be polite.

Lot of good that did.

The first thing he did was put his hand on the butt of his pistol and step up to the two of them with his teeth bared.

"Like what you see, cowboy? It ain't for sale."

"Grady!" It was the third time she'd admonished him in as many minutes. "Mr. Sampson was assisting me in finding the best place in town to purchase a new hat." Her blue eyes glittered behind the spectacles.

"And you don't have any idea how many men want to get in your drawers."

"Now see here, fella, you've no right to talk to this lady like that." The cowboy stepped up to Grady, all full of himself.

"The lady is my wife, mister." Grady snarled. "You can step back now, or we can make a mess all over this clean store." He kept his voice low, but his tone was hard as steel.

The cowboy didn't step back, and Grady tightened his grip on the pistol. Eliza was the one who stepped in to stop them.

"I've had quite enough of the foolishness. Grady, go back outside and wait for me. You wanted me to make some, ah, purchases, and I will do that. However I will not stand here and witness two grown men acting like little boys measuring the size of their sticks." She pushed them both back and walked away.

Grady had two reactions. First, he was angry with her for dismissing his anger over the cowboy trying to seduce her. Second, he was surprised she was suddenly not only standing up to him but telling him in no uncertain terms he'd been a fool.

"Helluva woman you got there, stranger."

Grady scowled at the cowboy. "Yeah and she's *mine*. Go find your own filly to sniff around."

"No offense meant. The lady had no ring on her finger." With that the cowboy left the store.

Grady watched Eliza as she looked through the clothing section. She had more confidence, more life in her. Much more than when he'd met her and she seemed almost as meek as the horrible clothes she wore.

It wasn't the first time someone had mentioned the lack of a wedding ring. Grady decided he'd do something about that.

Eliza was furious with Grady. He'd embarrassed her in front of the man who'd offered her assistance, and made a fool out of both of them. He wanted her to act like his wife, yet he acted like a true wolf barking and growling at the other male wolves who dared stand within ten feet of her.

Deep down, beyond the frustration at the way Grady acted, she was flattered. No one had ever displayed jealousy because of her before. Perhaps it was simply Grady's way of keeping his lover to himself, but she interpreted it as jealousy and it did give her a little thrill.

She wouldn't forget though that she was angry with him. The embarrassment had not faded, and there were still a few ladies in the store watching her and whispering. Eliza was used to being talked about as if she weren't there, but that didn't mean she liked it.

There were nice cotton serviceable chemises in the pile,

some that would definitely fit her, but nothing silky. At least he couldn't say that she didn't look for one.

"Can I help you, ma'am?"

A young freckle-faced redheaded girl appeared at her elbow. Likely no more than sixteen, she had a bright smile and lovely blue eyes. Her youth reminded Eliza so much of Angeline, it made her heart pinch to look at her.

"I'm looking for a new chemise."

"Oh, we have plenty of stock in lots of sizes. They might be a little long on you, but you can hem one up in a jiffy." The girl reached for the pile Eliza had just gone through.

"You have lovely garments, miss. I was hoping for something a bit . . . er, softer." Eliza was at a loss to tell this sweet young girl she needed something sexy.

The young woman, however, nodded knowingly. "I understand, and we do have something a bit more in the back. Come with me and you can take a look." She led Eliza to a door on the left side of the rear of the store. "My name is Amy, by the way."

"Eliza Wolfe. Pleased to meet you, Amy." Eliza liked the girl, the openness and friendliness of her youthful face. "I appreciate your assistance as well."

"Oh, I'm glad to help you, Mrs. Wolfe. My grandparents own the store, and I help out when I'm not in school. I'm going to be a teacher."

They walked down a hallway where Amy opened a door to a storage room. There were lots of boxes and crates, but they were stacked neatly. Amy walked over to a box in the corner and pulled it from the shelf.

"Here they are. My grandmother thought some ladies might want something different for their undergarments. It turns out ranchers' wives don't buy much unless it's serviceable." Amy smiled. "I'm sure she'd be thrilled to know someone is interested in them."

The box itself had writing in gold script on it. When Amy opened the box, there were layers of tissue paper on top. She pulled them back to reveal undergarments of various colors ranging from red to purple; there was even a bright pink.

Eliza's eyes widened as she absorbed the idea women wore such things beneath their clothes. The vibrant colors reminded her of the bright flowers she'd seen growing wild in the woods.

"Oh, my."

"Yes, ma'am, they are bright, aren't they?" Amy was as cheerful as the colors. "We do have some cream-colored garments under here."

The young woman dug through the colored garments and pulled out two creamy silk chemises. One was simple with piping around the edges and a scoop neck and narrow straps. The other was almost entirely made of lace, which was also completely see-through.

Eliza's body reacted to the sexy garments because her mind imagined Grady's reaction to them. She swallowed and reminded herself that she was in a public store talking to a young woman who was no doubt as much a virgin as Eliza had been two weeks earlier.

"Do you like either of these, ma'am?"

Eliza nodded. "I like both of them." She reached out and picked up the lacy one first, holding it up to her body for fit. It appeared to be made for her. The second one was the same. Amy's grandmother could have ordered these custom-made for Eliza.

"How much are they?"

Amy shrugged. "Grandma bought these three years ago after a salesman gave her a good price, likely hoping folks would like them enough to buy more. I'm sure she'd take whatever you wanted to offer."

Eliza recognized the material was well made, as was the actual garment. They were probably more expensive than Amy would admit, but understood they might not ever be purchased because of the practical nature of the people in the area.

"I will pay whatever she paid for them." Eliza thought it

only fair to at least reimburse the shopkeeper for what she had paid.

"Oh, she might not even remember what she paid." Amy laughed. "What if we sell you both of them for three dollars?"

Eliza stared at the girl in surprise. "The fabric alone is worth more than that."

"It's a fair price. And I think you'll enjoy them, which is just as important." Amy smiled. "I saw your husband. He's a bit, um, intense."

"You have no idea." Eliza smiled back at the girl. "Then I will purchase both of them."

"Wonderful!" Amy took a few pieces of tissue paper, then closed the box and returned it to the shelf. She took both garments from Eliza and folded them quickly within the tissue.

As Eliza followed her back into the store, she couldn't help but feel as though everyone knew what the tissue paper held. Her cheeks heated, but she kept her head high, secure in the knowledge Amy had been right. Eliza, and Grady, would enjoy them.

Amy led her over to the counter. "Was there anything else you needed, Mrs. Wolfe?"

"She needs a hat." Grady appeared at her elbow, scaring a year off Eliza's life.

"We have some bonnets up in front." Amy stared at Grady with wide eyes.

"Not a bonnet. Something for being on the trail, not a piece of frippery." He glanced at the tissue-wrapped parcel, but said nothing about it.

"We don't have anything like that in stock right now. I could order something, but it will take a couple weeks to get here." Amy managed to smile, although Eliza could tell the girl was nervous around Grady.

"Mr. Sampson said the livery sometimes carried hats for sale." Eliza had been about to find out where the livery was before Grady decided to jump in and act like a caveman.

"Oh, that's true." Amy eagerly agreed with her. "The folks

that own the livery do leather work and make hats for customers sometimes. Elsa and Helmut Johanssen are their names."

"That's wonderful. Thank you, Amy." Eliza smiled at the girl, trying to put her at ease. "Where is the livery located?"

"Straight down the street at the south end. You can't miss it." She wrapped up the garments in brown paper and secured it with twine. "That'll be three dollars."

Grady raised his brow but pulled the money from his pouch to pay her. "What did you buy, buttons and thread?"

"No, I purchased what you wanted me to." Eliza took the package from the girl. "Thank you so much for all your assistance, Amy."

"Y-you're welcome, Mrs. Wolfe." Amy kept her gaze on Grady, looking like a deer in a hunter's sights.

Eliza elbowed him. "You need to stop scaring children and small animals, Grady."

He grunted and took her elbow. "Where's the fun in that?"

Eliza thought she heard Amy chuckle, but it may have been simply a cough. The two of them walked out of the store with the small package beneath Eliza's arm. It felt hot against her skin, as if the beautiful garments were reacting to their new owner.

A silly bit of imagination, but she couldn't help it. Grady had opened up a new world to her, and Eliza found herself a changed person because of it.

The ring burned against his leg as it sat in the bottom of his pocket. He sure as hell shouldn't have bought it. She wasn't even his real wife. Oh, he could justify the twenty dollars he'd spent by telling her he didn't want people to ask questions why they were traveling together when clearly she didn't sport a wedding ring. It was for her comfort as well.

A big fat pack of lies and he knew it. Eliza was too smart to believe it, too, but she might allow him to lie about it. Maybe even enjoy the lie as much as he apparently was going to.

When he'd been paying for the ring, he'd at least taken the time to ask about Angeline. From what he could find out, she had been in town only to pass through within a few hours. The jeweler barely remembered her, but when he mentioned her white blond hair, he mentioned she'd been heading toward Montgomery.

Grady knew Montgomery was the largest town between where he was and the mountains. No doubt his quarry would be either in town or not far from it. It was good news, one he wished he could share with someone, but his wife wasn't really his wife. She would not understand what he was doing, and for that reason he'd never tell her exactly why he was on the trail. He figured if he didn't push her for information, she had no right to ask him any.

As he followed Eliza out the mercantile, he watched her round ass in the ugly brown dress. She had a deliciously curvy body under all that—she'd be a perfect wife if he were honest with himself. However, Grady never intended on having a wife, ever. He wasn't the kind to get married and couldn't imagine actually changing his mind. Yet he'd bought the damn ring anyway.

He had to force himself to keep his hand out of his pocket. It was bad enough he'd actually bought the fucking ring; he didn't need to be feeling it constantly. Instead he focused on the package she had under her arm. He'd told her to buy something to wear under her clothes, and he sure as hell wanted to know what he'd just paid three dollars for.

Grady was no expert in ladies underthings, but it seemed that cotton was the cheapest fabric used. He hoped she'd bought something other than cotton, but for only a few dollars, he doubted she had.

He shouldn't be disappointed, but he was. Eliza had willingly become his lover, and he was enjoying each second he spent under the blanket with her. But her damn clothes were dog ugly on the outside, which didn't exactly match with her passionate inside.

They mounted the horses and rode down the street to the livery. He'd noted a restaurant along the way where they could get a basket of food for dinner. Grady didn't deny he was selfish enough to want to see what she'd bought and would avoid eating in the restaurant to find out sooner rather than later what was in the brown-paper package.

The livery was in a long, narrow building sandwiched between a furniture maker and the undertaker. An odd spot to be sure, but a businessman could only use what he could get.

Eliza was off her horse before Grady even stopped Bullseye. She was obviously still annoyed with him, judging by the way she was leaving him behind intentionally. Grady hoped she would stop acting like a foolish woman since she was anything but.

The livery had a small office in front. A blond middle-aged woman sat at a workbench, small hand tools scattered around the table. She was deep in conversation with Eliza, who sat on a stool beside her. Grady had no idea his sometimes wife was able to be friendly with strangers. Of course, it was one of the reasons, if not the main reason, he allowed her to travel with him.

"I'm so glad you're such a skilled craftswoman, Mrs. Johanssen." Eliza gestured to the small leather pieces on the workbench. "Your talent is outstanding."

How the hell did Eliza know that already?

"I recognized the quality of the work on the walls just as soon as I came in." Eliza smiled at the blond woman. "If you have a hat that fits me, I'm sure my husband would be pleased to pay for it." This time when she smiled, it was more of a dare than a sweet gesture to him.

She was daring him to contradict her, to embarrass himself in front of the leather-loving Mrs. Johanssen. Eliza was in for a surprise then.

"I'll be happy to pay for whatever you want for a hat, honey." He grinned at Eliza, and she stopped smiling.

With a perverse satisfaction, he let the smugness show in his face. When Mrs. Johanssen stood up, Eliza stuck out her tongue at him. Grady laughed, surprising all of them.

"Mr. Wolfe?"

"I'm just happy is all. Let's see what you've got for hats." Grady struggled not to let another laugh escape. He didn't ever remember being so amused or enjoying sparring with anyone before he met Eliza.

"Of course. Follow me." Mrs. Johanssen led them into the livery to a stall she obviously used to display her leather work.

Despite his strange mood, and the fact he was annoyed by his own obsession with the ring in his pocket, he was impressed by the quality of the blond woman's leather work. Detailed décor shone in the polished leather pieces, everything from hats to belts, even shoes.

He turned to look at the livery owner's wife with new eyes. "Liz is right, you have a real talent here, ma'am."

"Why, thank you." Mrs. Johanssen's pale cheeks flushed a light pink color. "Please try on the hats and see what fits you."

Eliza took her time looking at each hat, the brim, the inside, and the decoration added to it. He leaned against the wall and watched her, particularly when she reached up to pull down a hat and her dress strained against her breasts.

Damned if he wasn't getting aroused watching her pick out a goddamn hat. What an idiot he was. He frowned at her as she finished looking at the last hat, then started with the first again.

"For pity's sake, Liz, pick a hat already."

"Don't rush my decision, husband. I'm the one who has to wear it, not you."

"I have to look at it every day."

"Then watch something else."

He could, and did, watch something else, but that's what got him tangled up with Eliza in the first place. Her breasts were positively distracting.

Grady plucked a medium brown hat and plopped it on her head. It landed near her eyes. "Well that one is too big."

"What gave you that idea?" she said dryly as he took the hat off her.

"Shut up and pick one." He bit his lip to keep from grinning.

"I like the light one, but I'm afraid it will show things too quickly."

"What does that mean?" He picked up the hat she liked and looked at it. "Show what?"

She rolled her eyes and took it from him. "Perspiration."

"Oh, but I will line the hat for you with some soft material, then the sweat will not stain." Mrs. Johanssen was obviously eager to make a sale.

"Sold." He handed the blond woman the hat. "Put the material in, and we'll take it."

"B-but—" Eliza tried to protest.

Grady pulled Eliza toward him, effectively cutting off her complaint. He kissed her hard.

"Don't argue with your husband. Now let's get out of here."

Eliza shook her finger at him. "You're deliberately being annoying and trying to distract me."

They walked out of the stall and toward the front of the livery. "Is it working?"

She smacked his arm. "Yes, you incorrigible man."

"Then I'm doing my job right."

Eliza held his hand as he paid Mrs. Johanssen ten dollars for the hat. She mentally calculated how much he'd spent on her clothes so far and wondered how she'd be able to repay him for all of it. She had no money at all and no means to earn any at the moment. Perhaps she could be a schoolmarm after all; however, it likely didn't pay a great deal. It would take her years to get enough to pay him the huge amount of funds she owed him.

Eliza's excitement over a new hat, her first new hat, began to wane. They agreed to come back in fifteen minutes to pick up the hat, allowing Mrs. Johanssen to sew in the lining.

"Let's get some dinner from the restaurant to take with us." He tugged her across the street.

Her disappointment deepened. "You mean we're not eating there?"

"No need. It's not even eleven o'clock. We can get what we need, then stop in a few hours to eat." He glanced back at her. "This way we don't have to wash up and sit in a restaurant with a bunch of strangers."

Eliza wanted to sit in a restaurant, to see the strangers, to experience life. It was selfish of her, to be sure, but she couldn't help the way she felt. She ought to concentrate on helping Grady find Angeline, not the new experiences she was gifted during her journey.

With a sigh, she stood by his side while they purchased a basket of fried chicken, biscuits, and even milk. They were all foods she missed from home and were difficult to get while on the trail. She had to admit it would be nice to have a picnic of sorts together with Grady. The restaurant was nearly empty between breakfast and dinner, but she gazed at the empty tables, imagining people eating and talking. At least that's what she thought people did in restaurants.

They stepped back out into the sunshine and walked over to get her new hat. Eliza held on to the paper-wrapped package, unwilling to let the new purchase out of her hands. It was something to look forward to, other than cold fried chicken on a rock.

Grady went inside to get the hat, and Eliza waited beside Melba. She stroked the horse's neck and took pleasure in having him beside her. He was a familiar face, so to speak, in a world she didn't quite understand yet.

As she watched, Grady came out of the livery with her new hat in his hand. The buttermilk color gleamed in the sunlight, and she realized he'd chosen the right hat. It was a beautiful piece of craftsmanship, and the color complemented her dark hair nicely.

Interestingly enough, she also realized it was close in color to the new undergarments she'd purchased. It was an unexplainable coincidence that Grady had found the right shade of leather.

"It's tanned deer hide." He popped it on her head and kissed her before tossing her up in the saddle.

"Let's get moving."

Although she should be angry with him for bossing her around yet again, she was too fascinated with the new purchase. The hat felt perfect, as if it were made for her. The buttery softness was comfortable and lightweight.

"If you don't stop feeling that hat, I might get jealous." Grady sounded a bit annoyed with her.

"You picked it out."

"Not so you could feel it like it was my dick."

Eliza's mouth dropped open. "Grady!" He seemed to like to shock her as much as he could, to keep her on edge and uncomfortable. She refused to let him. "You're going to have to ask nicely for that."

He made a choking noise, and she was pleased to have made him shut up. For some reason Grady was in a very odd mood, and she didn't quite understand it. Eliza had seen him angry, grumpy, and distant, but today he'd been something completely different.

They rode in silence for a while. Eliza's mind drifted back to replay the time they'd spent in Emerson. He'd hurried them out of town, and she wondered why. Maybe he'd come across some information about Angeline.

She wished she could ask him.

They stopped to eat two hours later. By then Eliza had spent far too much time thinking about why Grady did the things he did. She was only making suppositions of course, and without being able to ask specific questions, she could only guess.

The food allowed her to think about other things, such as how hungry she actually was. They stopped in a meadow with a small copse of trees. With the sun shining and birds twittering, it was an ideal spot. Eliza set out the food while Grady took care of the horses.

When he sat down and picked up a piece of chicken, he stared at her while he gnawed on it until she started to feel uncomfortable.

"Why are you staring at me, Grady? Have I got chicken in my teeth?"

"What did you buy in Emerson?"

His question knocked her out of her strange mood, and butterflies took up residence within her. "Undergarments."

He threw the bone into the meadow and moved toward her. Inching back his hat, his gaze met hers, intense and full of heat.

"What did you buy?"

This time the question wasn't playful—it was demanding. She swallowed the bite of chicken and took a drink of the cool milk. He watched her, waiting like a predator and prey.

"I bought two chemises."

He took off his hat and narrowed his gaze. "Show me."

"They're in the paper-wrapped package in my satchel." Eliza's heart thumped a steady rhythm as the air between them crackled with arousal.

"Put them on and show me." He inched toward her, eyeing her dress as if he were going to tear it off her body.

The heat of the sun mixed with the heat in her body, and suddenly she was in desperate need to take off her dress. Eliza wasn't sure what possessed her, but she set aside the food, wiped her mouth, and stood.

He looked surprised, then sat back to watch her, a hunger in his gaze that she felt all the way to her core. Eliza walked over to the horses, standing between them so he couldn't see her. She glanced down at herself and wondered how she had come to be there, her body already buzzing with a need to make love with Grady. He was a potent addiction, one she found herself wanting more with each time they joined.

What she was about to do was exciting and a bit naughty, considering they were in a meadow in broad daylight. Anyone could ride along and see what she was doing, what they were about to do. She tingled with the excitement of both.

Eliza unbuttoned her dress and slipped it off, followed by her drawers. She took off the old cotton chemise with more courage than she thought she possessed. The warm afternoon breeze caressed her bare skin, and her nipples hardened. She glanced behind her, but he hadn't followed, for which she didn't know if she was glad or not.

Unwrapping the twine and paper, she pulled out the creamy one first. The fabric was soft and cool against her warm skin. It fell nearly to her knees and swayed softly. She felt marvelously sexy as she stepped out from between the horses, very conscious of her undressed state.

Grady was chewing on a blade of grass when he saw her. He dropped the grass and watched her as she walked toward him. His heated gaze raked her up and down.

"Now that's better than that old rag you had."

Her entire body clenched at not only the desire in his gaze, but because she actually felt it on her skin as if he'd touched her.

"I'm glad you approve of my purchase."

"What does the other one look like?"

"The other one?"

"You said you bought two, now show me the other." He leaned back against a large boulder, and she was surprised to see he already had an erection.

Power surged through her. It was her body in the beautiful undergarment that made his body react so strongly. She finally felt like a woman, a sexy woman. As she walked back to her "dressing room," she swung her hips, making the chemise slide on her skin, likely exciting him as much as it excited her.

Then she pulled off the silky chemise and pulled on the lacy one. It scraped nicely against her erect nipples, making her shiver at the contact. She couldn't wait for Grady to see her. If she closed her eyes and ignored her logical side, she might even pretend this was her wedding night.

Fanciful notions, of course, but it put a smile on her face as she walked back toward Grady. This time he actually got to his feet and met her halfway.

"Jesus, that's, ah, damn, Liz." He walked around her, looking at her from all angles.

She had a hard time not blushing.

His fingers brushed along her back. "That little redhead had this in the back, hm?"

"This was the tamest of her selection." Eliza's voice was husky, filled with need.

"Tamest one? I'd like to have seen the rest of them." He walked around to face her and cupped her unfettered breasts encased in the lace. "I can see your nipples."

A pulse slammed into her, and wetness gathered between her nether lips. In a moment, she might have to seduce him.

"They can see you, too."

He chuckled. "You know I don't remember laughing for a long time, Liz. You have made me break all my rules." His thumbs brushed her erect nipples, and she shuddered.

"I've broken all my own rules, as well. That makes us a pair of rule breakers." She put her hands on his, pressing them against her aching breasts.

"Do you want something, Liz?"

"You."

He picked her up and she wrapped her legs around him. Her pussy slammed against his erection through his trousers. As her lips found his, he stepped toward their campsite. Tongues dueling, Eliza barely paid attention to what he was doing as his hands dug into her buttocks.

Suddenly he was sitting with her legs spread on his lap. She met his gaze. "I don't understand."

"You're going to ride me, Liz."

She didn't know what that meant, but she was willing to try. Her entire body pulsed with the need to be with him, to join with him.

"Show me."

He captured her lips again and managed to unbutton his trousers to free his staff. When he brought her hand to him, she closed her fingers around it, familiar and beautiful. She squeezed, running her hand up and down the length of him. A drop of moisture appeared at the top, and she had the insane urge to taste him.

Grady popped her breasts out the top of the chemise. They sat on the seam like two apples waiting to be picked. He cupped them, bringing them to his mouth. Eliza shuddered at the rasp of his tongue, the bite of his teeth, the suck of his lips. She squeezed him harder and he groaned.

"Feel good?"

"Yes, it feels tremendously good." Eliza reveled in sitting on his lap while he pleasured her breasts, she pleasured his cock, and the cool breeze teased her bare pussy. It was pure bliss.

"I can smell you."

She could hardly understand him. "Smell me?"

"Your cunt. I can smell you because you're wet." He bit at a nipple, and a jolt shot straight to the area of discussion and she clenched.

"Rub my dick on you, coat it with your juices. Tease me, tease you."

Grady's instruction left her breathless again. It was like they were in the woods again and he'd told her to touch herself. The idea of touching both of them at once brought her the same level of intense arousal.

With hesitation at first, she moved forward just enough. As she pulled him toward her pussy, her thumb brushed against her clit and she hissed in a breath.

"That's it, honey, keep going."

Encouraged by his words, and her own pounding desire, she used the head of his cock like a big finger. She rubbed it up and down her pussy, landing near the entrance where she forgot what she was supposed to be doing and pushed him in an inch.

"Jesus fucking Christ." Grady groaned against her breast. "Don't stop there, c'mon, Liz, fuck me."

Grady was the opposite of everything Eliza had ever known. His dirty words, his sexiness, his body gave her more pleasure than she could absorb at once. He was the other side of herself, a perfect match.

As she pressed down farther on him, inch by inch he entered her, and that's when Eliza saw the value in "riding" him. She controlled their lovemaking, the pace, the depth, everything.

She loved it.

"I quite like this."

He bit her nipple hard. She yelped at the pain and pleasure, pushing him farther inside her.

"Me, too, now fuck me, Liz. I'm done teasing."

Eliza rose on her knees until he was almost out of her, then plunged down. Her slick folds made the passage smooth and wet, deliciously exciting. Her rhythm was awkward at first, then she found one that worked for her and him.

He never let go of her breasts, never stopped pleasuring them with his mouth and his hands. Eliza didn't realize how much it heightened her bliss until then. She rode him up and down, pulling him deep within her body, until he touched her womb, her heart.

Eliza moaned as her pleasure grew, as the spiral within her tightened with each plunge. He thrust up inside her as she pushed down, then must have realized if he bit her nipple as she slammed herself onto him, she would gasp.

So he did it every time.

Soon Eliza was mindless with joy, her body pulsing for a

release. Grady shook beneath her, and his hot breath coated her already slick skin.

"I'm gonna come. Jesus, I can't hold back. Come, Liz, come, come, come." He chanted through his teeth as they were clamped on to her nipple.

Her body tightened to its breaking point, then exploded with the greatest ecstasy she'd ever experienced. She screamed his name, and as the echo of her voice rang in her ears, the echo of the orgasm rippled through her. She buried his cock deep inside her as he pulsed with his own release.

Eliza saw stars behind her eyes as she held on to his shoulders and rode the waves of pleasure. As it began to subside, she shook with the power of their joining, with the intensity of it.

He lapped at her nipples, causing her to clench around his still hard staff within her. She giggled, more happy at that moment than she'd ever been.

"It's as if I'm a windup toy, I think. You've discovered the button to make me go."

He kissed her breasts and looked up at her. In his gaze, she saw what she thought was love, but it might have been the remnants of the amazing sex they'd just had.

"I'll remember that because these are my buttons to make me go, too."

She cupped his face and kissed him. "I'll remember that."

They extricated themselves and used the water from the canteen to clean up. Eliza felt as if she were floating on air. Her body still buzzed from the bliss she'd achieved in Grady's arms.

By the time she'd gotten herself dressed, he was eating chicken again. His dark gaze locked on her as she walked back. A shiver snaked up her spine, and she wondered what he was thinking about and whether she'd be happy to know.

She managed a small smile as she sat down. He didn't return the smile. In fact, he threw the chicken bone into the meadow again and rose.

"Is there anything wrong, Grady?"

He put his hands in his pockets. "Yeah, there's something wrong."

She swallowed hard and decided against eating any more chicken. "Please tell me what it is. Perhaps I can help."

He snorted. "You can't help because you are the problem."

Eliza frowned and tried to swallow down any fear over Grady's odd behavior. "If you could stop talking in circles and simply tell me what is wrong. I deserve that much from you."

He sat back down with his hands in his lap, now clutching a small piece of burlap. "Every town we go into, folks say something about you not having a ring, doubt we're married."

"We're not."

"I know that, Liz. That's not my point. We both need folks to believe we're man and wife." He fiddled with the piece of burlap.

"Why?" She had enjoyed the idea of having a husband, of being Mrs. Wolfe. Yet she never thought Grady had thought much of it.

"Well, for one thing, if you are traveling around with me, sleeping in my bed, folks will think the worst of you if they find out we ain't married. And folks won't talk to me about who I'm looking for if they think I've got a whore traveling with me."

Eliza flinched at the word whore. "That's a harsh judgment and uncalled for."

"I didn't say I believe it, just that others might. I want you to feel, well, safe traveling with me." He cleared his throat, and Eliza was amazed to realize he was struggling with what to say to her.

"I appreciate your concern, Grady, but I'm not sure how we can solve the problem without actually getting married."

As soon as the words were out of her mouth, she regretted them. His face hardened.

"That ain't happening."

"I never expected it to. I was simply stating a fact." Eliza wasn't lying, although she maybe harbored the tiniest hope it might actually happen. One day.

"Okay, good. Just wanted to make sure you understood that." He opened the burlap. "I thought of something else."

A ring sat on the brown material, winking in the sunlight. Eliza's breath caught in her throat, but she kept her expression normal, even if her stomach was trembling.

"It's quite lovely. Did you purchase the ring in Emerson?" She peered at the ring, imagining it was a real wedding band and not a solution to a problem. Nervously, she pushed her glasses up on her nose.

"Yep, I was right surprised they even had one." He held out the ring to her. "You want to wear it?"

She told herself to not be too enthusiastic as she took the ring. The metal was heavier than she expected and it was warm, likely from being in his pocket. As she slipped it on her ring finger, she was surprised to find it was a perfect fit.

"Fit okay?"

She held it up for him to see. "It's quite comfortable as well. I would be glad to wear it until we part ways. Then perhaps you can sell it to get the money back that you've spent."

He stared at the ring, then looked at her. She would give anything to know what he was thinking.

"Let's get moving then."

Eliza nodded and started cleaning up, her gaze continually returning to the newcomer on her finger.

Chapter Eleven

He'd spent too much valuable time thinking about Eliza, and the damn ring. What the hell was he doing? It was bad enough he'd given her a birthday present even if the soap was something he'd bought back in Bellman. When he realized it was her birthday, he thought she might like something to wash with other than sand. Besides, God knew he never got birthday gifts, and obviously she didn't, either.

The look on her face still shimmered in his memory. He could hardly allow himself to remember when he pleasured her, only to experience the most powerful orgasm of his life. Hell, it made him hard just thinking about it.

Then there was the damn ring he'd bought. Twenty dollars was more than he intended to spend in a month on food and supplies, much less in one minute on a ring for the wife he really didn't have.

Yet he'd gone and done it anyway. Her expression when he put the ring on her finger was enough to make him forget she really wasn't his wife. She'd acted as if they had said their "I dos" and gotten hitched instead of making the pretend marriage look more real to the people they met along the trail. His intention was to hide their imaginary marriage, not make it more real.

"Grady, I don't believe you're paying attention."

Eliza's schoolmarm tone yanked him out of his fascination with her lips. Damn. He was acting like a complete lovesick calf around her. If only they didn't have sex every goddamn night, if only he hadn't kept her so close to his body when they slept, if only, if only.

None of it mattered worth a spit now. Done was done. He had to focus on who and what he was after, not the distracting Eliza. He knew he'd leave her in the next town they found.

Grady could have left her in the wild, but he wanted to be sure she was at least in civilization before leaving her behind. There was a small town about ten miles from them. It was the nearest to them, in the direction his quarry was headed, and the perfect place to rid himself of his distraction before he completely lost himself in her arms. He couldn't fail at this job even if he'd never hunted a woman before.

Eliza would be furious, not annoyed as she was right now as she attempted to teach him how to make cornpone in the skillet for supper. Truth was, he wasn't ever going to make his own, so he didn't pay much attention to her. Damned if he wasn't actually humoring the woman.

Definitely time to part ways.

"I ain't a cook, Liz." He poked at the fire with a stick. "I eat in restaurants or make do with stuff I ain't gotta cook, except coffee of course."

She tutted and continued her lesson, pushing her spectacles up her nose. The way she explained things made him wonder if she really was a schoolmarm. If she wasn't, she sure as hell could be. Every detail, boring or not, was covered in how to cook cornpone. She might even have it written down in her journal somewhere.

"You sure you ain't a schoolteacher gone loco?" He knew she'd get past annoyed and into angry with him, which is why he said it. " 'Cause, woman, you are just spending too much of your time thinking about it."

"Good gracious, Grady, you're deliberately inciting my temper. I hate to admit it's working." She huffed and puffed at the fire, shooting him dark glances as the cornpone's delicious aroma wafted past his nose.

Eliza riled up was a sight to see. He preferred her over the mousy spinster. If he were smart, he'd wire the old man in Tolson that he didn't find his quarry and quit looking. If he were smart, he'd hold on to Eliza and find a small corner of nowhere to be with her for good.

However, Grady would be the first to admit he wasn't always the smart one and didn't always do what he should. He'd never given up on a job before, and he wasn't about to start. His work depended on his reputation, one he'd built up from years of being successful at finding what he set out to hunt.

He wouldn't throw all of it away because of Eliza. Or perhaps he couldn't because the possibility of giving up the one thing he had been good at scared the shit out of him. Hunting and killing were part of who he was, not just what he did. Eliza couldn't change him any more than she could tame a cougar.

"I'm not going to share the cornpone with you, by the way. You misbehaved intentionally, so I will do you the same in kind and not feed you the fruits of my labor." No matter how much he tried to teach her different, she kept talking like a thick textbook on a dusty shelf. Eliza would not change her ways.

Neither would Grady.

Decision made, even if he didn't want to think about what he'd do tomorrow, Grady poured himself a cup of coffee and sat back, watching her fuss around the fire. He should leave her be for the night without complicating his weakness for her body. Yet each time she moved, her unbound hair flashed in the firelight.

He was already aroused, much to his consternation. There were two things he could do, either strip her naked and fuck her silly, or walk away until she fell asleep, then spend the night thinking about how he wanted to wake her up.

Grady had already had sex with her too many times, and he shouldn't have touched her even once. Although it nearly made him weak in the knees, he stood up and stretched his legs.

"I won't ask you for any then." He turned and walked toward the trees behind them, his steps almost dragging.

"Wait, Grady, where are you going?" She sounded confused, something he had to nip in the bud.

"Away from you for a while. I ain't used to being around people much."

She sucked in a breath, audible even from fifteen feet away. Grady felt the force of it, and he almost tripped.

"Damn it to hell." He gritted his teeth and kept walking.

Eliza stared at the spot Grady disappeared into until the cornpone began to smoke. She pulled the pan off the fire and tried to pull her attention back to her supper.

It didn't matter that he left her alone. Since his horse was still tethered to the tree, he'd be back. Of course, he'd still walked away without an apology, and only a cryptic explanation. She wanted to be angry with him, but she was disappointed in herself instead.

There was no future for the two of them, she knew that. They were walking a very fine line between reality and fantasy, and sooner or later it would become razor sharp, enough to wound both of them. The ring was as fake as their marriage, even if it felt real on her finger.

Yet she wanted him to come back, wanted more of his touch, wanted to sleep by his side, and for that she was disappointed in herself. If only he wasn't hunting Angeline, she'd be free to pursue a future with Grady, to convince him they were perfect for each other.

Pipe dreams, that's all they were. Dreaming could lead to wonderful things, like books and inventions, but in her case dreams of Grady would bring her nothing but heartache.

She couldn't help how she felt, though. Eliza knew she was

in love with him, and that would never change, no matter what happened. She recognized the deep feelings for what they were, and she had hoped he felt the same way.

Maybe he did. The thought made her heart thump hard enough to make her chest hurt. Perhaps putting distance between them was his way of denying his feelings. She could only hope it was true, or perhaps she shouldn't hope for it at all.

If they loved each other, though, Eliza liked to believe anything was possible. Even resolving the impossible situation they were in, on two sides of a situation made even murkier by the untruths she'd contributed to it.

Eliza used to think she was trapped in her life at home, like a bird in a cage. Now that she was free, flying on her own, soaring in the sky, she found her life to be just as constraining. There were rules to everything, even living in sin with a bounty hunter on the trail of her runaway sister.

If she weren't experiencing it firsthand, she might even think it was a story from a book. She wished it was, and then she could write a happy ending for herself.

Eliza sighed and forced herself to focus on the meal rather than the missing companion. Truthfully she was surprised he hadn't left her behind again. It made her believe Grady had feelings for her. It was a circle of confusion that made her head and heart hurt.

She ate without tasting much, but her belly was full, and after the day's activities, her body was exhausted. She left the pan with a cloth over it for Grady despite her warning she wouldn't share it with him, then cleaned up everything she'd used to cook with.

With a yearning for his company she had trouble setting aside, Eliza laid down on her bedroll and watched the dancing flames in the fire until her eyes grew heavy. She fell asleep to the sound of the crickets singing her a lullaby.

Grady stood in the trees, smoking a cheroot and watching her. Damn fool that he was, he couldn't even be away from her without actually being away from her. He told himself it was because he wanted to be sure she was safe.

He was a fucking liar.

When she laid down to sleep, he snuffed out the cheroot and leaned against the nearest tree. Eliza was so innocent, still trusting of the world around her. She hadn't even checked to be sure it was safe before she slept.

He waited another thirty minutes before he returned to the fire. To his surprise, she'd left the cornpone for him to eat. As he sat down and pulled a piece from the pan, she made a noise in her sleep. It was almost a moan.

Grady's blood began pumping through him, and every small hair on his body stood up. He didn't even want to consider what his reaction meant. His body knew hers from top to toe, each dip, curve, and sweet spot.

His dick pulsed, pressing against his trousers. She was asleep for God's sake. What the hell was wrong with him? He'd just made a vow to leave her alone, to literally leave her behind, and yet one small peep out of her and he was as hard as an oak.

Maybe he should have fucked her silly, then walked away, but that would have been selfish and stupid. Although he never claimed not to be either of those things, he hadn't felt right about taking her body when he had decided to leave her.

Eliza rolled over, her blanket dipping down to reveal one breast. She wore her not-quite-white chemise, the one he wanted to rip to pieces but she wouldn't let him. It wasn't the ratty chemise that caught his attention, though.

It was the hard nipple beneath it.

If there was one thing he could hardly resist, it was Eliza's tits. They were perfectly shaped, with raspberry nipples that drove him nearly insane. The right one was just visible above the edge of the blanket.

He swallowed hard, instantly and completely so aroused he almost forgot he had cornpone in his mouth. After successfully getting the food down his gullet without choking, he licked his lips. He couldn't tear his gaze away from that nipple.

She moaned again, and Grady fisted his hands to keep from touching her. Obviously he couldn't keep his hands or his body from wanting her. He had to keep himself in check or risk the plan he'd already decided to follow. Yet there was no way in hell he could sleep with the tent pole in his trousers.

That left him only one option.

Grady didn't want to think about what he was doing, so instead he focused on relieving the arousal that had slammed into him. He unbuttoned his trousers and slid down to lean against the tree behind him.

He opened his drawers to pull out his pulsing dick. His hand closed around his hardness and squeezed. He imagined it was Eliza's hand instead of his own callused one. His gaze never left her, watching her sleep, perhaps dream of him. She moaned again, and he responded, low and deep in his throat.

Grady stroked the hardened flesh, squeezing the tip, then did it again. His other hand dug into the ground beside him, the loamy earth substituting for the perfectness of her breast. Her lips parted with a breathy sigh and he sucked in a breath.

As the fire crackled beside him, Grady quickened his pace, his hand moving faster, squeezing the base, then the tip. His balls tightened and he imagined plunging in deep within her body, finding the perfect place where he belonged.

As the orgasm swept over him, he didn't close his eyes, but kept focus on Eliza, on the woman who owned him but didn't know it. Pleasure mixed with sadness accompanied his release, and then it was over.

His arousal quenched, Grady rose and used the canteen to wash himself. The cool water helped to finish the job his hand had completed. He buttoned up his trousers, then took his bedroll from beside Eliza.

Grady couldn't look at her any longer. Not that he expected to become horny again, although he might, but because he was pulling away from her again. He needed to re-gain control of himself no matter what.

As he laid the bedroll where his feet would be near hers, but he couldn't see her, Grady refused to think about the fact it was the first night in weeks he hadn't slept beside her. Sleep was a very long time coming.

Eliza slept deeply and heard nothing until Grady's voice yanked her out of a deep sleep.

"Liz, for pity's sake, get your ass up. The sun's been up for half an hour." He banged some loud items together, startling her into full wakefulness.

She rose quickly, readying herself within ten minutes, only to find Grady had already saddled and loaded the horses. He sat on Bullseye with both sets of reins in his hands, the standard scowl marring his features. Eliza noted he had dark circles under his eyes, and his cheeks looked gaunt. There was obviously something bothering him, and she had a feeling it was her presence.

A bounty hunter was a lonely creature, due to the nature of his business. Eliza knew it was only a matter of time before he fell back fully into his habits as that solitary being.

She could only hope it was later rather than sooner, which was selfish of her for more than one reason.

Using a rock, she mounted Melba, very conscious of the fact he'd not offered assistance. This was another bad sign.

It took another hour before he spoke again. "We're heading into a town named Montgomery later, likely get a hotel room for the night."

She hated to admit that a bed, any bed, was more appealing than anything she could imagine. The hard ground, the cold nights, were all taking a toll on her body and her mind. It sounded positively indulgent.

"I've not stayed in a hotel before. I must admit to being intrigued to do so." She grinned at the top of Melba's head. "Does that mean the horses also stay in guest facilities?"

"I don't even know what facilities are, but I'm sure there'll be a livery for the horses." He pointed toward some low rolling hills in the distance, dwarfed by the towering mountains farther out. "Montgomery is in that valley up yonder. We'll be there near dinnertime."

Eliza didn't want Grady to think her a fool for being excited about the hotel, not to mention the dinner in a restaurant she hadn't been able to enjoy. She kept quiet while they rode, amazed to realize that being on top of the horse was now completely comfortable. Although riding for long periods of time still made her numb, it no longer caused pain.

She was thrilled with her horsemanship and rode with her shoulders thrown back and the wind in her hair. Eliza was free from the ghost of who she used to be.

The town grew larger with each passing minute. When they rode through the outskirts, bruised-looking clouds filled the sky.

"The sky's gonna open up any minute. Let's move a little faster, Liz." He spurred his horse into action, and Eliza followed close behind.

The scattering of houses and small buildings gave way to a moderately sized town. There were wooden sidewalks, groups of people walking to and fro, a mercantile, a saloon called "Dog's Leg," a restaurant, and a hotel. A much different place than Black Rock, for which she was entirely grateful. Montgomery looked inviting and well kept.

Eliza nearly bounced on the saddle as they stopped in front of the restaurant, aptly named "Ana's Plate." It had blue gingham curtains in the windows and a set of chairs with a checkers set between them on a crate.

"It looks wonderful." She dismounted without hesitation and didn't realize until her feet touched the ground that her anomalous dismount wasn't so unique after all. She'd done it again.

"You act like a kid on Christmas. It's just a place to get some vittles." Grady was his usual chipper self.

"Well, I'm going to enjoy Montgomery and all it has to offer." She took his arm, which a moment after they touched she realized was a big mistake. He was stiffer than the wood beneath her feet.

"That ain't a whole hell of a lot." He didn't pull away from her, but he didn't seem to welcome her touch, either. Something had happened after Black Rock, after her birthday when he had shown her true pleasure. It was as if he was deliberately putting the distance between them again. She didn't like it, nor did she welcome it. Eliza would do her best to stop his nefarious plan, even if it meant throwing herself in his arms.

Of course, that would be what she wanted to do anyway. She'd had another dream of him last night, one where they had pleasured themselves in full view of each other. It was incredibly erotic and left her needing his touch even more. Then of course, he'd woken her rudely and had barely said three words to her all day.

Grady was two people inside one. The trick would be finding the one who was gentle, considerate, and protective. It appeared the grumpy, mean, and taciturn side had control. Eliza would find a way, no matter what the cost.

They stepped into Ana's Plate, and the scents of many different things washed over her. There were apples, cinnamon, fresh bread, perhaps gravy or beef stew. She closed her eyes and reveled in the scents, most of which reminded her of home. The kitchen was the place she missed, and the satisfaction of making a wonderful meal. There were few things other than her inventions that Eliza took pride in—cooking was one of them.

A plump, matronly looking woman with gray hair in a tight bun approached them. "Afternoon, folks. Sit where you'd like. We've got rabbit stew, taters, and apple pie for dessert."

She pointed to the tables peppering the room. Only two of ten had people at them.

Eliza drank in the wooden tables with mismatched chairs

around them. On a table by the window someone had put wildflowers in a tin cup.

"That one there by the window will be lovely." She bounded over, a spring in her step.

"Your wife sure is chipper." The woman must have remarked to Grady.

"You have no idea." Grady's response made Eliza's grin wider.

"We'll take two plates and coffee."

"I'd rather have water." Eliza waited by the table until the two of them caught up.

"Okay, water and a coffee." Grady sat down with a thump, and without pulling out her chair. She knew a gentleman would have done so, but she reminded herself again her companion was no gentleman.

"Be right back." The older woman winked at Eliza before she turned away.

Eliza didn't know how to react because she'd never had anyone wink at her before. This town of Montgomery was obviously a much friendlier place than the awful town they'd escaped days earlier.

The wildflowers were a bright blue with white flecks in the delicate petals. Eliza ran her fingers down the side and smiled at the softness. This was exactly what she needed, to take another step toward a new life away from the LDS community.

She wouldn't think about what would happen after Grady found her sister. That time would come soon enough, and she would decide how to proceed then. A coward's way out, but at that moment, she would accept being a coward.

The food arrived quickly, for which Eliza was grateful. She'd had too much time with her thoughts already that day. The stew was thick and rich with potatoes and vegetables, salty and simply delicious. Eliza swallowed the first bite with a groan of pure satisfaction.

She glanced up at Grady's face and stopped with the spoon

halfway to the bowl. His dark eyes were fixed on her, glittering with what she could only describe as hunger. She had not expected his primal reaction to her pleasure with the food, but something within her responded to him.

Goose bumps danced up and down her skin as they stared at one another. She couldn't look away or reach across the table and kiss him. This was what she wanted; the connection between them was just as strong as it had been.

Her breath came in short, slow bursts while her heart thundered crazily. The moment stretched out as Grady's intense stare made her nipples rise and press against her blouse.

"Is it good?" The older woman's voice made Eliza startle so badly, she dropped her spoon with a clatter and a splash into the bowl. "Oh, dear, I'm sorry." She pulled out a towel from her apron and wiped up the spill.

"I was clumsy. There's no need for you to apologize." Eliza wasn't surprised to hear a tremor in her voice. Her body was still yearning for and oddly reactive to Grady's.

"I surely hope you're enjoying your dinner. Save room for pie now." The woman refilled Grady's coffee from a tin pot before ambling off to another table to service other guests.

Eliza managed a deep, cleansing breath before she picked up her spoon and began eating again. Grady watched her still, yet it was surreptitiously, out of the corner of his eye rather than the intense gaze. The strangeness of what happened wasn't lost on her. No matter how much he tried to push her away, she knew now he could never push her far enough.

The intensity of his reaction and of hers was exactly the indication that what they shared was much more than a pair of casual traveling companions. Much, much more.

The childlike excitement in Eliza's eyes almost made Grady look away. She was too damn innocent to be stuck with someone as dark as he was. It had been so long since he'd even been around someone with her naïve view of the world, it was as sweet as it was painful. Little did she know of the shadows around her, of the task he had been hired to carry out. Even he had to do some heavy thinking before he accepted the job to hunt and kill Angeline Brown. It made every moment with Eliza that much harder.

Then there was the attraction between them, which was out of control. He should have never allowed her to travel with him, should have left her the day she stumbled into his life for the second time. Hell, he didn't even know her story beyond the vague explanations she'd given him.

He didn't know her reasons for meandering around the territory with him, and she didn't know his. In fact, he needed to focus on what he was getting paid to do, not on being distracted by the little wren who'd latched on to him.

"What is your schedule after you finish dinner?"

He frowned. "I don't have a schedule, Liz. I just do what I have to."

She took a sip of water. "Well, then, what is it you have to do?"

"That ain't none of your concern. Just eat." He meant to sound rude and was rewarded with disappointment in her gaze.

Exactly what he wanted. Grady needed to disappoint her so she'd stay away the next time he left her. Eliza was going to destroy him if he didn't.

They ate the rest of their meal in silence with only a few sidelong glances from Eliza. He kept his focus on the rabbit stew, which was actually real good, and the bread he used to sop up the gravy. He had a feeling if he asked, she'd tell him her cooking was just as good, yet another fact he did not want to know.

"You folks want that pie now?" The older woman reappeared with huge slices of pie on two tin plates. The sight of the decadent dessert was enough to make him forget how full his belly was.

"I sure do. Thank you, ma'am." He took the plate from her, but Eliza shook her head.

"I'm quite full. Are there facilities nearby? I mean, do you have an outhouse or something similar?" Eliza's cheeks flamed up pink, and he figured he was the cause of her discomfort.

"A'course. Right through that door there is the back of the building." She pointed for Eliza down a hallway. "The outhouse sits to the right. Can't miss it. And there's some soap and a bucket of water, too, if you've a mind to wash up."

Eliza murmured her thanks and disappeared through the door. Grady couldn't have timed it better.

"She okay?"

"Yeah, she's fine, just feeling a bit poorly. We had to leave home quick 'cause my mama's sick. My sister and aunt were riding a few days ahead of us, and we haven't caught up to them yet." He put a forkful of pie in his mouth, and the explosion of flavor was incredible. "This is delicious."

"Why, thank you, sir. My mama taught me that recipe." She sat down in Eliza's empty chair. "Yours is sickly?"

"Oh, yes, ma'am, with a fever. We got a wire that she didn't have much time left, so Liz and I left as soon as we heard." He shook his head dramatically. "We haven't got much sleep on the trail, especially her. The hotel will be right nice for her tonight."

"Bless her heart." The older woman tutted. "She looks plumb worn out."

It really was too bad he couldn't keep Eliza with him, but her kindness and innocence didn't mix with a cold-blooded killer like him. She would hate him if she knew what he'd done in his life for money, what he was about to do. He could not accept her hate.

"I'm worried about my sister and aunt, too. They didn't wait for me to stop and get them, being so worried about Mama and all." He took another bite of pie and forced himself to sound overly concerned about a woman he didn't know from the woman he rode with.

"Maybe I've seen them. What do they look like?"

It was easier than expected, yet again. Eliza had opened so

many doors to him he hadn't been able to breach in years past.

"My sister has long blond hair, seventeen, and pretty. My aunt has brown hair, about thirty, kind of short. They likely headed through here three or four days ago." He gripped the fork so tightly the metal cut into his finger, but Grady kept his worried gaze on the older woman in front of him.

"I remember them! Yes, they were here about two days past, looking just as tired as your lady there. Oh, now I know why. I wish I'd known then, I would've packed some good vittles when they left."

"Two days you say? Then we're closer than I thought. I'm sure we'll catch up with them soon." He took a sip of the lukewarm coffee while inside he was howling with satisfaction as the knowledge he'd not only been on the right trail, but he had caught up. "Did they rent a buggy or get a ride with a wagon heading west? They didn't have horses and have been making their way to Mama that way."

The gray eyebrows slammed together, and she tapped her cheek with one finger. "I don't rightly know, but I'm betting Tim at the livery would."

"Much obliged, ma'am. I'll speak to Tim when I put the horses up for the night." He finished the pie with his belly close to bursting and his mind whirling with the possibility of being within two days of his quarry. The thrill of the hunt was best when he got close enough to smell the prey.

In this case, it meant the end of his time with Eliza was upon him. The job would be over, and he could disappear into the Colorado wilds again. Eliza could find her own way to whatever she needed. Life would return to normal.

He almost snorted at the thought, then remembered he had company at the table with him. Grady was not usually so careless.

She pushed the other plate toward him. "You may as well enjoy this one, too, and I'll get you some fresh coffee."

The last thing he wanted was to eat more food, but he

smiled pleasantly and pulled the plate close. "Don't mind if I do."

Eliza made her way back to the table feeling better. He barely glanced up at her as he stuffed her piece of pie in his mouth. She wanted to smack him for being deliberately rude to her again. It was as if he didn't intend to let down his guard and be nice, because as soon as he realized what happened, up went that wall of ice.

She was tired of it and wished fervently he'd stop doing it. Of course she could ask the sun not to shine and it would have as much effect. Grady was as solid as the mountains in the distance—unmovable and hard.

He was hunting her sister and picking up pieces of information as they traveled. She ascertained he'd found out something useful from the woman who'd served them lunch. The matron had hugged her profusely and held her hands as if they were long-lost friends.

"Y'all come back for supper if'n you're staying in town tonight. I'll have fried chicken and dumplings, your man's favorite." Another hug, and the woman walked them to the restaurant door.

Eliza should ask Grady what that was all about, and how in the world the woman knew what his favorite dish was. However, she didn't want him to lie to her, and likely he would if she asked. She'd already done enough lying for both of them. All he'd done was lie by omission, which may be a less serious sin in the eyes of the world; it was in her eyes. Everything she'd done in the past couple of weeks would condemn her to hell in the opinion of her former church, so why not continue to lie. It wasn't as if she hadn't already sinned profusely.

They stepped outside to a light rain, but the purple black clouds looked even more ominous, if that were possible.

"It's fixin' to come down something fierce. Why don't we get you to the hotel, and I'll get the horses down to the livery?" He didn't give her a chance to answer, but rather took her by the elbow and walked her two doors down to the building marked MONTGOMERY HOTEL.

Eliza was annoyed with his high-handedness, but also completely fascinated to step into a hotel for the first time. This entire adventure was a series of first times and she wouldn't ever forget a moment of it.

The lobby had two arm chairs, a small table, and a rather large rag rug on the floor. A fireplace with ashes and half-burned logs was to the left, a set of stairs to the right. In front of them was a long wooden desk with a cowbell sitting atop it. There was no one about, so she picked up the bell and rang it merrily.

Grady snatched the bell from her hand and growled at her. "You don't need to keep acting like an idiot."

She sucked in a breath of pure pain and stared at him with her mouth open. He'd never been deliberately cruel before, and she could hardly believe her ears.

He slammed the bell back onto the counter and braced his hands against it. "Damn it, Liz, why the hell do you have to tie me into knots?"

She tied him into knots? What was that all about? The man treated her with gentleness one moment and nastiness the next. He was a conundrum she would likely never puzzle out.

"I beg your pardon?" she managed to say without her voice shaking.

This time when he looked at her, she saw naked agony in the depths of his gaze. It shocked her more than the cruelty did. Before she could absorb what she saw, he turned away.

"Can I help you folks?" A balding, tall man with kind eyes appeared behind the desk. He wore a nicely pressed blue shirt and a small bowtie.

"Grady Wolfe and my wife Liz. We need a room for the night." Grady's tone was hoarse, but calm.

Eliza felt as if she'd just lived through a thunderstorm named Grady.

"Welcome to Montgomery, Mr. and Mrs. Wolfe. Name's John Fowler. I own the hotel with my wife Maisie. You'll meet her in the morning." He smiled at Eliza, who was still trying to get her bearings. "We've got a nice big tub in the bathing room if you've a mind to take a bath later."

"That would be lovely, Mr. Fowler." Eliza felt her cheeks tremble as she attempted a smile. "I'm afraid I am travel weary."

Grady put money on the desk. "Heat up the water for her, and give her whatever she needs."

When he turned to Eliza, his eyes were cool as the rain outside. "I'll go get your things."

With that, he left her alone in the hotel, her excitement smashed beneath the heels of his boots.

After dropping the bags at their room in the hotel, Grady set off for the livery. He didn't want to feel guilty about being curt with Eliza. She shouldn't have any expectations of him being sweet or polite. However, that didn't mean anything when he saw the stricken, pale face sitting on the bed.

He rode down to the livery, Eliza's horse in tow, with the idea he'd be riding away within twelve hours without her, or the old nag she loved. As he arrived at the weathered-looking building with a hand-painted sign, HANSEN'S LIVERY, Grady set aside every thought of Eliza or his entanglement with her.

It was time to do what he did best.

He dismounted and secured the horses to the post outside. After a deep breath, he stepped into the gloom of the building. Before his eyes adjusted, he kept his hand on the butt of his gun.

"Help you?"

Grady turned and found a muscular man with wide shoulders and ginger-colored hair, two or three inches shorter, but thirty pounds heavier. He kept his weight on the balls of his feet and his hand exactly where it was.

"My wife and I need to put up the horses for the night."

The man relaxed his stance and nodded. "Sure thing. Got two stalls next to each other in the back there. Three dollars for both of them, includes feed and fresh hay."

Grady paid the man and backed out the door to get the horses. He wasn't about to turn his back on the stranger.

"You Tim?"

"Ayup, Tim Hansen. This place was started by my pa, and I took over when he passed." The man's voice changed pitch as they walked out into the street to get the horses. "The gelding is nice, but that nag looks like he's gonna fall down dead before he gets to the stall." The man obviously knew his horses because Grady thought the same thing about Melba each morning.

"Liz loves that horse, for whatever reason. He's got a good heart, I'll give him that." Grady took his horse's reins while the other man led Melba into the barn ahead of him. "My horse needs new shoes, too. Can you do that today?"

"Sure can. Be happy to."

A quick look around the barn showed three other horses, four empty stalls, and plenty of horse shit. Nothing surprised him, which was a very good thing.

The two men unsaddled the horses, rubbed them down, and got them settled with freshwater and feed. It seemed as though Bullseye sighed with relief when Grady used the curry brush on his coat.

"My wife and I are staying at the hotel down the street. Fowler sent me down here with the horses." Grady took his time to give the horse more attention than he'd had in a week.

"John's a good man; sends business my way whenever he can." Hansen sounded genuine enough.

"Folks in town seem to be good people. Ana is right

friendly, too." The restaurant owner had been as transparent as a pane of glass.

"She's friends with my ma." Hansen sounded even more open.

"Her apple pie was like a slice of heaven after being on the trail for a week." In that, Grady was telling the absolute truth.

"Where are you and your wife headed?"

It was a friendly question, one anyone would ask. "Raymer Falls. My ma took sick, and we're pushing to get there. My sister and aunt are headed there, too, a couple days ahead of us." He leaned his forehead into the horse's neck and felt the warmth from the only companion he'd had for years. Until Eliza.

"The rain gave us an excuse to stay here for the rest of the day. Liz was tuckered out." Another truth, strangely enough.

"Ah, that's too bad. Your ma gonna be okay?" Tim poked his head into the stall and smiled when he saw Grady with his horse.

"Probably not. That's why we're running the horses so hard. Ana told me you may have seen my sister and aunt." He described them again, keeping his tone even but concerned. "They didn't have horses to ride, so they've been renting wagons or relying on the kindness of strangers. I need to catch up to them to keep them out of danger."

Tim frowned. "What are their names?"

"Angeline and Lettie." The names he carefully memorized rolled off his tongue as if he knew them intimately.

"Ayup, they was here two days ago. They rode over to Bowson with Randy Burns. He was delivering a load of lumber just outside of town."

"I appreciate your helping them. This Randy a man to trust with your sister?" Grady peered at him with a narrowed gaze, exactly what a worried brother would do.

"Absolutely. He'll make sure they get to Bowson and then help them find a safe place to stay." Tim closed Melba's stall door, and Grady did the same with his own horse's.

"Then I'm obliged to you for finding someone to look out for them. God only knows she never listened to me, stubborn little cuss." Grady wanted to rub his hands together with satisfaction.

He was closing in on his prey.

Eliza stared at the steam wisps rising from the bath and tried not to sigh again. She should be enjoying the deepest, hottest bath she had ever had. The hip tub she grew up with didn't allow for a deep soaking. The hotel's luxury was unexpected and should have pulled her from her doldrums.

It didn't.

Grady was nearly ready to get rid of her, and she knew it all too well. He was deliberately cruel, driving a wedge between their relationship, or whatever it was they had together. She had a choice to either allow him to do it or fight him.

The old Eliza would have allowed him to do what he pleased. However, the new Liz would not.

Decision made, she would enjoy the bath no matter what self-pitiful nonsense she'd been wallowing in. With a smile, she soaped up the wash rag with the lavender bar she'd found in the bathing room.

The sweet scent filled the air as she scrubbed off the dirt and grime from the trail. Then she scrubbed her hair, delighting in dunking her head beneath the hot water to rinse it. She washed her hair again and felt cleaner than she had since she couldn't remember when.

She remained in the bath a few more minutes until the water grew cool. Her fingers were wrinkled, and she felt indulgent for having not only used so much water for bathing, but had been the only one to use it.

With a grin, she stood up and reached for a towel. That's when the door to the bathing room opened and Grady stood in the doorway.

Eliza was completely naked.

His eyes widened as his gaze wandered up and down her wet form. She felt frozen in place, her heart pounding so hard she thought her ribs might crack. Then he closed the door behind him.

She swallowed the lump in her throat and reached down to find her courage again. Her decision had been made; now she had to keep to it. After all, she'd made a promise to herself and no one else.

Instead of covering up, she stepped out of the tub, sluicing water on the floor; a few drops landed on his dusty boots. The air between them crackled, and every small hair on her body rose. Although she was wet from the bath, a different kind of moisture gathered between her legs. She knew it meant she was ready to be with Grady.

Judging by the erection clearly visible in his pants, so was he. She actually heard him swallow, and his Adam's apple bobbed up and down. She smiled and gestured to the tub.

"Would you like a bath now, Grady?"

The corner of his mouth twitched. "Later."

"The water is cooled down now, but we can probably request a bucket of hot water." She knew she was pushing him now, acting as if she wasn't standing there naked as the day she was born. Eliza trembled with arousal and nervousness.

"I'm hot enough." He stepped toward her, and she managed not to jump.

Eliza reached for the towel on the stool and stopped when a growl sounded from his throat. She licked her lips and waited to see what he would do.

"Come here, Liz."

It was an order, one she could either follow and be the same old girl she always was. Or she could seize the moment to take control.

"Come here, Grady." The words echoed in the small space.

One of his brows went up as he regarded her with his blazing gaze. She expected him to crook his finger and disregard her.

What she didn't expect was for him to cross the few feet between them and grab her by the waist. As his mouth came down on hers, she closed her eyes and swallowed the small smile that threatened.

After a hard kiss, he stepped back and looked down at her body. He was dusty, and her clean skin was now peppered with smears of mud.

"Maybe I should've taken that bath."

Eliza grinned. "Let's get your clothes off then."

With a courage she didn't know she had, she slowly removed his hat and shirt. As she ran her hands down his chest, the crinkly hairs tickled her palms and she loved the difference between them. When her fingernails scraped his copper-colored nipples, he groaned.

She knew enough about him to recognize it wasn't a groan of pain but rather of pleasure. Her education continued as she pushed him onto the stool to take off his boots.

"You're getting all dirty," he remarked as she knelt in front of him.

Eliza tugged off his boots, very conscious of her naked breasts brushing close to his canvas trousers. "I think I've been dirty since I met you."

He barked out a rusty laugh. "That's the truth if I ever heard it."

When he was barefoot, she pulled him to his feet. He watched her as her hands drifted toward the buttons on the trousers. Eliza knew he was waiting to see what she would do, if she could finish what she started. Her blood pounded through her veins as she reached for him.

The trail of dark hair led from his belly button down. Something possessed her as she traced the line with her finger, and his body jerked.

"You learn something new today, woman?" His voice was laced with tension.

"I learn with every moment I spend with you." She met his gaze and kept it as she unbuttoned his trousers.

His staff sprang free and thumped against her hand. Satin-covered steel and hotter than a blazing fire, she hesitantly touched him with her fingertips.

"You ready to keep on with that education?"

His question was laced with so much more than a simple request. There was so much she didn't know about the relations between men and women. Prior to meeting Grady, all she knew was what she'd observed with farm animals, which of course told her nothing. With animals, the male bit and forced the female to do his bidding.

Grady was offering her the power to control their relations. She shook with the possibility of moving past the simple sexual actions they'd shared.

Swallowing the fear, she leaned forward and kissed him while her hands closed around his staff and squeezed.

"Mmmm, yeah, Liz, more."

She tickled his lips with her tongue as her hands continued to explore his manhood. He opened his mouth, and she mimicked what he'd done and found his willing tongue. They slid against each other, exploring the recesses of his mouth, his teeth, and her arousal.

He groaned low and deep in his throat. She felt hot and cold all over, on pins and needles. She was new to seduction and wasn't sure what to do next. He saved her the trouble of deciding.

"Lay that towel on the floor, and let's get busy, woman."

She shook with the arousal that coursed through her, amazed he was there with her even after all they'd been through. Eliza loved him, too much, so much, she could hardly take a breath.

With trembling hands she laid the towel on the floor and then watched as he stripped completely. He was such a wonderful specimen of man, and hers for the taking, at least for this precious now.

She took hold of his cock and pulled him close until they both sank to the floor onto the towel. As she pressed her breasts into his chest, he made a sound of approval. His chest hair tickled her nipples, making them tingle deliciously.

He lifted her leg and slid forward until he was nudging her entrance. Before she could fathom what he was about, he'd entered her in one quick thrust. She gasped at the sensation, the fullness from his penetration.

They'd made love in many places, in many positions, but never like this. It was as if they were on level positions, rather than one on top of another. His dark gaze found hers, and then he started to move.

She pulled him close enough to kiss, his lips just as hot as the rest of him. Sweet, sensual, wet kisses as he thrust in and out of her grasping pussy. She could hardly believe how arousing just facing him was. Grady's hand held her leg up even as he kept a steady rhythm with his lower half.

"Feel good?"

"Mm, feels wonderful." She nibbled his earlobe and he sucked in a breath. Obviously another ticklish spot. Deliberately she did it again and he growled at her.

Eliza was surprised how quickly her body responded to his, perhaps because they knew each other's triggers, likes, and desires. Or perhaps because she loved him, wanted to spend her life making love with him.

He nibbled at her lip. "You look different without your spectacles. Sexier. Your eyes are so damn blue. Like blue-bonnets."

Eliza vowed to take them off each time they were intimate. It was the first time he'd complimented more than her breasts, and she found a little voice inside her who very much enjoyed it.

His slow pace was creating a storm within her, a hunger she wanted to be slaked. Although she tried to thrust back against him, because she was on her side, she had no leverage.

"Faster." She bit his shoulder as he buried himself inside her.

"Pushy."

"Desperate."

He chuckled, and suddenly she was on her back with her legs in the air. Eliza forgot to breathe as he pounded into her, deep, so deep. She closed her eyes and scratched at his back, pulling him toward her, to fly with her, be with her.

"Yessss."

Her body tightened in its familiar rhythm of release, like a spring being wound up. She felt herself sliding into the vast reaches of space, amongst the stars. Eliza whispered his name as she exploded into a million points of light, shining against the blackness behind her lids.

His fingers dug into her hips as he found his own release, joining her as she soared high above the earth. He collapsed against her, his heart thumping hard against her.

For that brief moment, they were one. He was hers and she was his. She loved him.

Chapter Twelve

Grady stared down at Eliza as she slept. She looked so damn innocent, so naïve with her dark hair spread over the pillow. He should have left long ago, and made sure she couldn't find him.

He turned away, unable to look at her anymore. Since he'd already broken his vow never to touch her again, he wouldn't do it even one more time.

Grady had a job to do, and he was determined to do it even if it meant killing a woman. He left two golden eagles on her bag, hoping she wouldn't think of it as payment for services rendered. Then he picked up his saddlebags and slipped out the door without a sound.

The predawn sky was slate gray as he walked down the sidewalk to the livery. He'd make sure to leave extra money for Hansen if the man wasn't awake yet. Eliza should head back to where she came from or where she needed to be, but he didn't want to rush her. Hell, she could even decide to stay in town.

Just as the hotel lobby was deserted, so was the livery. He saddled his horse quickly and left five dollars in the slat of Melba's stall. As he walked out into the murky light, his mood couldn't have been darker.

Considering he'd tracked his quarry and caught up to her

within two days, he should be in a good mood. Or at least not ready to snap somebody's neck at the least provocation.

The streets were quiet except for an occasional bird call and a dog bark. He mounted the horse and against his better judgment, looked back at the hotel. If luck was with him, Eliza would let him go without following him.

Grady turned and left town, letting the wind erase his tracks. It was time to become the hunter again.

He rode until the horse was lathered and he had more sand in his eyes than he thought possible. The sun had risen in the clear blue sky, reminding him that the summer had not yet let loose its grip on the land. Sweat ran in a river down his back as he found shade near a creek.

The water was cool and inviting, and clear judging by how fast Bullseye pushed Grady out of the way to get to it. He patted the equine's great neck in silent apology. Normally he wouldn't push his horse so hard. He didn't know whether it was his desire to find the woman he hunted or to run from the one he left behind.

Grady didn't want to know.

He managed to get down a biscuit with ham he had gotten from Ana the day before. He drank water using his hand as a cup to wash it down. Within fifteen minutes, he was back on the trail somewhat refreshed and completely determined.

Eliza knew Grady was gone the moment she opened her eyes. The bed was completely cold on the right side, and so was her heart. She lay in the bed a few more minutes, feeling sorry for herself for waking up alone. Self-pity was going to get her nowhere of course. She gave herself a stern talking-to, then rose from the bed to dress. Perhaps he was down at Ana's restaurant drinking coffee.

Eliza nearly forgot she was naked, and there were numerous places on her skin where the flesh was slightly reddened, particularly around her nipples. Her cheeks flared as she realized it was whisker burn from Grady.

She wished he had stayed in bed with her and woken her in the morning to make love. Now that she'd had a taste of what pure bliss was, she wanted it with him over and over again.

Her heart sank to her knees when she realized his saddlebags were missing. She had hoped that what they shared the night before would be enough to bind him to her.

It appeared she was completely mistaken.

Eliza didn't allow herself to cry until she saw the golden eagles on her bag. The two of them sparkled in the sunlight that came through the lacy curtains on the windows. The coins stared at her, nearly sneering at her naïveté and her inability to accept that a wolf cannot change his nature.

She wanted to hurl them into the street and howl at the cruel trick fate had played on her. Instead, she sat on the edge of the bed with the coins in her hands and wept.

Once the tears had subsided, Eliza's heart was still just as heavy and just as broken. However, her logical side took over and forced her to recognize her own stupidity. The old Eliza would have wired her father and waited to be retrieved, then punished.

The new Eliza, who became a true westerner under Grady's tutelage and a woman under the starry night sky, would never return to Silas's house. It was time to find her man and fight for him.

Eliza washed and dressed with speed, then almost flew downstairs with her bags. Although she shouldn't accept the money he'd left for her, she took it anyway. She wasn't quite sure what he'd meant when he left it behind. Perhaps he'd thought of her well-being with no money in hand, or perhaps he wanted to give her the means to begin again without him.

Either way she wasn't going to give him up without a fight. She'd tracked him once, she could do it again.

After asking Mr. Fowler to watch her bags, she walked down to the livery to retrieve Melba. Although she hadn't accompanied Grady the day before, she knew where the building was. The ginger-haired man was shoeing a horse when she arrived.

"Good morning, sir. Are you Mr. Hansen?"

He stopped and wiped his brow on his rather dirty sleeve. "Morning, ma'am. Yep, I'm Tim Hansen. Can I help you?"

"Yes, I am hoping you can. My, er, husband boarded my horse here yesterday along with his own." She managed a smile, although it hurt her face to do so. "I would like to retrieve Melba now."

Eliza didn't know if Grady had paid for the boarding or not, but she had the golden eagles tucked into her gloves if she needed them.

"Melba? What kind of horse is it?"

For once, she didn't know the answer. "Brown with a white blaze on his nose and white stockings."

"Oh, you mean that old fella in the back. I saw your husband's horse was gone this morning, but he left more money." Mr. Hansen scratched his arm. "I figured you was staying here a few more days."

Grady had left more money? She didn't know what that meant, either.

"Could we retrieve Melba now? I'd like to get started with a morning ride." She stepped toward the barn and he followed.

"Sure thing, Mrs. Wolfe. I'll be glad to saddle him for you. He's got a good temperament."

The interior gloom of the barn was barely touched by the bright sunlight outside. Mr. Hansen picked up a lantern by the door, which threw a warm glow ahead of them.

"Did my husband mention to you where he went this morning?" She strangled out a chuckle. "He left so early I thought perhaps he'd have been back by now."

"I don't rightly know where he's gone, ma'am. He left afore I even got up." Mr. Hansen led her to the corner stall. "If you want to wait right there, it'll only take me a few minutes to get him ready."

Eliza rubbed Melba's neck. "Yes, thank you. That would be lovely."

She tried not to think about the fact Grady had left before the livery was open or that he'd left even more funds for her. The man had to remember she would try to follow him, or maybe he was hoping if he left enough money, she wouldn't.

He'd be very surprised, then, when she found him.

"Here you go, ma'am." Mr. Hansen handed Melba's reins to her and they walked out of the barn together.

The sunlight hurt her eyes, and she blinked against the pain. It wasn't tears for Grady again, that was for certain. She only had one emotion when it came to the Wolfe who'd stolen her heart.

Determination.

"Thank you for your assistance, Mr. Hansen." She noted a mounting block and walked over to make use of it. "I need to go retrieve my bags from the hotel, then I'll be on my way."

"Wait, Mrs. Wolfe, take the money your husband left. It ain't right me keeping it and all, especially with his Ma being so sick."

Eliza took the proffered money from the livery man. "Yes, it's a shame, isn't it? He's been worried sick." What kind of game was Grady playing?

"I expect he was trying to catch up to his sister and aunt. Way he tells it, they're stubborn enough to try to travel alone." Mr. Hansen shook his head. "If I were them, I'd be worried about what he's going to do to them when he does find them."

Dread coiled in the pit of her stomach at the reminder of exactly what Grady was doing and who he was chasing. He had obviously found Angeline's trail and she was still traveling with Lettie, Josiah's second wife. She'd suspected they had left together, but given Mr. Hansen's retelling of Grady's tall tale, now she was sure they had.

"Mr. Wolfe is simply worried about them. I-I'm sure they'll be glad of his assistance as they travel to the family homestead." She didn't know what she was talking about but knew she had to find out as much information as she could.

"Yep, he did look right worried. I was glad I knew they'd gotten a ride with Randy over to Bowson." He tucked his hands in his trouser pockets. "He's a good man, but your husband is right to be worried about his kin."

His kin. Wasn't that a twist of the information? She wanted to shout it was *her* sister that was in danger, but didn't want to cause any more issues for herself.

"Again, thank you for your help, Mr. Hansen." Eliza mounted Melba with ease using the block of wood. Amazing how far she'd come in less than a month.

"You're welcome, Mrs. Wolfe. Hey, you're not planning on following your husband alone, are you?"

Eliza's grin was more like a feral baring of her teeth. "Of course I am. What wife wouldn't follow her husband when he needed her most?"

She left the sputtering livery man and headed back to the hotel. Then she'd get some food supplies using the money Grady had left her and be on her way within thirty minutes.

It was time for the apprentice to surprise the teacher.

Grady stopped only two more times to rest the horse, riding until it was too dark to see his hand in front of his face. Only a fool would risk injuring his horse in the rough terrain. He could act like a fool sometimes, but when it came to his horse, he'd temper it with logic.

Logic told him to stop and sleep. If he was able to sleep, of course. There was a little shelter behind a large group of boulders ahead. It would provide protection from the wind and allow him a vantage point to see anyone approaching the camp.

As he unsaddled his horse, his mind wandered to Eliza. Even though he didn't want to think about her, apparently he had no choice in the matter. He wondered how Eliza had handled his departure, whether she'd gotten angry or sad, maybe even taken the money and rode in the other direction.

His worse fear was her hieing off after him as she'd done before. This time he had anticipated the woman's resourcefulness and rode through terrain that would leave no tracks to follow. The horse also had new shoes, which meant she couldn't use the trick of following the shoe prints with a nick.

He was impressed; it took a lot of effort to actually throw Eliza off his trail. She was damn smart, and not just book smart, either; she had good instincts and a sharp eye for detail. If he wasn't hired to kill the people he tracked, they could be very good together in the bounty-hunting business.

That was neither here nor there. The truth was, he'd left her behind and that was that. Grady would never see Eliza again.

The realization hit him like a gut punch, and he sat on a smaller rock reeling from the impact. He hadn't said goodbye, or even kissed her sleeping cheek. It proved what kind of man he was, that was for sure. Not the kind to marry a woman like Eliza.

Jesus, he needed to stop thinking about her and start thinking about who he was supposed to be hunting. Angeline Brown was a wily target for a woman, but the fact she'd stuck with the older woman proved she wasn't as wily as she should have been. They would have done better by splitting up, but considering her age and lack of experience, he understood the need to rely on each other.

From what he knew, they had headed to Bowson two days earlier. It was a smaller town than most, and the number of folks riding in and out would be fewer, which meant less opportunity for someone to offer them a ride. He assumed the women had little funds, so perhaps they would stay in town for a while, maybe earn some money in one way or another. Bowson was a three-day ride, which meant they'd be getting there tomorrow.

He'd ridden so hard, he'd get there in just over two days, and hopefully surprise them. That's what Grady was counting on. From what Tim Hansen had told him, the fugitives had relied on others for help and settled for a meal they'd split between them at Ana's. No doubt they were hungry, scared, and nearing on desperation.

Perfect opportunity for the wolf to catch his prey.

After taking care of his horse, he laid out his bedroll without starting a fire. No need to advertise where he was camping for the night. Yet another precaution against the resourceful Eliza, and any other two-legged or four-legged creature that might be about in the blackness of the night.

When his head finally hit the bedroll, Eliza's scent surrounded him. He cursed loud and long as he realized there was almost no escape from her. She had crawled under his skin, and dammit all the hell, into his heart.

He didn't want to love Eliza, didn't want to believe he was capable of such a weak emotion. Women and trust didn't mix; there wasn't much else to offer her. Yet he'd gone and done something so monumentally stupid, he wanted to kick his own ass.

Grady rubbed his bedroll up and down the horse's withers, then in the sand to rid himself of her scent. He shook it to get rid of the excess gravel, then took a whiff. His loco idea took care of the scent and added a ripe, not-so-sweet one instead.

By the time he lay down for the second time, his eyes were as gritty as the blanket. His heart, however, was beating again. An organ he'd long since given up on had come to life over a mousy spinster schoolmarm with beautiful blue eyes and the courage of a lion.

He ground his fists against his eyes, telling himself the stinging was due to the sand and nothing else. Grady wrapped himself up in his now smelly bedroll and closed his eyes.

It was a long, lonely night for the lone wolf.

*   *   *

Eliza rode Melba at a steady pace toward Bowson. With directions from Ana, and a sack full of food, she set out after Grady. She had to find him before he found Angeline, before everything crumbled into dust, before she lost him for good.

Oh, she wasn't fooling herself into thinking a happy ending was possible. Even if she had indulged in one of those romantic books, which lay at the bottom of the bag if she were honest, she had no qualms about accepting that there was a very slim chance at a future with Grady.

First, he was a bounty hunter. Second, she'd lied to him from the moment she met him. Obviously he'd been doing his fair share of lying, too, but what they did with their bodies, what she felt in her heart, was no lie.

She loved Grady Wolfe, and she was certain he loved her in return. If he hadn't, he wouldn't have left her all that money, or made sure she was taken care of before he rode off. Oh, no, his actions told her there was hope, and she was holding on to it for dear life.

Angeline's return to Josiah Brown would prove to be a sticking point between them. Grady would need to agree to give up whatever he'd been paid or would be paid for bringing her back. She wasn't sure if Lettie had a bounty on her head as well, but regardless of that, he was sent to find Angeline. If he loved Eliza, he would understand why he couldn't bring her sister back.

Josiah Brown was a monster who pretended to be human. He had beaten Angeline from the moment he'd married her, leaving her bruised and bloody on their wedding night. When Eliza had arrived the next morning, she'd been heartbroken to see what had been done to her beautiful, vivacious sister. Eliza had tried to think of a way to undo what had been done when Angeline and Josiah spoke their vows, but hadn't yet come up with a solution.

Then Angeline had run with Lettie, and everything had changed. Eliza had found out quite by accident that Josiah had hired Grady Wolfe to find her. Eavesdropping was a bad habit, but she considered it to be a necessary device when she was dealing with someone as evil as Josiah.

Eliza had to make Grady understand just how much danger Angeline would be in if he brought her back to Josiah. There was no doubt in Eliza's mind that her sister would die within a few days of her return to the Brown household. No one would dare stand up to the great Josiah who held sway across all men in the ward.

However, Eliza dared that and more. She had thrown away her entire life to help her sister and along the way discovered who she really was, and had fallen in love with a man she should have never met.

Life had been so simple, so uncomplicated, and so stifling. Leaving Tolson had been like a metamorphosis for Eliza. She was no longer the ugly caterpillar living on a tree branch and waiting to be something else. Instead she'd become a butterfly, a thing of beauty with wings to soar above the drudgery and escape the misery.

For that, Eliza would be grateful to her teacher, who had given her the books and instruction to survive. And to Grady, who taught her to fly.

Eliza's determination drove her to ride Melba alone all day and into the night. She didn't see a fire or even a single speck of evidence that Grady had passed the same way. Yet she knew deep down in her heart, he'd been there.

Exhausted but proud of her journey, she stopped for the night near a stream with cool, clear water. The fresh shoe prints in the mud told her someone had been there earlier that day. She could only hope it was Grady and her path was the right one.

After making Melba comfortable, she put her bedroll down on a bed of pine needles and lay down to rest. As soon as her head touched the blanket, Grady's scent surrounded her. She breathed in deeply, bringing him into her lungs, into her body. The strength and purpose she had started with that day only grew greater within her.

As she closed her eyes, she imagined it was his arms around her, and not the blanket that held the ghost of his scent. Sleep came easy as she felt secure within the circle of the man she loved.

Grady woke with a start, feeling as though he'd just closed his eyes. The sun was just painting the horizon pink, and dawn was only a few minutes away. He dragged himself up and broke camp quickly, eager to be on his way.

As he saddled his horse, he had vague recollections of dreaming about Eliza, about holding her in his arms and pressing his nose into her hair. If only the damn bedroll hadn't smelled like her, he wouldn't be in such a fix.

He rode hard again, trying to outrun his thoughts and his memories—not that it worked. He exhausted himself again, yet when he finally slept again the next night, he again dreamed of Eliza.

By the time he woke up on the third day, he was almost relieved to see her standing in front of him. Her old brown dress was now in rags, her face lined with dirt, and she sported bags under her exhausted looking eyes. Her hair had seen better days and was currently sticking every which way under her battered hat.

She stood with her hands on her hips and a look of pure satisfaction on her face. "I thought maybe you forgot something." She tossed the two golden eagles in the dirt in front of him. "I am not for sale and I won't accept payment for sharing your bed."

Grady thought at first he was dreaming, but then the coins kicked up a cloud of dust that tickled his nose. Jesus Christ, how the hell had she found him?

"Liz, go home." He rose to his feet, ignoring the coins.

Having Eliza stand over him gave him an uneasy feeling he didn't like.

"I have no home to return to. You are currently the closest thing I have to a family in this world, and you left me behind as if I was a saloon whore you had sex with." She sucked in a breath, which sounded more like a sob. "I gave you my trust, my body, and my heart. All of which you just threw back in my face as if it were worthless. To make matters worse, instead of being completely angry with you, I find myself wishing you would take me in your arms and kiss me."

Grady should have turned his back, should have made tracks away from her. But he didn't. In fact, he was so stupidly happy to see her, he did exactly what she wanted.

He took her in his arms and kissed her.

They were both dirty, covered with two or three days of dried sweat, but it was the sweetest kiss he'd ever shared with her.

She tucked her head into the crook of his neck and he realized she was crying. Eliza had shed tears for him.

He was completely dumbfounded by the notion. This woman who had braved hell and back to not only ride by herself, but track him twice, was crying over *him*. Grady had never had anyone shed even a single tear for him.

Eliza was crying buckets.

His throat closed up as he sat down on the rock with Eliza firmly attached to his side. Leaving her behind had been a mistake, his heart and mind finally agreed on that. He'd left because he wanted to find his quarry, finish the job, and get his money. Yet he had abandoned the one person in the world who cared if he lived or died. The one person who cried for him.

"I'm quite angry with you." Her voice was muffled against his neck.

"I realize that."

"You've got a lot of explaining and, I daresay, apologizing to do." She swiped at her cheeks, and he saw the dirt and water mixture coat her hand. "We had an agreement, you and I, and you broke it. I did everything you asked, including cooking, cleaning, and sharing your bed. Although I didn't expect a marriage proposal, I did expect common courtesy."

He cringed at the tongue lashing she was meting out. "Okay, enough already. I get it, Liz. I am a poor excuse for a pretend husband and a lousy son of a bitch."

She was quiet for a moment. "Well, I don't know if I'd sink so low as to call you derogatory names."

"Then I did it for you." He pulled her to a sitting position and tugged off her hat so he could look her in the eyes, watery as they were. "You have to know I ain't one of the good guys."

"I never thought you were a knight on a white steed." She sniffed. "I did think you were good at heart, though, or rather I do believe it."

He could hardly swallow that bit of information. She thought he was good at heart? What the hell ever gave her that idea? He was a nasty bastard, literally and figuratively, who did what he could to survive, including killing people for money.

"Then that makes one of you." He tucked a strand of hair behind her ear. "Liz, I ain't worth your tears." If he'd ever told her the truth, this was the most honest he'd ever been.

"I'll be the judge of that. You continue to be my traveling companion, promise not to leave me behind ever again, and I will forgive you." She shook her head. "I cannot explain the whys of how things occur, but I will accept them if all evidence points to them as the truth."

"What the hell does that mean? Don't rattle my brain with your fancy talk, woman, just tell me in plain words." He hated feeling dumb around her, but every time she opened her mouth, every other word was lost on him.

"What I'm trying to say, unsuccessfully of course, is that I've fallen in love with you."

Grady didn't even remember getting up, but suddenly he

was ten feet from her and her mouth was open in an "O" of surprise.

"What?"

"You heard me quite well apparently judging by how quickly you just moved." She rose and walked toward him with deliberate, slow steps. "I love you, Grady Wolfe, whether or not you want to accept my words. There is absolutely nothing you can do to change how I feel. I accept it as the truth and trust that my heart knows what it's doing."

"Oh, sure as hell it doesn't know a damn thing if it's fallen in love with me." Grady could hardly swallow the gigantic lump in his throat. He didn't want her love, the responsibility of it, the realization he likely felt the same way about her.

He stumbled over some loose stones as he backed away from her. "Liz, honey, you need to set your sights on someone a little more reputable. Some farmer with a nice couple of acres, have a passel of kids, grow old and safe with him."

She pressed her palm against his frantic heart, and his body cried out for more of her touch. He felt as if he'd fallen head-first into a twister, and he'd be lucky to get out alive and in one piece.

"I don't want to live on a farm with some other man. The only man I want in my bed, or my bedroll, is you. As for children, the same holds true. I cannot imagine holding any baby unless they had your eyes."

This time he fell on his ass into the dirt, his mouth opening and closing but no sound coming out. Eliza was loco, plain and simple. He couldn't be the man she wanted.

"I can't," was all he managed to whisper hoarsely.

She knelt beside him and cupped his face with her small hands. "Oh, yes you can. We can do anything our minds and hearts want us to do. I love you, Grady, and I believe you love me. Whether we're riding through the prairie, or tucked beside a fire in a small mountain cabin, I want to be with you for the rest of my life."

This time when she kissed him, Grady felt something inside him burst, as if a dam of hurt and fear and fury had burst. It careened through him, leaving behind a shell of a man whose heart beat for the woman in front of him.

This time when their cheeks pressed together, he couldn't tell who the tears came from.

They slept for a few hours, spooned together and content. Grady needed the sleep. Considering he'd spent two days in the saddle, he was beyond exhausted. She was obviously just as tired because she'd caught up to him, which meant she rode harder than he did.

The sun was high in the sky before they woke. After some simple ablutions, he built a fire so they could have a proper meal. After he had the fire blazing, he couldn't find Eliza. He knew she hadn't gone far, but she wasn't within sight.

He walked around until he found her on her knees fiddling with her bag of books again. Beside her on a flat rock lay her journal, and a quill pen dipped into an inkwell. Judging by the amount of ink on the page, she'd been at it since she'd left him by the fire.

"What are you doing?"

She looked at him and smiled as she pushed the glasses up on her nose. The smile lit up her entire face, reminding him of just how pretty she was beneath all the layers of learning. "I needed to work with my hands a bit. It helps me, ah, relax. So I'm developing a pulley system to allow me to raise and lower the travel bags from Melba's saddle without straining myself."

He grunted. "You ain't the only one straining yourself. I've been hauling that bag up and down, too."

"Well, then it will assist you as well." She stood up and showed him a series of ropes, loops, and two metal rings all hooked to the saddle horn and the bag.

"Where did you get all that stuff?" He knew she didn't have it in her bag, and he sure as hell didn't.

"I found it in the alley behind Ana's restaurant near the outhouse. She told me it was trash and I could take whatever I wanted." She smiled. "I can't imagine throwing away such things. These are all completely useable pieces of equipment. A veritable treasure trove."

He didn't want to know what she'd been doing—he wanted to be on their way as soon as possible. They were close to catching up to Angeline Brown, and he didn't want to lose the scent.

"We've got to eat and get going, Liz. Just pack up your things so we can eat."

She looked down at the ground. "I've been told many times to stop my inventions." With determination in her eyes he recognized, she shook her head. "I'm going to finish this and verify it functions correctly."

He frowned at her. "What?"

"I said I am going to spend an additional ten minutes to finish this. My notes are incomplete." She knelt back down on the ground and started fiddling with the bits and pieces again.

He'd seen her in many different moods including scared, angry, exhausted, and happy. Even when they'd been intimate, she had kept a piece of herself tucked away. This was the piece. Obviously her passion knew no bounds when it came to her inventions.

Grady ran his hand down Bullseye's withers as he watched her work. He was going to leave her to whatever she was trying to do, but Eliza's enthusiasm coupled with his own curiosity about what made her tick made him stop.

"How does it work?" He leaned against the horse and watched her.

She grinned again and went back to work. "I'll be able to show you shortly." After writing something else in the journal, she made a few more adjustments to the parts.

"I believe it's ready to be tested." She placed one bag on either side of her horse on the ground, then looped it all together. "Ready?"

Her eyes shone in the early afternoon light. He felt the corners of his mouth tug as if he actually might smile at her.

"Go ahead, Liz."

With a flourish, she took the two metal rings in her hands, and with a whoosh, the bags were up to the top of the saddle. He was so astonished his mouth fell open. She whooped with delight and secured the rings to the bags.

"It worked." He walked over and examined what she'd done. Grady was no smart person like her by any means, but it seemed like she had invented something folks would pay good money for.

"Yes, it worked! Grady, I'm so excited to have done this. No more straining either of our backs with my books. We can simply use the pulleys to raise the bags up and down." She strutted around like a tiny peacock, her voice full of wonder and joy.

It was almost too painful to watch. He touched the rings, avoiding looking at her for too long. Eliza was meant for better things than a man like Grady Wolfe. She deserved better that was for damn sure. His dreams to keep her by his side were nothing more than smoke in the wind.

"You should sell your inventions, you know."

She stopped walking in circles. "What do you mean?"

"There's companies in big cities like New York or Chicago would pay you money for your inventions. Likely make a good living on your own." She didn't need a man to support her that way; although he didn't condone it, it sure was possible.

"Truly?" She put her hands on her cheeks. "I never thought, well, I never considered it anyway. That's a wonderful idea, Grady. I must look into that possibility in the very next town we stop in."

Oh, yes, that was a wonderful idea. He wanted to snatch it back out of the air and stuff it back down his lousy throat. What did he care, though? She wasn't his responsibility, hell she wasn't even his wife, although they told everyone they'd met she was. Eliza could and should ride to the nearest train depot and leave his sorry ass behind.

If she wanted to leave, Grady wouldn't ask her not to go. He swallowed the lie and turned to walk away from her.

Eliza was tired and dirty enough to beg for hot water to wash. Yet she was also deliriously happy. Although he hadn't said the words "I love you," she knew Grady had finally accepted her love. And to make the day even more perfect, her invention had worked. The first time she'd been able to create something useful for herself and use it openly. The jangling of the rings would be a constant reminder of her triumph. She'd been so glad Grady had been there to share it with her.

Even with three days of dirt and grit, they could only wash up using the meager water in the canteens. They feasted on the food Eliza had managed to mete out over the past several days. The stale biscuits and apples were more delicious than she thought possible. Grady even kissed her as he put her back up on Melba.

She knew Bowson must be close, and they could hopefully get a real bath in town to truly get clean. Eliza swore she could even taste dirt in her teeth.

As they rode, she was more than happy to be beside him again. He didn't look as happy as she felt, but that was all right. He'd accepted her arrival back in his life as if she were meant to be beside him. Her joy at that development knew no bounds.

There wasn't much that could break the bond between them now. Except of course, finding Angeline. From what

Eliza had learned from Tim Hansen, Grady was very close to finding her sister. In fact, she might even be in Bowson.

Eliza didn't know if she wanted to get there faster or not. If they arrived to find Angeline there, it would be a quick knife into the center of their relationship. Too soon after they had developed the fragile bond between them.

However, if they arrived and Angeline had already gone, they could ride together past Bowson, which would give her ample opportunity to solidify the connection between the two of them.

She was torn with the knowledge her happiness could cost her sister much, and vice versa. Things were quite complicated in Eliza's world, much more so than they had ever been. Yet she wouldn't trade it for anything in the world.

Eliza didn't realize how much love would change her, how she would feel simply looking at him riding beside her. He wasn't classically handsome with the harsh planes of his face or the sharp chin, yet put together, he was simply perfect.

Grady turned to look at her and raised one brow. "Something you want to say, Liz?"

She never considered herself as a Liz, but when she was with him, she became Liz, a woman who'd been born on the trail beside him.

"Just thinking that although you're not handsome, you're perfect." She hadn't intended on blurting that out, but it was too late to retrieve it.

His mouth almost curved into a grin. "And you, Liz, are not beautiful, but you're perfect, too."

Absurdly enough, Eliza felt her heart thump at the compliment, simply because he sounded sincere and because Grady didn't say nice things about anyone.

"Thank you, Grady." She smiled broadly at him, and he turned away.

"If we want to make Bowson by nightfall, we'll need to

ride a bit harder." He slid her a sidelong glance. "Are you ready?"

She couldn't stop the grin from spreading wider. "No, but let's go!"

Eliza spurred Melba into a faster gait, and unbelievably, he managed to not only keep up with Grady's bay, but did so with seeming ease. It appeared this adventure, these life-changing weeks, had been enough to reinvigorate her old horse into a new life as well.

They rode for miles, sometimes side by side, sometimes single file, toward the mountains. Bowson was nestled in the valley at the foot of the largest mountain ahead. The air had cooled enough that the extra speed made her cheeks sting a bit. She didn't care, of course, because she felt alive and happy.

The happiness would be put to the test, as would her love for Grady, when they found Angeline. However, she was as confident as she could be that their relationship would survive.

As the sun began to set, the peaks of buildings came into view and she knew they'd arrived in Bowson. Grady's jaw tightened with each step closer to the town. Eliza's bubble of happiness popped as she realized the time had actually arrived. It was time to test their love.

The town was a bit smaller than Montgomery, but large enough to have a hotel with a restaurant, a jail, and a blacksmith. There were numerous houses, well kept and clean, and some with flowers in the yards.

Bowson seemed ideal, a haven for someone looking to hide where danger didn't lurk around every corner. If Angeline had come there, she would feel safe, Eliza was sure of that. If they were lucky, they would find her sister there and put an end to the furious tension that existed between her and Grady.

He stopped at the hotel and helped her down off Melba. As her feet hit the ground, her body brushed against his, loosening dirt and some gravel. She almost laughed, but his expression was far from amused.

His eyes glittered with that dark intensity she'd come to expect from him. He touched her cheek with two fingers.

"What are you doing here with me?"

She swallowed, unsure of how to answer him. "Being with the man I love."

He closed his eyes for a moment and pressed his forehead into hers. "Somebody has a twisted sense of humor because I can't even think of a good answer to that."

She kissed his hand. "You know the answer."

"Damn, woman." He shook his head. "You don't play fair."

"When it comes to us, I have discovered playing fair gets me left behind alone. I refuse to go through that again." She kissed him quickly.

"Somehow I don't want to go through that again, either." He kissed her forehead. "Let's go eat."

"I need to wash up before I sit down for a meal." She glanced down at the dirt caked on her shirt. "In fact, I may have to burn this."

He snorted. "Hm, I think we could probably both create a new wallow for the local pigs." He peered down the street in the twilight. "I see a bathing house down the street. Let's go."

He grabbed his saddlebags and her smaller bag, and they walked down to the bathing house. Eliza had never used a public facility like it before and didn't know exactly what to expect. Grady obviously had because he marched in as if he knew exactly what to do.

It was a bit larger than the other buildings. When she stepped in she realized it was much longer than she thought. There were three long wooden tubs with a green curtain in the center. Beyond that, there must have been more tubs perhaps for women.

A middle-aged woman with frizzy curls was sitting on a

stool in the corner with a small table beside her. She had an apron with large pockets covering her not so small girth.

"Ma'am," Grady nodded in greeting. "You have a private room?"

She looked between them. "That your wife?"

Grady squeezed her arm. "Yes, ma'am."

"You got money to pay for a private room?" She narrowed her gaze at them. "Judging by the look of you, you still got no money."

Grady managed a small grin. "We've got money." He reached into his pocket. "How much for a private room with freshwater."

The proprietor made a face as if she was mentally calculating the price, or perhaps determining how much she could charge them to get what she could from them. "Five dollars."

Eliza gasped. "We are willing to pay for a hot bath, but not for the entire town."

Grady made a choking sound that might have been a laugh.

"Okay then, three dollars for the private room and fresh water." The woman got up from the stool, which creaked in protest. "You pay me up front or you ain't getting nowhere near the tub."

Grady handed her the money. "Fresh water." His tone told her in no uncertain terms he expected her to follow through on that particular requirement.

"Sonny! C'mere and empty the tub in the private room." A lumbering giant of a man, perhaps her son or husband, appeared from behind the green curtain. He had dark curly hair and a low forehead. Eliza ascertained he was one of those people who did not have the average intelligence most people did. He smiled at Eliza, so she smiled back.

"My son is an idiot but he's big, so's he works for his food."

Eliza frowned at the woman. "He cannot help how his

brain was formed, ma'am. If anyone is to blame, it might even be you."

"Excuse me?"

"Never mind." Grady took Eliza's arm and herded her toward the green curtain. "Sometimes you just need to shut up, Liz."

"But she was being cruel and to her own son!" She had to make Grady understand. "Your own parents should be the ones who take care of you, not push you down like that."

Grady shook his head. "I ain't saying I don't think you're right, just that nothing you say will change his life or his mother's mind."

Eliza didn't want to accept that, although it had the ring of truth to it. She looked around the room and realized it was clean and surprisingly cozy. Sonny reappeared with the large wooden tub in his arms, then set it in the center of the room. He smiled again at Eliza before he left the room.

"You gonna make him fall in love with you, too?"

Eliza turned to him, her mouth open in complete surprise. His face was a mask of confusion and pain.

"Too?" Did that mean he loved her?

"You have no idea what you've done, do you?"

"Tell me, Grady. Please."

As they waited for the hot water, he paced the room with Eliza watching his progress. "You think a parent should take care of a child, right? So do I, but it don't always happen that way, does it? My father used to own a store, did you know that? I used to love coming in there to sit beside him while he helped people." He looked far away, as though he'd left the room temporarily.

"No, I didn't know that. Where did you live?"

"Missouri, south of Kansas City. The store was everything to him, and he kept it neat and stocked for his customers." Grady shook his head. "There wasn't a person who came in his store that didn't leave with what they needed, even if they couldn't pay for it. He must have had so many people who owed him money, we barely scraped by ourselves, but he managed to do it. Even at the age of five, I knew there was a satisfaction in doing something he loved."

Sonny came in with two huge buckets of steaming water and poured them in the tub, then with another smile at Eliza, he disappeared again.

"What happened to your father?" Eliza had a feeling Grady's father was a very important part of what made him who and what he was.

"He let the wrong person get what they needed."

"I don't understand." Eliza touched his arm, and he flinched. "What happened?"

"He didn't open the store on Sundays, even in the afternoons, because it was family time. One Sunday when he was cleaning the store, somebody banged on the door." He paused, and Eliza could have shaken him.

However, Sonny appeared for a third time with more hot water. Only a few more buckets of hot and they'd be ready for the cold. This time when he smiled, Grady growled at him and the man-boy stumbled out of the room with his buckets smacking against his legs.

Although she wanted to scold Grady, Eliza simply waited for him to continue. She needed to know what happened.

"A man said he needed something, I never knew what, and my father, being the shopkeeper he was, let the man in. I was behind the counter playing, and I heard them talking." He swallowed audibly, then met Eliza's gaze. "It took me ten minutes to come around the counter to look for my father, and I found him lying in his own blood."

She gasped at the image. No five-year-old boy should see his own father murdered. What a horrible thing to have happened to him. "I'm so sorry." She tried to take his hand, but he again flinched.

"It was my mother's lover."

Eliza could hardly believe her ears. Before she could even absorb that information, Sonny came in with the last two buckets of hot water and dumped them in the tub. He kept a wary gaze on a tense Grady and moved much more quickly this time. After the young man left, the wisps of steam rose from the half-full tub.

"Grady, I can't tell you how so—"

"You know why he killed my father? Because she told him my father had raped her." His dark gaze was nearly feral with hate and fury.

Eliza realized it wasn't his father who had shaped him, but his mother.

"I don't understand."

"My mother was a fucking slut, a widow who had me years after her first husband died, then had her lover murder her second, the man who had become my father." His hands were clenched so tight, she heard his knuckles pop.

This time when Sonny came back in, Eliza was glad of it. He was a distraction they both needed. She had to have time to absorb the information she'd learned about Grady. There were of course bad people in the world, doing bad things every moment, but to imagine a woman would deliberately kill her husband was unthinkable.

"How many more buckets?" Grady barked at Sonny.

The poor young man jumped. "Four."

"Then let's get them. I'm done watching you ogle my wife, boy."

"I ain't oglaling nobody." Sonny looked so afraid of Grady, she was afraid he would actually soil himself.

"It's all right, Sonny. My husband is simply tired. He won't hurt you." She touched Grady's arm, and this time he didn't pull away, although he was tightly strung. Hopefully he wouldn't snap into pieces.

When Sonny left the room, Eliza let Grady be without asking him any more questions. There were so many she wanted to put to him, but knew he had revealed a great deal about himself, more than he likely ever did. She could be patient enough to wait until another time, another day, to hear more.

By the time the tub was ready, Sonny ran out of the room as if Grady was going to shoot him. She shook her head and vowed to talk to him about his intimidation tactics another time. Perhaps he didn't understand Sonny had the mind of a child trapped in a man's body.

Instead she needed to bring Grady back from the horrible memories, back to her side. After she took the bar of lavender soap from her bag, she began undressing while he watched her. The fierce expression on his face began to soften as she took off each article of clothing. By the time she was down to the chemise, he was now intently looking at her with that familiar hunger.

"I hate that chemise."

She looked down at the serviceable, nearly gray undergarment. "It serves its purpose."

"It's ugly as shit."

Eliza let loose a laugh. "I'm glad you're not reticent or shy about telling me how you feel."

He walked toward her and she managed to stand her ground, although she felt like a bird beings stalked by a big cat. He was tall enough to tower over her when he got close enough. His finger ran across the top of the chemise. Her nipples immediately popped.

"I love your tits."

She didn't flinch from the crude name. In fact, it felt even a bit deliciously naughty. "Thank you."

He brought his other hand up and cupped them. She closed her eyes as his thumbs ran across the turgid peaks. When she heard fabric ripping, she opened her eyes to find her chemise torn asunder.

"Grady!"

"Now you can throw that fucking thing away." He leaned

down and took one breast in his mouth, and she forgot to scold him for tearing her chemise.

In fact, she forgot everything except for the steam-filled room, the hot mouth on her breast, and the amazing sensations coursing through her body. His hand nudged between her legs and found her pleasure button.

Pure bliss zipped through her as he stroked her slick folds. He slid two fingers up inside her even as his palm continued to rub circles on her clit.

Then he bit her nipple and she jumped. She moaned and admitted to herself the fact she actually enjoyed his teeth on her. It heightened her pleasure, which likely meant something about her, but she didn't want to examine it. She just wanted to feel.

He scooped her up and carried her to the tub, standing her up so the wisps of steam circled her nude body. Then as she waited, he took off his clothes without his gaze ever leaving hers. Excitement curled in her belly as he stepped into the tub, turned her around, then they both sank in together.

The tub was long enough for her, but Grady's knees poked out the top of the water. It was positively decadent to be lying in a tub with her lover, taking a bath in a public bathing house. It was a good thing she didn't care who knew or she might be embarrassed. However, she was enjoying herself too much to feel ashamed of what they were doing.

She lathered up the soap and started washing both of their legs. He twitched when she washed his foot, a ticklish spot apparently.

Eliza tilted her head back and wet her hair thoroughly, then she heard him do the same to himself.

"Here give me that." He took the soap from her and washed her hair, massaging her scalp with his big fingers. The scent of the lavender surrounded them, its beauty winding around the steam wisps with each movement of his hands.

"I love it when you do that."

"Wait until I really get started."

After rinsing her hair, he washed his own quickly while she squeezed the water out of her black locks.

"Now I get to wash the rest of you."

He sounded positively delighted by the prospect, and she was more than excited to have him do just that. After lathering his hands again, he washed her back and arms, then reached around to cup her breasts. His hands slid in and around them, the soap making it feel as though he was gliding across her skin.

With splayed fingers he did the same to her nipples, the peaks popping through between each digit. It was incredibly arousing.

"That feels . . . amazing." Her voice was husky with desire.

"They sure do. I could play with them for hours."

"The water would get cool."

"Oh, don't worry, we could set it to boiling if we wanted."

She smiled and leaned back into him, recognizing the item poking her backside was not the tub. His erection was impressive and tempting.

"My turn."

Before he could stop her, she turned around to face him. The steam had made his hair curl up on the ends, and his whiskered face was near feral with desire. She kissed him, a fierce mating of lips, teeth, and tongue that left her a bit breathless.

She kneeled and took the bar from him, lathering her own hands even as he continued to touch her soapy breasts. As she leaned over to kiss him again, her hands dove into the water to find his turgid cock. The soap made her hands slick enough to glide effortlessly over his skin.

Their tongues rasped together even as they pleasured each other with their hands. Each time she was with Grady, her experience and her desire increased. She broke the kiss and sucked in some much-needed air.

Grady was breathing just as hard as she was. The only sound in the room was their labored breath and the frantic beating of her heart.

"I need to fuck you."

Eliza's body clenched at his bald statement. She needed him, too, the question was how.

"The tub's too small for that. Perhaps we can wait—"

"No, I ain't waiting, woman." He grabbed her by the waist. "Turn around and get on all fours."

He rose from the water, his cock mere inches from her face. She couldn't help herself, she reached out and licked him from top to bottom. He shuddered and touched her head.

"God, Liz."

He tasted like man, like Grady, like pure desire. She cupped his wet balls and pulled him deep into her mouth, sucking as he'd done to her. Although unskilled, she continued licking him, bringing him into her mouth, then releasing him with a pop. She nibbled at him, too, making him shiver.

His essence coated her tongue, and she recognized it as Grady's taste, the life within him. He suddenly pulled away from her and blew out a breath.

"I ain't ready to finish yet. Get on your knees."

She cocked one brow at him.

"Okay, please get on your knees."

Eliza did as he asked, eager to try whatever he had in mind. He knelt behind her, his knees on either side of her calves. She felt his dick nudge her entrance, and she closed her eyes.

As he slid into her waiting pussy, tingles spread through her. Inch by inch he filled her until finally he was joined with her completely. The sensation was beyond words, beyond anything she'd experienced.

They were two people joined as one.

"Liz." He sounded as amazed as she felt.

"I love you, Grady."

He gripped her hips and began to move. His speed was unhurried and maddeningly slow. She pushed against him, needing more than the leisurely pace he'd set. With an evil chuckle, he smacked her fanny.

Far from being angry or hurt, she found the slight stinging sensation to be as arousing as his teeth on her nipple. Eliza didn't know what any of it meant, or if it meant her proclivities were odd. All she knew is, it felt right and only with Grady.

"Do it again."

He paused for just a moment before he smacked her again. The combination of her wet skin and his callused hand made the stinging that much more intense. Apparently it also sparked an interest in Grady because his pace finally quickened.

As he plunged in, one hand would spank while the other tugged her closer. Deeper, then deeper still. His balls tickled her clit, heightening her pleasure that much more.

Eliza closed her eyes, her fingers digging into the bottom of the tub. As Grady went faster, the water began splashing up around them, but she didn't care one whit. All her focus was on him, his cock, his hand, her pussy.

Her pleasure began to spiral tighter and tighter in her lower abdomen. He was now thrusting so hard, she was having to hang on to the tub to avoid getting pushed out of it. One more slap, one more thrust.

Yes, more, now.

Eliza could hardly form a coherent thought as the steam and the water surrounded her. She clenched her eyes shut as a veritable tidal wave of sheer bliss roared through her. She bit her lip to avoid screaming his name aloud as the ripples of ecstasy took over her body, turning her into a liquid puddle of heat.

His fingers bit into her hips as he plunged in so deeply, he touched her soul. His body shuddered above her as he reached his release, prolonging hers to an intensity she hadn't known existed. Stars exploded behind her eyes, and it was several minutes before she could catch her breath.

"Holy shit."

Eliza hung on to the side of the tub. "Indeed."

He chuckled and bent down to kiss the nape of her neck as he withdrew from her body. She smiled and managed to get to her feet. Grady took her in his arms and they embraced while their hearts beat hard against each other.

They had been intimate numerous times, in various places, and now a bathtub in a public bathhouse. Yet this time had been different; it had been much more intense, and not just the pleasure, either. Perhaps it was because she'd confessed her love to Grady, or perhaps because he had accepted that love.

She kissed his shoulder and stood back to look at him. He was a fine specimen of man, and he was all hers. With a grin, she kissed him and stepped out of the tub.

"Now I'm quite famished."

He smiled and shook his head. Grady didn't smile often, but when he did, it transformed his face from forbidding to joyful. His beauty shone through with it. Not that she'd tell him that, so she simply enjoyed looking at her man.

Yes, he was definitely her man.

They wrapped their dirty clothes into the sack Eliza had brought food in, then put on clean ones before leaving the bathing house. She wore her purple dress, and it suited her mood well. It was as if the bath and their mating had rejuvenated both of them. Eliza almost felt like a different person, more hopeful and stronger.

Grady took her hand in his as they stepped onto the sidewalk to walk back to the hotel. Eliza didn't remember ever holding hands with him before and was absurdly pleased at how well they fit together.

The hotel was bigger than the one in Montgomery, but the restaurant took up most of the first level. Since it was near suppertime, there were quite a few people dining. Eliza looked around at the diners, releasing a breath after confirming none of them was Angeline.

"There's a table over by the kitchen door." He pointed to a small cozy corner with a lamp burning warmly on the table.

She took his arm as they made their way through the restaurant. He pulled out her chair, another first occurrence and entirely unexpected. Eliza could get spoiled very easily by his sudden gentlemanly attention.

He sat down with his back to the corner, affording Eliza a clear view of the kitchen door. As he looked around at each of the diners, the kitchen door swung open and Angeline walked out with two plates in her hands.

Eliza's heart stopped as she watched her sister walk past the man who hunted her. At first panic seized control of Eliza's brain as she saw the rest of her life disappear in a puff of smoke. Her muscles froze as her heart lodged in her throat.

No.

Her logical side took over and forcibly pushed the panic aside. This was no time to lose all semblance of intelligence. She managed to smile at him. "I left the extra money from Mr. Hansen in my bag with the books. Would you please go retrieve it for me? I don't want anyone to walk away with it since it belongs to you."

"Why the hell would you leave it in your bag? Jesus, Liz, you're smarter than that." He grumbled as he rose to his feet.

She watched out of the corner of her eye as Angeline served a family at another table. Her mouth was drier than the dirt she'd recently cleaned off her skin. Raw fear raced through her.

Too soon. It was just too soon. She needed another week with him alone.

"The money is in a small pouch; it's brown with two buttons on it." She squeezed his hand. "Thank you, Grady."

"Order me coffee, steak, and potatoes if they've got it." He walked out of the restaurant without looking behind him at Angeline.

Eliza trembled with more fear than she thought possible. When Grady was out of sight, she leaped to her feet and made her way on very shaky legs through the tables to her sister. Without a word, she took her sister's arm and pulled her toward the kitchen.

"Excuse me, ma'am, I—" Angeline's blue eyes widened as she realized who was yanking at her arm. "Eliza!"

"Shhh, just come with me quickly." They went into the kitchen to find Lettie at the stove cooking. The brunette had always been quiet, never venturing beyond the shadow of her father, marrying later in life into the shadow of a monster.

"Eliza?"

"Both of you listen to me now." She hugged her sister quickly, tears pricking her eyes. "Josiah hired a bounty hunter to find you. He's outside the hotel right now. You must get out of town immediately. There's no time to waste."

"A bounty hunter?" Angeline's face paled. "I thought someone might come after us, but a cold-blooded killer?"

"He's not cold-blooded or a killer, but he will take you back." Eliza tried to make Angeline understand. She had to realize the danger she was in. "You know what Josiah will do if you return to his house. This bounty hunter knows nothing of his cruelty, and even if he did, he'd being paid to bring you back, nothing more."

"How did you get here, Eliza? I can't believe you're standing here." Angeline had tears in her own eyes now.

"I left and set out to find you, to save you from the bounty hunter." It sounded so simple, but there had been so much that had happened since she'd left home. It hadn't been a month yet, but Eliza was no longer the same person.

"Alone?"

Eliza smiled. "Yes, alone."

"B-but how did you survive? Heavens, you even look clean, and that dress is so, well, purple." Angeline's eyes widened as she gazed at her older sister's frock.

"Angeline, there is no more time to discuss my clothes or my journey. You have to leave before he sees you." Eliza gripped her sister's arms and pushed her toward the door. "I must return to the table before he notices I'm gone."

"Why would he notice you're gone? Eliza, what is happening?" Angeline's voice had started to rise in panic.

"Please be quiet." Eliza shushed her again. "Listen to me, you must go now. Take whatever belongings you have and leave Bowson."

"But I don't understand—"

"You don't need to, just listen to me and do as I say." Eliza glanced at Lettie who nodded at her. "I'll meet you in a few minutes behind the hotel."

She went back out into the restaurant, eager to find a way to help Angeline escape without alerting Grady what she was up to. Fortunately, Grady had not returned to the table yet. Another waitress brought her a water and coffee for Grady. As Eliza nearly bounced with anticipation, she sat alone waiting for him. She waited another five excruciating minutes, but he still didn't return.

She didn't know where he'd gone, but she was becoming more scared with each passing moment. Eliza argued with herself for another minute before she rose and left the restaurant to look for him. Her stomach jumped as if a dozen frogs had taken up residence inside her.

He wasn't in the small lobby, and when she stepped outside, the horses stood still secured to the hitching rail in front of the hotel. She didn't have to be nervous he'd left her again. Where would he go without Bullseye? Perhaps he had to use the outhouse. She walked back into the hotel lobby, then into the restaurant without seeing him.

Dread wound its way around Eliza's heart as she headed

for the kitchen. When she opened the door, only Lettie stood there. Eliza's dread turned into terror when she saw how pale the other woman's face was.

"Where is she?"

"I don't know." Lettie's voice was husky for a woman, even huskier given the current state of fear. "She went out the back door and disappeared."

Eliza abandoned all decorum and turned and ran through the restaurant. When she reached the sidewalk, she wanted to shout in agony, but it was no use. Grady's horse was gone.

Chapter Thirteen

Grady held the blonde belly-down on the horse in front of him. He'd knocked her out by pinching off the blood on her neck, then got her on the horse before anyone saw him. It was definitely Angeline; he'd made certain of that before he took her. She not only responded to her name being called, she had a strawberry birthmark on the back of her neck in the shape of a heart. The telltale sign he'd been told to look for.

He didn't want Eliza to know that he'd found who he was after. No doubt she had already noticed he was gone, but he couldn't go back to town. He never did his killing in plain view of anyone and never left the body where it would be found.

Eliza would be angry and probably hurt, but it couldn't be helped. Besides it wasn't the first time he'd disappointed her or caused her pain. It was in his nature.

Grady wanted to finish what he'd set out to do, to get free of the yoke he wore. For the first time in his life, he had something to live for, but he couldn't do that until he finished what he had to do. He had no idea how he would explain to Eliza why he disappeared. Right now he had to focus on his mission, then he'd worry about her.

Eliza would be looking for him, and he tried not to think about the fact she was probably worried about him. She made it clear she wouldn't be abandoned again, and he'd done it on the same day. If he wasn't a piece of shit human being, he didn't know who was.

The truth would be too ugly to tell her, so he would have to lie. Not the best way to start off a life with the woman who'd captured his heart, but he didn't know what else to do. He had accepted the job to hunt and kill Angeline. What did that say about him? He was a broken man living on the edge of nothingness. This sweet young girl was about to lose her life because he tracked her—because some lousy son of a bitch gave him two hundred dollars.

What the hell was wrong with him?

The air had cooled to the point where his breath puffed out in white clouds as he rode out of town. He'd seen a few likely places to bury a body just outside town. If he could get there, kill the blonde, then return to town quickly, his life might just begin in earnest. Tears stung his eyes and he told himself it was the cold, even if he knew that was a lie.

It would have been easier if Eliza hadn't told him he was a good person, that she loved him. The damn woman had woken up his conscience and his heart. Grady didn't want to deal with either, and he didn't know how to turn them off. Their sex in the bathing house had been the most powerful experience of his life. He was still shaking from it if he were honest with himself.

Grady shook his head to clear his thoughts before they made him foolish or careless. His fascination with Eliza had to be tucked aside until later.

As he left the lights of the town behind, the inky darkness closed around him. The moon was high and bright in the sky, guiding him to a clearing in the woods two miles outside of town. It was private and quiet, exactly what he needed.

He pulled his horse to a stop and dismounted, keeping his hand on the blonde lest she wake up suddenly. The last thing he needed was to be chasing her through the woods in the dark.

He pulled Angeline down off the horse, and she moaned as she hit the ground. Grady stared down at the woman and realized just how young and beautiful she was, with fresh-faced creamy cheeks and bow-shaped lips.

No wonder that old man was angry with her. She was a treasure he'd let slip through his fingers, and now Grady had her life in his hands.

He squatted beside her and pulled out his gun.

Eliza rode like a mad woman after Grady. Logically, he would go back the way they had traveled, being familiar with the terrain. She didn't believe he knew the area well enough to select a different direction to return to Tolson.

All she could think of was that Angeline would return to Josiah, to a certain death by his hands. She couldn't let Grady do that to her sister, no matter how much she loved him. Josiah wasn't the forgiving type as evidenced by the fact he'd hired a bounty hunter within a few days of her disappearance.

Eliza was fortunate the moon was bright enough to see where she was going. Melba, good-hearted horse that he was, ran for all he was worth. It was as if he knew what Eliza was trying to do, to rescue her sister. Desperation coated her tongue as she realized the horse couldn't run like that for long, and Eliza's current state of mind could hinder her ability to find him.

The wind whistled past her ears as the cold night air made her nose numb. A bright patch ahead revealed a clearing, and a single horse, riderless. Eliza didn't know if she believed in God, or who to believe in, but at that moment she knew something had given her wings. She blinked away tears of gratitude for whatever guided her to the right spot.

She slowed down and approached slowly, recognizing Grady's bay Bullseye, but not seeing any sign of him or Angeline. Her heart still thumped madly in her chest, but she was able to take a breath for the first time since she realized they were both missing from Bowson.

Eliza dismounted and left the horses to graze on the cool, sweet grass while she followed the sound of his voice from up ahead. When she got closer, she realized Angeline was on the ground and Grady stood above her, his pistol aimed at her sister's head.

Bile coated the back of Eliza's throat as she realized exactly what Grady had been hired to do. He wasn't a bounty hunter, he was a killer sent to rid Josiah of the wife who dared to run from him. How stupid had she been to think he was a simple bounty hunter? He wouldn't return her sister to Josiah, he would bring back evidence of her death.

Grady told her over and over he wasn't a good person, and she didn't listen. She was convinced deep down that he was more than he believed himself to be. Yet there he stood, ready to murder her sister because a madman in the guise of a church elder paid him coin to do so.

Perhaps even the golden eagles he had left for her.

She swallowed back the urge to vomit and forced herself to think of a way to stop him. He was too skilled to sneak up on, particularly given his current state of heightened awareness. Perhaps she could surprise him by knocking him unconscious with something.

After feeling around the area, she located a rock a bit larger than her fist. She scrambled quietly across the pine needles to a vantage point above him as quickly as she could, took aim, and threw it as hard as she could.

Her aim was true enough to knock him sideways where he landed on a much larger rock and lay still, his gun in the dirt beside him. A sob tore from her throat as Eliza ran to him and picked up the gun. She had never hurt another human being in her life, yet she might have killed the man she loved to save her sister.

She put her hand on his neck and felt a strong steady pulse, although blood was sliding down his forehead.

"Did you kill him?" Angeline's raspy voice startled Eliza so badly she almost dropped the gun.

"I don't know. Are you all right?" Eliza knelt in front of her sister and examined her. She didn't appear to have any wounds, thank goodness.

"My head aches and my stomach is sore, but otherwise I'm fine." Angeline got to her knees and pulled Eliza into a fierce embrace. "Thank you, sister. Thank you."

Eliza allowed herself a moment or two, then pulled back from Angeline. "I need to tie him up."

Her sister nodded. "I don't know how to do much but a simple knot, but I'll help."

Eliza tried not to sound bitter, but it was difficult. "He taught me how to tie several different kinds. How perverse that fate has now given me the opportunity to use those skills on him."

Angeline held the gun on his inert form while Eliza searched for rope in his saddlebags. Although she didn't want to acknowledge her love for Grady was still in her heart, she also brought the medical kit and the canteen.

After securing his hands behind his back with the rope, then binding his ankles, she examined the damage she'd inflicted on him. Eliza had much better aim than she thought, judging by the ragged wound on his head. She cleaned it as best she could with water and a rag. The blood had nearly stopped so she just placed a piece of gauze to soak up any additional seepage.

When Eliza finally looked up from tending to Grady, Angeline sat on a rock, watching her with wide eyes and the gun in her hand. Suddenly Eliza felt decades older than her younger sister.

"Who is he?"

Eliza gathered up the supplies and sat beside Angeline, then took Grady's gun from her. "He's the man who's been hunting you."

"You know him." It wasn't a question. Although young, Angeline was very bright and had always been observant.

"I'm afraid it is a very long and complicated story." Eliza put her arm around her sister's slender shoulders. "Right now I want to enjoy the fact that you're sitting beside me, safe and alive."

"It's amazing!" Angeline smiled as she hugged Eliza hard. "I never expected to see you again and here you are, so far away from Tolson. What are you doing here, Eliza?"

"Rescuing you."

Grady heard the women's voices first, a soft murmur that was soothing. Then a hammer started pounding on his head, and the soft murmur resembled a screaming mob. Survival instincts kicked in, and he didn't open his eyes until he knew what his situation was.

He determined that he was lying on the ground with pine needles, dirt, and a host of insects beneath and around him. A tug on his hands and feet let him know he'd been tied up. The excruciating pain in his head told him whoever had tied him up had also conked him on the head with something.

His memory was still a bit gray around the edges, but he remembered finding who he'd been searching for, and then, nothing. What the hell happened? Someone had managed to sneak up on Grady, and he had to figure out who.

He heard an unfamiliar voice ask what Eliza was doing there, and when Eliza responded "Rescuing you" he opened his eyes.

At first he didn't quite understand what he saw. Eliza was holding his gun and sitting on a rock beside the blonde he'd been chasing. Their heads were close together, and Eliza's arm was around the other girl's shoulders.

Holy shit.

He must've made a noise, because both women turned their gaze on him. That's when he noticed the similarities between them, in stature, in the curve of their cheeks, in their identical bright blue eyes. His stomach clenched up so hard, it threw bile up his throat.

The blonde was her fucking *sister*.

In Eliza's gaze, he saw anger, betrayal, and pain. The same emotions catapulted through him like a mule kick to the balls. Eliza had more skill than he'd given her credit for. She'd been playing with him all along, waiting for him to find her sister. He'd done exactly what she wanted, believing every damn lie she fed him as if he were a complete and utter fool.

Grady's faith in humanity's lowest form of life, a female, had been reaffirmed yet again. This time, he'd let himself believe in Eliza, in what she felt for him. Jesus Christ, he thought she loved him. He should have known better than to believe a woman, to believe she could love him of all people.

His heart shattered into a million pieces, this time for good. There was no chance in hell it would ever be whole again, nor did he want it to be. To think he had wrestled with his conscience about killing Angeline, when the entire time her sister was playing her own game with him. What a fool he'd been.

Grady wanted to howl in fury at her, to shake her until she told him exactly why she'd just destroyed him. It wasn't enough that she managed to ride along with him while he found her sister, but she also had to play with his emotions.

The bitter taste of betrayal filled his mouth, and he spat toward her, startling both women. "I guess you got what you came for, eh Liz?"

"Liz?" The blonde sounded completely confused.

Eliza swallowed visibly. "You were going to murder her."

Grady pushed her comment aside. "I was getting paid to do what I had to."

"There was nothing you had to do, you chose to do it."

"Fuck you, Eliza whatever the hell your name is. You used

me to find your sister, and don't tell me you didn't." He struggled against the bonds. "You're a conniving, lying bitch."

She flinched at the words, but didn't deny them. "And you are a cold-blooded killer."

"Never said I wasn't."

Eliza narrowed her gaze. "You lied each and every day we traveled together. Don't cast stones when you've been practicing the same deceit."

"You traveled together?" The blonde was like an echo to everything Eliza said.

"My lying wasn't going to hurt anyone."

"Except Angeline." She pointed his gun at him, the barrel looking a lot larger when he was at the receiving end.

Grady didn't know how to respond to that. The two of them were bald-faced liars who deserved the pain they'd caused each other. He had known what might happen if he let Eliza into his life, so he shouldn't place all the blame on her. But, oh, how he wanted to.

Eliza had done what no woman had in many, many years—she had brought Grady Wolfe to his knees.

"I am not proud of being disingenuous with you. My conscience was constantly pricked by the way I kept information from you." Eliza looked at the gun in her hand. "My intention was to save my sister from returning to a certain death at Josiah's hands. What I didn't know was he'd already ordered that through yours."

"I don't even know what disin—whatever you said means. All I know is you were just as bad as I was, lying to me, and to everyone we met." If only Grady could get free, he'd take his damn horse and leave. The money from Brown wasn't worth what he was going through—no amount was.

Eliza had the grace to nod. "I was deceitful and I've wronged many people along the way, but I did it to save my sister." She took the blonde's hand in her own, holding up the clasped hands for him to see. "She is all I have in the world, the only person who cares if I live or die." Her voice caught on the last word.

Grady refused to feel anything but anger and contempt for Eliza. She had made her choice, and he'd made his. "Until you had me convinced you had me. You should be an actress, y'know."

Eliza's face blanched. "I wasn't lying about that."

He hooted. "Oh, of course you weren't. Pardon me if I don't believe your lying ass."

They locked gazes, staring at each other across the moonlight ground. He didn't want to believe what he saw in her gaze, so he looked away. Whatever they'd shared together was dead. He had no desire to resurrect it.

"Let's start a fire and get the camp set up." Eliza rose, pulling her sister to her feet. "You must first start with a level surface and put together a ring of stones to contain the blaze."

As Grady watched, the unbelievable Eliza taught her sister how to start a goddamn fire while he lay on the ground like a trussed-up turkey. If he wasn't there to witness it, he'd never have believed it. She ignored him, left him in the dirt with beetles tickling his ear and a headache the size of Texas.

Before he could open his mouth and tell her a thing or two, she'd come back to him. She grabbed his feet and started pulling him across the soft pine needles. He was surprised she had the strength.

"What the hell are you doing?"

She grunted out a word with each foot she managed to move him. "Pulling. you. into. a. safe. spot."

Perversely, he tried to be dead weight, unmovable by the resourceful, deceitful Eliza. She wasn't deterred, and while her sister gathered rocks, she yanked and pulled Grady until he was beneath the shade of a pine that seemed to be taller than God. Its branches reached out twenty feet in each direction, providing ample shelter and warmth from the elements.

Damn, he wished he could find fault in what she'd done. Eliza had been paying attention to him and her goddamn books. Was there nothing she couldn't do well?

She pushed him into a sitting position, and he pushed against her as she did it. "Stop it, Grady, or you'll have to lie on your side all night. I'm certain you do not want insects to be depositing larvae in your orifices."

"Depositing what in my what?" He stopped fighting her and let her push him upright.

"Insects put their young inside warm holes." She touched his ear and pulled out a beetle. "Such as this one."

He scowled at her and the bug. "Untie me."

"I can't, not until we can come to an agreement, and I fear you're far too angry to have an unemotional conversation." She got to her feet and looked down at him, the shade of the tree making her face dance with shadows. "Whatever you believe, Grady Wolfe, I do love you, but I also love my sister. This situation is untenable, and we must find a way to resolve it amicably."

With that, she left him sitting there while she gathered wood for the fire. She started using words again that he didn't understand, maybe to confuse him, maybe because she was as upset as he was. Either way, he didn't understand half of what she said.

His anger simmered down to a low boil as the sisters worked. Eliza was definitely the older sibling and more efficient in everything she did, but the blonde had a grace that her sister lacked. It was as if the girl had received Eliza's share of the beauty and Eliza had gotten her sister's common sense. It must've been the other woman, Lettie Brown, who had carried the burden of decisions for Angeline, because it sure as hell wasn't her.

The fire was crackling merrily within ten minutes. Grady had a chance to really look at the two of them while he busily picked at the ropes binding his wrists. He recognized the knots he'd taught Eliza and silently cursed his own foolishness.

The women talked quietly by the fire for a few minutes, then Eliza came back over to him. She carried a canteen and what appeared to be another stale biscuit.

"I ain't hungry."

She shrugged. "Very well, but you may become hungry in the near future."

He thought she'd return to her sister, but instead she sat down so they were facing each other. The firelight flitted across the right side of her face.

"You're very angry with me."

Grady gritted his teeth. "You got that right."

She nodded. "Deservedly angry. I wanted to speak with you and hope you understand my actions. You see, Angeline and I grew up without a mother; she died shortly after Angeline was born. Our father, Silas, was a dictator, a cold man whose only concern was the ward. Before you ask, the ward is the place we live, as part of the church. You may have heard of the Mormons or the Latter-day Saints, followers of Brigham Young."

Grady had spent time in Utah; he couldn't help but know about the Mormons and their strange ways. "What of it?"

"The church is quite strict about many things, including the teaching of girls, yet lenient in others, such as allowing men to have multiple wives."

"Multiple? As in more than one? What kinda fool would want that?" Grady couldn't imagine wanting one wife, much less more than one.

"Yes, and each wife must serve and service her husband as needed, without question. Women are veritable prisoners in our faith with very little freedoms." She reached out to touch him, but he jerked away. "I deserved that."

"Damn right you did." He was curious to know the rest of the story but unwilling to allow her to trick him again.

"Angeline is seventeen, so very young and innocent. She was given as third wife to a much older man, Josiah Brown, in marriage by my father. She had a beau, a man she loved who was off completing his mission, a requirement for all young men in our faith. Father wouldn't listen and saw the marriage as a way to further his position in the ward." Eliza sounded bitter and angry, two emotions Grady knew well. "Within a week of the marriage, Josiah was beating her every day. I tried to tell Father, but again he would not listen to me. Angeline and his second wife ran away the month after her wedding."

Eliza's eyes glittered with pain for her sister and fury at the man who had harmed her. "I overheard Josiah speaking to Father about you, the man he'd hired to find her. I packed my belongings and went into Tolson to find you."

Grady stared at her face, trying to find some sign she was lying. He'd known she wasn't being truthful from the moment he'd slammed into her, but he never imagined all of this. The fool woman took off on her own with nothing but a sack of books and a mission to save her sister.

If he wasn't so furious with her, he might actually be proud of her.

"I am truly sorry for deceiving you, Grady, and for causing you pain." She reached up to touch his head, then stopped and sighed. "I tried desperately to think of a way to tell you before today. I never expected you to find Angeline so quickly, and I never"—she cleared her throat—"I never expected you to be the harbinger of death for her."

Grady's hands started to go numb; the damn woman had tied the knots too well. "I was paid to find her and kill her. It ain't the first time, either. I told you more than once I ain't a nice man, or a good man. You didn't believe me."

She shook her head. "I still don't." This time when she reached for him, he didn't pull away for some loco reason. Eliza cupped his cheeks. "Inside that gruff, prickly exterior is a good man with a giving heart, and it's that man I fell in love with."

"Stop saying that." He twisted away again, unwilling to hear her lie to him anymore.

"Even if you don't believe me, I know it's the truth. I love you, Grady."

"Shut up! Shut up! Jesus fucking Christ, woman, shut up!" Rage poured through him as he jerked at the ropes, flailing around and smashing his head into the tree. She didn't love him; she never did. Warm blood coated his hands as the rope bit into his skin.

"Grady, stop, please!" Eliza tried to keep him still, but he shouldered her back. She landed on her behind and stared up at him with frightened eyes.

"You should be afraid of me, woman. I told you more than once, I ain't a nice man," he snarled, full of so much hate and pain, he could almost taste it. "I found out long ago from my own mother not to trust a woman. After my sweet mother had my father killed, she married, then murdered three more fools."

The memory of the funerals, the grieving widow pretending to sob by each grave site, made his stomach cramp so hard he nearly vomited. "By the time I was fifteen, I'd had four different fathers, five broken bones from her beatings, and the know-how to kill. The bitch drank herself to death, so I burned the house down with her body in it and left. I've been killing, hunting, and surviving." He felt himself slipping into a frenzy of hurt and pain, unable and unwilling to let the past go. It had been his constant companion, his cross to bear for so long. Until Eliza.

She jumped on him, straddling his legs and leaning onto his shoulders. He bucked, trying to shake her off, but she held fast.

"I'm not going to let you do this. I love you, Grady, no matter what you've done, or who you've killed. You could have killed Angeline when you found her in Bowson, but you didn't. Inside you is a good man, one who is capable of so many things. The man I love." Her tears fell onto his cheeks. "Do you hear me? I won't let you go."

"Let me be." He sounded so small even to his own ears. The life he'd led had brought him nothing but darkness, until Eliza. His heart had never beaten before, until Eliza.

Grady didn't understand any of it. He was trapped in a twister whirling around and around until he lurched to the side and vomited. Eliza's soothing voice murmured to him as she brought his head to her lap where he buried his head and wept the darkness away.

Chapter Fourteen

Grady slept beneath the tree, exhausted by the emotional storm he'd endured. Eliza felt shaken by the experience, by witnessing him exorcise the personal demons that lurked inside him. He'd had some horrible things happen to him, and for that she cried for him.

Angeline sat by the fire and watched her. "You're different."

"It's that obvious, I'm sure." Eliza smiled sadly. "I can hardly believe it's been less than a month since I left Tolson."

"Is it him? I mean, was it him that changed you?"

"Yes and no." Eliza gazed into the fire, memories of being with Grady, of learning from him, loving him flashed through her mind. "I found an inner well of strength I didn't know I had. There is so much I want to tell you, but now isn't the time."

"I don't understand what's happening." Angeline took Eliza's hands. "Please let's just leave here together."

"I can't. I know you don't understand, and I wish I had time to explain it to you. The situation is making me choose between the two of you. By helping you escape, I've already chosen you. Yet I can't simply leave him. I love him."

Angeline's mouth opened and closed. "You what?"

Eliza had to make Angeline understand. "I love him, and I

know deep down he loves me, too. Believe me, I performed a ridiculous amount of arguing with myself about what I've done, what he's done, and what we did together. After all of that, I decided I must stay with Grady because I love him. It doesn't matter if we're together for one night or thousands of nights. My place is by his side for however long we both live."

"I'm scared for you." Angeline took Eliza's hands. "He's a dark man, Eliza, and scary, too."

"He doesn't scare me any longer. I can see underneath that mask he shows everyone else. Believe me, there is a good man in there and I love him." Eliza knew she was risking everything, including her life, on her feelings for Grady.

"Are you sure? Really, really sure?" Angeline might appear to others as pretty but empty headed, but she wasn't. She was simply soft spoken and kept her thoughts to herself, unlike Eliza who spoke too much.

Eliza hugged her sister. "I'm very sure. Now you must be on your way before he wakes up."

Angeline walked over to Melba, wringing her hands and looking scared. Eliza took all the food supplies and the full canteen and followed her sister. Reluctantly, she used her pulley system to remove the bag of books and her own traveling bag from the saddle and set them on the ground. Then she removed the contraption and tucked that into her bag. The saddle was ready for Angeline.

"You must go now. Ride toward Bowson and find Lettie, then keep going as far as you can. I'll find you, I promise, but you can't stay here now." Eliza didn't want to let her sister go so soon, but she had to.

"I still wish you would leave with me." Angeline peered at the inert form beneath the tree. "We can send someone back from town to help him later."

Eliza's throat tightened as she realized she was about to be separated from her sister again. "Now let's get you on your way. Melba is an old horse, but he's got a good heart. He's been nothing short of amazing the past weeks. I know he'll be your trusty steed as well."

Angeline eyed the horse with skepticism. "All right, but I hope he makes it back to Bowson."

Eliza patted the horse's neck. "Melba has more heart than ten thoroughbreds. He'll take you where you need to go."

She tied the bag of food and canteen to the saddle, then turned to her sister. "Please be safe. You and Lettie need to be so careful because I don't think Josiah is done yet."

Angeline nodded, her eyes huge in the moonlight. "We've done pretty well so far, until today anyway. We even got jobs at the restaurant in Bowson. Never thought serving food to Father would give me enough practice to work at a restaurant."

Eliza managed a shaky smile. "I love you, Angeline. I will find you again."

"I love you, too." Angeline let loose a little sob as they embraced.

Eliza held on to her sister for a few minutes, savoring the knowledge she'd succeeded in what she'd set out to do—save her sister's life. Now it was up to Angeline to be vigilant and keep herself safe.

She cupped her hand as Grady had done for her numerous times. "Here, use my hand to mount."

Angeline stepped on her hands and made it up onto Melba's back with grace. Eliza had always envied that about her sister, but now she was glad of it. Whereas horsemanship had always been hard for Eliza, it had come easily to her younger sister.

"Thank you for everything." Angeline glanced toward Grady. "Be careful."

"You, too. Good-bye for now." Eliza's throat grew tight as her sister rode off into the darkness and soon she was swallowed by the night.

It was time to wake Grady and convince him the rest of their lives awaited, together.

* * *

Grady listened to the sisters say good-bye, then to the sound of the woman he'd been chasing for weeks as she rode away on the ancient nag. He lay there and did nothing.

Nothing.

He felt wrung out from going loco earlier and had even closed his eyes to try to find his way back. Grady wasn't used to being out of control, and he sure as hell didn't like it. Eliza hadn't untied him, dammit to hell, and he lay there like a crying fool.

Embarrassment didn't sit well, and he wanted it over, now. When she walked back to him, he heard her soft footsteps in the pine needles, slightly stirring the leaves scattered throughout. Her scent, that of lavender and Eliza, caressed him as she sat down beside him.

"I know you're not sleeping, Grady. There are signs when a body is conscious rather than unconscious." Her matter-of-fact tone irked him.

"Aren't you the smart one?" he mumbled. "You don't need to keep reminding me of how much you know and how much I don't."

She touched his cheek. "I only know what I read in books. Everything else I've learned from you." Her fingers were cool against his hot skin.

He snorted. "I don't know if I believe that."

She lay down and faced him, her breath gently brushed his mouth as she spoke. "You spend a great deal of time making sure everyone knows what a terrible person you are."

"It's the truth." Over and over again.

"Open your eyes, Grady."

He didn't want to, really didn't want to.

"Please."

Her entreaty plucked at his battered heart, so he complied with her request.

Eliza's deep blue eyes seemed almost black in the shadows

of the firelight. Within the depths, he saw so many things, he wanted to shut his eyes again.

"I can't be who you want me to."

"You already are. Please understand that I don't expect you to change." She ran a finger along his brow. "I never knew what being alive felt like until I met you. The man I fell in love with is right in front of me."

His chest hurt as he tried to absorb what she was telling him. "I'm not going to love you."

"Oh, Grady." She sighed and kissed his forehead. "You already do."

He didn't answer, not that he could have even if he wanted to. There was no answer he would accept. He couldn't love her, because it wasn't possible for him to love anyone. Grady lost the ability long ago, if he ever had it. Yet he had been content with Eliza when they traveled together. She fit beside him, under him, and with him.

She'd betrayed his trust by lying to him about her sister. He didn't know if he'd ever forgive her for that. He'd done many things in his life that qualified as unforgivable, so he was something of an expert. Eliza had deliberately deceived him for weeks, even to the point of knocking him out and tying him up.

Betrayal was so damn bitter.

"I was in an untenable position. I love my sister and had to help her, but then I fell in love with you. I had the unenviable task of picking her or you." Eliza started unbuttoning her shirt. "I made sure she survived, and then I picked you."

His heart started thumping harder with each button she freed. Her words started to echo through his ears. "You picked me?"

"Yes, I did. You see, I gave her Melba and sent her away to hide from Josiah. Now that she knows what he's capable of, she can protect herself." Eliza leaned forward and kissed him.

Her lips were soft, warm, and wet, and felt like an angel's kiss.

"Stop." A feeble and ridiculous response.

"No, I won't stop. I need to prove to you that I am yours, that I have given up everything to be with you." She met his gaze. "I even left my bag of books in the dirt."

Her books? She left her books in the dirt for *him*? The beloved books she carried across the Utah terrain instead of practical things she could have used?

He could hardly believe it.

"You'll go back and get them."

"And then what? I don't have a horse. There's just you and your bay. If you don't give me a ride, then I walk." As she pulled her shirt from her skirt, his entire body clenched.

He wanted to tell her to stop again, but found that his mouth would not form the words.

"Don't give them up for me. Jesus, Liz, can't you see there's no future for us? I'm a gun for hire, a man who kills people for money." His voice was hoarse from shouting, from the emotions that overwhelmed him.

"Oh, Grady, we can do anything, live anywhere. It doesn't matter where or what, as long as we're together." She licked her lips, and he moaned deep in his throat.

"What are you doing?" he managed to say.

"Seducing you, giving you my love and my body, to start our future together." She took off her shirt, and he began trembling. "Is it working?"

"No."

She stepped out of her skirt, and he realized she wore only the lacy chemise, the one she'd worn the day he'd given her the ring. Blood rushed through him, making him light-headed.

"I think it is working. Let me in, Grady."

"Isn't that what I'm supposed to say?" He wanted to run, to tell her he hated her, to escape from the onslaught of her gentle seduction.

He couldn't.

She nodded. "Perhaps it is, but you don't need to ask me at all. What I have, what I am, is already open to you."

Eliza pulled off her chemise until she was completely naked in front of him. She was beautiful, ethereal in the moonlight like a fairy creature in front of him.

"Untie me." He didn't want to be seduced while he was her prisoner.

"Not yet. I want you to accept my love, to understand that I am giving you everything I am."

"What does that mean? Liz, untie me."

"No."

Grady wanted to scream at her, to tell her to put her clothes back on. Truthfully he didn't want her to stop, he just didn't want to be at her mercy tied up. It still rubbed him the wrong way that she was able to tie him up in the first place.

He hated her for making him weak.

He loved her for making him feel.

Eliza rose from the ground, naked, and walked over to pick up the knife from Grady's pile of things. She had to let him loose, had to take the chance he would accept the gift of her love.

He watched her with a dark, glittering gaze. The firelight had burned down to embers, casting him in deep shadows. His clothes were askew after all he'd been through, including being dragged. She wanted to straighten them, but knew he would protest loudly if she tried.

She cut the ropes binding his feet first, then set the knife down and knelt behind him. Her skin broke out in a clammy sweat as she helped him to a sitting position. What he did when he was free would determine what happened in their lives.

Did she go too far? Did her deceit destroy any chance they had together? Had his?

Too many questions and no answers. With her mouth as dry as the desert, she reached for the ropes on his wrists.

They were covered with blood, and she sucked in a breath of pain for him.

"Oh, Grady, I'm so sorry. I didn't know." Tears pricked her eyes as she tried to untie the knots without hurting him any further.

"Just cut them." His voice was strained, harsh.

"I don't want to hurt you."

"It's too late for that, Liz. Just cut the goddamn ropes."

With a sob stuck in her throat, she picked up the knife and carefully cut through the knots she'd tied. Eliza had no idea just how tight she'd made them, or how well she had secured him. Her anger had made her cruel.

He flexed his hands as she freed them. Eliza stood and returned the knife to the scabbard. She heard him rise and fix his clothes.

Nude, she had no defenses, no way to stop him from doing whatever he wanted. She had to give herself over, body, heart, and soul to him.

She trembled before the fire, her back to him as she waited for him. He walked toward her, and her heart stopped beating when his hands closed around her throat.

His hands rested on her skin, the blood making them tacky against her neck. He could kill her in a split second. There was nothing stopping him except himself.

"I love you," she whispered.

"Eliza."

He fell to his knees, letting go of her neck, letting go of his anger. She turned to face him, and he wrapped his arms around her waist. Tears fell freely down her face as Eliza accepted his love in return.

Grady Wolfe had found his mate.

Epilogue

The cabin was nestled in a perfect valley covered with rich green grass in the summer and a foot of snow in the winter. Guardians of towering trees protected the brook that meandered through the property. A small barn with a new corral completed the picture.

Eliza stepped outside of the house and shivered against the cold. She pressed her scarf to her mouth, and still puffs of her breath sneaked through into the blue wool. The scarf wasn't thick enough, but Grady had purchased it for her to match her eyes, so it was her favorite.

Her boots crunched on the snow as she walked slowly to the barn with a pail of water dangling from her hand. It was the day before Christmas, another holiday she hadn't celebrated in her life. Truthfully being with Grady was like a holiday every day.

She slid the barn door open and stepped in, closing it quickly behind her. It wasn't snowing yet, but the sky was threatening to start any moment. Eliza wanted to get the animals fed and watered before she had to shovel her way to get to them.

"Good morning, Daisy." She stopped at the cow's stall first and rubbed her nose. "I'll milk you in just a bit."

The brown-eyed milk cow had been their first purchase after settling in their house. Eliza had missed having fresh butter, cream, and cheese. Although he listened when she taught him how to do farm chores, she knew he really didn't want to touch Daisy's teats. That was okay with Eliza because her own were much more interested in his touch.

With a smile born of contentment, Eliza went to Bullseye's stall first. The bay had seemed to adjust nicely to being off the trail. She filled his water trough, then moved to the next.

Grady had surprised her with a new horse, a mare with a sweet disposition and a mane as dark as her own. The white blaze on her nose was the only color Midnight sported. She came right over to Eliza and nuzzled her as she filled the water trough.

"Good morning to you too, girl. Hungry?" Eliza checked to be sure the blanket was secure on Midnight's back before she stepped back out to get the feed.

As she filled a scoop from the sack on the crate in the corner, she couldn't help but think of how different her life was. A year ago, she had been living under the iron fist of her father, unhappy and trapped. Now she was married to the man she loved, living in a cozy cabin, spending her days cooking and enjoying life, and her nights making love.

Nothing could be more perfect except for one thing. She had a Christmas gift for her husband and couldn't wait to give it to him.

After she fed and checked on the horses, she took the now empty bucket to Daisy's stall. The cow was lowing with impatience to be milked. Eliza didn't ever think she'd enjoy milking a cow, but she did now.

The milk steamed in the cold morning air as it hit the bucket. She finished as quickly as she could to get back into the cabin before Grady woke. The coffee and biscuits were probably ready as well.

She left the barn, and the cold made her eyes nearly freeze. It was colder than she ever remembered it being, and the air was sharp with the threat of snow. The gunmetal sky had gotten darker. As she stepped onto the front porch, a snowflake landed on her nose.

Christmas snow was special, a blanket of white to bring in the day where there was peace and joy everywhere. Eliza stepped into the cabin and closed the door against the icy cold.

"Snowing yet?" Grady sat at the table with coffee and a biscuit, with his shirt unbuttoned and barefoot. He looked good enough to eat.

"Just started." She slipped off her boots, coat, hat, and scarf, then went to stand by the fire to warm her hands. Her skin prickled from the sudden heat, and she rubbed them briskly. Grady came up behind her and pressed his body against hers. He jumped when they touched.

"Jesus Christ, Liz, you're colder than a wi—um, really cold." He wrapped his arms around her waist and nuzzled her. "I can warm you up."

Although they'd made love the night before, her body was instantly and completely aroused. Her nipples peaked against her chemise, a silk one he'd insisted she wear because it was sexy.

"Oh, I think I'd like that."

He kissed her neck up to her ear.

"Do you find yourself with any regrets?" She couldn't help but ask because she'd been wondering.

"Not one."

"Restless perhaps?"

"No, there's too much to do around here, and you keep wanting to get me into bed."

Eliza smiled. "You did give up your life and career."

He turned her around until she could stare into his beloved dark eyes. "No, I gave up nothing. When I married you, I started my life."

Eliza's heart skipped a beat at the honesty and love in his gaze. "Me, too. Are you happy?"

"Damn happy."

She giggled. "Me, too." Christmas day was too far away, she had to tell him. "I have a gift for you."

He kissed her while he continued to rub his body against hers. "Tomorrow is for gifts."

"I can't wait until tomorrow. I want to give it to you now."

Grady looked at her with a puzzled expression. "Okay, if you really want to."

She couldn't help the smile on her face, so wide it actually hurt her cheeks. "Grady, we're going to—"

A knock at the door stopped her. He scowled at it. "Who the hell is that?"

Eliza kissed him quick. "It's Christmas Eve, be nice. Now get yourself dressed while I answer the door."

"Fine, I'll get dressed, but I only have to be nice to you." He pinched her fanny as she walked away from him.

Laughing, she opened the door to find her sister on her doorstep. She hadn't seen Angeline since the night in the woods more than a year earlier.

"Merry Christmas, Eliza."

Eliza turned to look at her husband who stood there with a gun in his hand. Her sister had almost ended their relationship, and now it appeared she would step back into it.

"Merry Christmas, Angeline."

And try Cynthia Eden's latest, I'LL BE SLAYING YOU,
out now from Brava!

The music was terrible, the food was shit, and the crowd of dancers were all but screwing on the floor.

Dee leaned against the bar, trying to ignore the throbbing in her temples and letting her gaze sweep past the throng inside Onyx.

This was the eighth club she'd been in since she'd hit the streets. Humans only. Well, mostly humans. Onyx catered to the unaware, and that made the place perfect for vamps. So much easier to pick up prey when the humans didn't realize the danger they faced.

They didn't realize it, not until their dates stopped seducing them and started feeding from them.

By then, it was too late to scream.

Her nails drummed on the bar. Zane lounged in the back corner, his emerald gaze sweeping over the room. Some bigbreasted blonde was at his side. Typical.

Jude hadn't made an appearance yet. But he would soon. She'd use his nose to sniff out the place. See if he could detect the rot of the undead and—

"Let me buy you a drink."

She'd ignored the men beside her. Greeted the few comeons she'd gotten with silence. But that voice—

Dee glanced to the left. Tall, Dark, and Sexy was back.

And he was smiling down at her. A big, wide grin that showed off a weird little dent in his right cheek. Not a dimple, too hard for that. She hadn't noticed that curve last night, not with the hunt and kill distracting her.

Shit, but he was hot.

Thanks to the spotlights over the bar, she could see him so much better tonight. No shadows to hide behind now.

Hard angles, strong jaw, sexy man.

She licked her lips. "Already got one." Dee held up her glass.

"Babe, that's water." He motioned to the bartender. "Let me get you something with bite."

She'd spent the night looking for a bite. Hadn't found it yet. Her fingers snagged his. "I'm working." Booze couldn't slow her down. Not with the one she hunted.

Black brows shot up. Then he leaned in close. So close that she caught the scent of his aftershave. "You gonna kill another woman tonight?" A whisper that blew against her.

Her lips tightened. "Vampire," she said quietly and dropped his hand.

He blinked. Those eyes of his were eerie. Like a smoky fog staring back at her.

"I hunted a vampire last night," Dee told him, keeping her voice hushed because in a place like this, you never knew who was listening. "And, technically, she'd already been killed once before I got to her."

His fingers locked around her upper arm. She'd yanked on a black T-shirt before heading out, and his fingertips skimmed her flesh. "Guess you're right," he murmured and leaned in even closer.

His lips were about two inches—maybe just one—away from hers.

What would he taste like?

Try THE PIRATE, the latest in Katherine Garbera's Savage Seven series, available now from Brava!

"Excited about your trip?" he asked, stepping out of the shadows.

He was a rough looking man but still attractive. A light beard shadowed his strong, square jaw. His dark hair was shorn close to his head, revealing a scar twisting up the left side of his neck.

As a surgeon, she could tell that whoever had stitched up what she guessed to be a knife wound hadn't been to medical school. As a woman she guessed that Laz hadn't minded, since if the wound hadn't been stitched up he probably would have died.

She'd been single for almost two years now, but this man wasn't like any of the men she'd dated. An aura of danger hovered about him. It might be due to the fact that he led a crew of men who looked like they'd be better suited to crew Johnny Depp's *Black Pearl* in Disney's *Pirates of the Caribbean*. Or maybe it was due to the fact that when he looked at her, she had the feeling that he looked past the confines of her profession and saw the woman underneath.

"A little nervous, actually."

He laughed, a rough sound that carried on the wind. "Somalia—hell, all of Africa—has that effect on people."

The sea around the tanker seemed calm, and on this moonlit night with no one else on deck, she felt like . . . like they were alone in the world.

"On you?" she asked. She couldn't imagine this man being nervous in any situation. He radiated the calmness she always experienced when she was in the operating room. It was a calmness born of the fact that he knew what he was doing.

"Nah. I've been around this part of the world for a long time."

"Why is that? You're American, right?"

"Yes, I am. But I was never one for staying put. I wanted to see the world." There was a note in his voice that she easily recognized. It said that he was searching for something that he hadn't found. Something that he might never find. She understood that now.

It was funny, but before her divorce she would have thought he was unfocused or didn't know himself well. But now she understood that sometimes life threw a curve and dreams changed and your way was lost. Hers had been. She'd been drifting without a focus, and she hoped this summer in Africa would help her to find her way back to who she had been.

Did this rough looking man have dreams? Dreams that she'd be able to relate to? At one point in her not-so-distant past she would have seen Laz as a man she had nothing in common with—a man whose dreams would make absolutely no sense to her. She no longer looked at the world in the black and white terms she used to, and she guessed she had to thank Paul and his philandering ways for that.

"Well, you are certainly seeing parts of it that are off the beaten path," Daphne said.

She'd spent all of her life taking the safe route. College followed by medical school. Marriage to an up-and-coming lawyer who morphed his successful career into a successful Senate bid. She'd had two children with Paul Maxwell and raised them to be very successful teenagers before Paul decided that it was time to trade her in for a newer model. A microbiologist named Cyndy who didn't have stretch marks.

She shook her head. She wasn't bitter.

Really.

It was just that when Paul had walked away from their marriage he'd broken something that she'd always claimed as her destiny. He'd broken her dreams of a fifty-year wedding anniversary party. Her dreams of being married to the same man for her entire life. And she was still trying to figure out who she was if she wasn't going to be Mrs. Paul Maxwell.

She realized she'd let the conversation lag while she'd been lost in her thoughts of her ruined marriage. She looked over at Laz.

"Our group goes to the places that really need aid," she said.

He gave her a half-smile that showed her the dangerous looking man could also be sexy in a rough-hewn sort of way.

"Good for you."

She glanced over at him; it was hard to see much of his features in the dim lighting. "Are you being sarcastic?"

He shrugged. "Not really. I admire people who walk the walk."

She had no idea if he was sincere or not. But she'd always tried to be honest about who she was and what she wanted. She heard the sound of another engine. "Did you hear that?"

"Yes, ma'am. I think you should go below," Laz said, standing up straighter. He tossed his cigarette over the railing.

"Why?"

"Pirates operate in these waters, and Americans are some of their favorite targets. Go below where I know you'll be safe."

She hesitated for a moment but then saw him draw out a handgun. Moonlight glinted off the well-polished steel of his weapon. His entire demeanor changed. He no longer wore an aura of danger. He was danger. She'd think twice about talking to this man if she saw him on the street back home. In fact she'd do her best to avoid him.

Keep an eye out for BEDDING THE ENEMY
by Mary Wine, coming next month . . .

He was staring at her.

Helena looked through her lowered eyelashes at him. He was a Scot and no mistake about it. Held in place around his waist was a great kilt. Folded into pleats that fell longer in the back, his plaid was made up in heather, tan and green. She knew little of the different clans and their tartans but she could see how proud he was. The nobles she passed among scoffed at him but she didn't think he would even cringe if he were to hear their mutters. She didn't think the gossip would make an impact. He looked impenetrable. Strength radiating from him. There was nothing pompous about him, only pure brawn.

Her attention was captivated by him. She had seen other Scots wearing their kilts but there was something more about him. A warm ripple moved across her skin. His doublet had sleeves that were closed, making him look formal, in truth more formal than the brocade-clad men standing near her brother. There wasn't a single gold or silver bead sewn to that doublet but he looked ready to meet his king. It was the slant of his chin, the way he stood.

"You appear to have an admirer, Helena."

Edmund sounded conceited and his friends chuckled. Her brother's words surfaced in her mind and she shifted her gaze to the men standing near her brother. They were poised in perfect poses that showed off their new clothing. One even had a lace-edged handkerchief dangling from one hand.

She suddenly noticed how much of a fiction it was. Edmund didn't believe them to be his friends but he stood jesting with them. Each one of them would sell the other out for the right amount. It was so very sad. Like a sickness you knew would claim their lives but could do nothing about.

"A Scots, no less."

Edmund eyed her. She stared back, unwilling to allow him to see into her thoughts. Annoyance flickered in his eyes when she remained calm. He waved his hands, dismissing her.

She turned quickly before he heard the soft sound of a gasp. She hadn't realized she was holding her breath. It was such a curious reaction. Peeking back across the hall she found the man responsible for invading her thoughts completely. He had a rugged look to him, his cheekbones high and defined. No paint decorated his face. His skin was a healthy tone she hadn't realized she missed so much. He was clean-shaven in contrast to the rumors she'd heard of Scotland's men. Of course, many Englishmen wore beards. But his hair was longer, touching his shoulders and full of curl. It was dark as midnight and she found it quite rakish.

He caught her staring at him. She froze, her heartbeat accelerating. His dark eyes seemed alive even from across the room. His lips twitched up, flashing her a glimpse of strong teeth. He reached up to lightly tug on the corner of his knitted bonnet. She felt connected to him. Her body strangely aware of his, even from so great a distance. Sensations rippled down her spine and into her belly. She sank into a tiny curtsy without thought or consideration. It was a response, pure and simple. Her heart was thumping against her chest and she felt every beat as if time had slowed down.

A woman crossed between them, interrupting her staring. It was enough time for her mind to begin questioning what she was doing. Fluttering her eyelashes, she lowered her gaze, forcing herself to move through the court on slow steps. She ordered herself to not look back. She was warm, warmer than the day warranted. The reaction fascinated her but it also struck a warning bell inside her mind. She should not look back.

But a part of her didn't care for that. It clamored for her to turn and find him again. His eyes were as dark as his hair but lit with some manner of flame. She wanted to know if he was still watching her, wanted to know if she glimpsed the same flames in his eyes that she felt in her cheeks.

Ah yes, but fire burns . . .

Helena smiled. She enjoyed the way she felt, a silly little sort of enjoyment that made her want to giggle. The reason was actually quite simple. The way he looked at her made her feel pretty. Court was full of poetry and lavish compliments, but none of it had touched her. His eyes did. The flicker of appreciation was genuine.

She had never felt such before.

"Good day to ye."

She froze. The man must be half specter to move so quickly. But she wasn't afraid of him. Quite the opposite. Her gaze sought his, curious to see if his eyes continued to fascinate her up close.

She was not disappointed. Her breath froze in her lungs, excitement twisting her belly. His gaze roamed over her face and a pleased expression entered his eyes. In fact it looked a bit like relief.

She was suddenly grateful to Raelin all over again for having freed her of the heavy makeup. The way he looked at her made her feel pretty for the first time in her life.